Home

Amy Leah Magaw

Copyright © 2010 Victory Christian Publishing
All rights reserved.
Photographs courtesy of Amanda Joos Photography © 2010
All rights reserved.
ISBN:
978-0-615-45996-7

Dedication

This book is dedicated to first of all, my Lord and Saviour Jesus Christ. Without Him, life would be nothing. This is also dedicated to my husband, Brian, for all of his love and support throughout this journey. Finally, I dedicate this work to my good friend Hope, who showed me something new.

Acknowledgements

I would like to thank all of my friends and family who have assisted me with "Beta Testing" this book, with a special thank you to Mrs. Sherri Hendricks for her special advice on this project.

I would also like to thank Ms. Amanda Joos for her expert photography on the cover artwork.

Chapter 1

"Please, Susan, don't do this!" Cal pleaded as he reached for Sue's hand. Just as he reached for it, she pulled away.

"Cal, please don't make this any harder for me than it is already," Sue replied.

Cal grabbed Sue by her shoulders, "Harder for you? You're the one breaking it off! I don't understand! Sue, we've been together for a while! Just because we are graduating doesn't mean that it's over? It's just beginning! I've been planning and preparing for us. Please- I love you," Cal pleaded.

Sue stood there in the commons grove at Clover High School doing one of the hardest things that she had ever done-break up with her boyfriend of two years. She knew that it would be hard for her and Cal, but she also knew that to continue their relationship would be a lie.

"Cal, I love you too, just not the way that you need me to. I'm so sorry. I've enjoyed being with you, but I just don't see a future for us. I'm going away to college. My parents have worked really hard for me to be the first college graduate in our family, and I can't let them down. Besides, I want to go and see what it's like to live on my own," Sue replied.

"Susan, you don't have to live on your own. I want to marry you. I'd planned on asking you graduation night. You know that I've been working at the plant part-time; but what you don't know is that the boss has offered me a full-time job starting next month. I know that I didn't say anything; I wanted it to be a surprise." The horrific realization of Cal's anguish suddenly shone on Sue's face. She had no idea about of any of this, but it still didn't change anything.

"I thought you knew deep inside how I felt, and I thought that you felt that way too. Susan, please…" Cal said angrily as he gripped her arms tightly in desperation.

"Cal, let me go..." Sue said as she tried to pull away from him, trying not to cause more of a scene; but someone had already noticed her distress, and came just in time.

"Sue, is there a problem here?" asked Brady as he walked up behind Cal, placing his hand on his shoulder. Cal released his hold on Sue. Brady was an acquaintance of Sue's from her youth group at church. A lot of the girls at church really made over his good looks, but Sue had never noticed; she was Cal's girl. She and Brady barely knew each other, but right now, he seemed to be at her service.

"No, Brady, everything's gonna be fine. I was just leaving. Goodbye, Cal," Susan said sadly as she walked away from both young men, rattled, and headed towards her Ford Focus.

Small streams of tears fell down Sue's face as she walked to her car. She never meant to hurt Cal. They had had some good times together. As she had examined her life through much prayer and Bible study along with careful counsel from her parents, Sue felt like she was making the right decision. Her parents gave her Godly advice, but they realized that this was a decision only she could make. Sue wasn't ready to get married, and she knew how proud her parents would be when she became the first graduate of the Haybert family.

As Sue pulled out of the parking lot she felt stabbing pains of guilt as she replayed the scene in her mind. There was nothing wrong with Cal-he was strong, handsome and caring-she just didn't love him enough to spend the rest of her life with him; after the encounter she just had, she definitely felt sure that she had made the right decision. Cal had just shown her a side of himself that she had never seen before. Perhaps he would have become violent with her after they were married. Married! She couldn't even entertain the thought! She knew that she had made the right choice, and with that, she dismissed the matter for a while.

As Sue drove down the small country roads of Campbell's Grove, she took a good look around. In just three months, she would be leaving for college. There were some things that she would miss about her small hometown: her small country church, the supermarket where everyone knew everyone, and of course, her home; but, on the other hand, Sue really felt like she was ready to fly the coop right now! There was a whole world of opportunities available to her as she stepped out of the nest and spread her wings. She only hoped that she would be fortunate enough to fly, and not crash and burn! Yes, going away to college was indeed a scary thought for Sue, but she was sure that she could handled it with the Lord's help.

Then a thought occurred to her; she only needed the Lord's help, and not another man's! After her last encounter with Cal, Sue became only too aware of what a distraction a man could be. Sue determined in her heart, right then and there, that this excursion of education would be about just that-education. It would be difficult enough trying to study and keep up with all of her assignments while adjusting to living on her own. A man would just complicate things, and she didn't need any more complications. She was reliving her last complication in her mind as she drove down the highway, but not with regret. Sue wasn't going to college to find another man-definitely not!

Sue drove to her dad's family business to begin her afterschool shift. Sue ran the register for her dad's auto parts business, Max's Automotive World. She enjoyed working with her family, and she would miss it when she went away. Fortunately, her dad had given her register position to her best friend, Michelle. Having Michelle there to 'fill the gap' might help her parents make it through their empty nest syndrome-at least that's what Sue thought.

The business was thriving; The Haybert family had owned and operated Max's Automotive World for the past twenty-five years. In the tri-county area, Max's was known to be the best and most reliable place for auto parts. The store always smelled clean and glimmered with shiny chrome wheel covers that adorned the walls. From air fresheners to fuel injectors, Max had it; and if he didn't, he could get it.

Max had always honored God in all that he did, and his store was no exception. In twenty-five years of business, the store had never been opened on Sunday, and God had blessed Max for his stand for Him. God had provided enough money for a full four years of college for Sue, and then some. Max Haybert could not have been more thankful for what God had done for him and his family; and he could not have been prouder of his daughter. The very sight of his Sue brought smiles to his chubby cheeks! Max was a heavy set, hard working man, who loved the Lord; his dark receding hair line made him look quite 'distinguished', according to his wife Irene.

Irene Haybert was Max's angel. She worried as only a mother could and should, but her face never showed it. Her beautiful blond hair showed no signs of gray, not that she would ever color it if a few gray sprigs had appeared. She vowed that if God ever allowed her to have grays, that they would be her trophies of survival!

Max and Irene had worked and saved all of their lives to put their only daughter through four years of college. The burden Sue carried was tremendous, as she certainly did not want to disappoint them. Sue had often talked with her *'Daddy'*, as she affectionately called him, and he had assured her that they only expected her to do her best. "God tells us in His Word that, *'Moreover it is required in stewards that a man be found faithful.'* That's all we ask of you, Sue. Just be faithful to the Lord, to your studies and whatever the Lord leads you to do with your life," Max told his daughter.

Sue had thought about her parents on the way home, and what they might think about the breakup. Truly, how did they expect her to go to college and marry Cal? Irene had always known of Max and Sue's dream of college, but she secretly hoped that Sue would marry and stay in town. The funds that were saved for her education would make a wonderful wedding gift to give her daughter, a good solid start with her new husband.

Sue then thought specifically about her Daddy. She remembered how he told her that God only expected her to be faithful in the task that He had given her to do. She loved the talks with her Daddy and gleaned so much from them. Sue had been saved at the early age of five. She asked God to forgive her of her sins, and she accepted Him as her personal Saviour! She had heard in Sunday school how Jesus died on the cross to make it possible for all the people in the world to go to Heaven. No matter how bad those people were, they only had to believe that Jesus died for them, and that He arose on the third day, and is now living in Heaven, just waiting to come back and get His children! Sue felt very sad in her heart that Jesus had died just for her, and then she was happy that He was now alive, and she wanted Him to be her Friend! Now, not only would she go to Heaven when she died, but from that point on she could serve the Lord, and tell others about him! Pastor Creighton had explained that she would still have troubles in this life, but now she had a Friend to help her through those times-Jesus! Sue smiled as she remembered those Sunday school lessons, and how glad she was that someone had told her about Jesus. Sue and her Daddy were always able to talk about the Lord and share a special bond between Father and Daughter.

Sue had done her best to live a good Christian life. Noting the fact that she was human and no one's perfect, she had had her share of mistakes, but God had always been there to put the pieces together again. Her family, her faith, and her friends had all given her a full life until now. This chapter of her life was coming to an end, and Sue was excited and a little anxious about what lay ahead for her. She thought about this as she walked into the store.

"Hi, Sue" said Sue's mom, Irene.

"Hi, Mom!" she replied.

"How did it go?" Irene asked.

"At school? Great. I think I aced Mr. Johnson's exam, and I know that I passed Ms. Rogan's exam, I just don't know if it's an 'A' or not. As for Cal, that did not go so great."

"What do you mean?" she asked.

"I broke up with him," Sue replied, as she watched her mom's jaw drop in shock. "Mom, he was devastated. I had no idea that he thought we were so serious."

"Your Daddy did. Cal had asked for your hand last month, and your Daddy agreed," Irene replied as she felt her heart skipping a beat. She couldn't believe what she was hearing! She thought it was absolutely absurd for her daughter to go and throw away a perfectly good proposal to go off to college. But Irene did realize that Sue was practically an adult now, and she had to start making her own prayerful decisions.

"He did what?" Sue exclaimed. "Did Daddy really think that I loved Cal enough to marry him?"

"He honestly didn't know. He says that he's not been able to read you lately in that department. Actually, he's been kind of concerned about you, and now poor Cal. I can imagine how hurt he must feel," Irene answered.

"I'm sorry! It's just that I've been looking forward to college, and my new life! I never thought about getting married right now. Was Daddy really gonna let me forget all about college to get married, after all of the hard work that you both have done, saving and scraping for me to go?"

"He had peace that you would make the right choice, whatever that was. I thought that you'd choose Cal, but only you can know God's will for your life, Sue. That's something that your Daddy and I can't tell you. We can give you advice from the Bible and our experiences, but you're gonna have to really start praying hard and seeking His answers, not ours." Irene knew she was telling Sue the truth, but she didn't have to be happy about the decisions that Sue was making. She felt herself becoming irritated. She was so concerned about her daughter still being so young, and unsupervised. She just didn't know how it was all going to turn out. "So, you're gonna go on to college then, and do what? Get caught up with all of those partying drunk kids? Wouldn't you rather stay here and settle down and raise a family for the Lord?" asked Irene.

Sue caught the tone in her mother's voice; she was angry. Sue then realized that her mother really did think that she should've married Cal in lieu of going away to college. But why didn't her own mother want her to have this experience? *'Was she jealous of Sue and her opportunity? Was that the real issue here?'* Sue reluctantly thought to herself.

"Mama, Christians go to college, too. I plan on finding a good church when I go to Atlantic and serve the Lord there. You've raised me better than to run off and go wild, Mama, don't you know that?" answered a slightly disappointed Sue.

"Shh. Here comes your Daddy," said Irene.

Max walked up from his office with a stack of invoices on a clipboard. He looked a little flustered. "Has anyone seen my glasses?"

"They're on your head, Max," answered Irene.

"Oh, yeah, so they are!" he replied as he reached up and took down his glasses. He looked at Susan. "Hey, kiddo! What's up? How'd the exams go today?" Max asked.

"They went great Daddy. Everything's great!" Sue said as she walked past her mom, whispering in her ear, "I'll let you tell him the rest," as she assumed her position at the cashier's counter.

"Wimp!" Irene whispered back.

Max looked at the two of them, knowing that

something was up, but he simply said, "Whatever," and walked back to his office.

As Sue tied on her smock, she thought to herself how blessed she was to have parents like hers, even though her mom worried way too much. She knew that her mom was right on one aspect-she would have to learn to lean on the Lord more, being on her own. She wasn't worried; she was simply eager to see what God had in store for her.

As Sue took her place at the register, Irene walked to the back where Max sat in the office, filing receipts. "Max, she broke up with Cal today," explained Irene.

Max paused before he spoke, and Irene could see the wheels turning. "Well, everything will be alright. She'll go on to school, and things will be...okay," answered Max as he kept his nose in the receipts.

"But Max, I thought that she'd marry Cal and stay here. Who knows what she'll turn into when she leaves here! You know what college is like these days: wild parties, alcohol, drugs, sex! Max, how can we let her go?" rambled Irene as she sat down with tears in her eyes.

"Irene, I can't believe you. Sue has been saved since she was five years old. Now we both know that she hasn't been perfect, but we've raised her right. We've got to trust the Word that we've instilled in her, Irene. God will take care of her. She has to make the choices now. All we can do is pray for her; I've got peace about it. It'll be alright." explained Max, as he held his wife's hand.

*****

Later that evening, Sue was reading her Bible when her cell phone rang. It was her best friend, Michelle, according to the caller id. Sue and Michelle had been best friends since they both went to Nursery Sunday School class with pig tails! As far as Sue could remember Michelle had worn those same pig tails since then too, but she had graduated from ribbons to clips and all kinds of rhinestones and sparkles! Michelle was a high spirited young lady who had her own definite style and way of thinking, but, who also always sought the Lord in all that she did. She was the best 'country-fried girlfriend' that anyone could ever want, complete with neck and eye rolls and finger snaps to beat the band. She planned to stay there in Campbell's Grove and attend Beauty School while she waited on the Lord to give her further direction.

"Hey girl, what's up?" said Sue.

"Girl, it's all over town! What happened with you two?" Michelle started off without even breathing. "Didn't you know what was going on?"

"Hello, Sue- and how are you? Did you have a good day today?" Sue replied in a mocking tone. Michelle had not even stopped to say 'hello' to her friend. She simply wanted answers.

"Point taken. Again-what's going on with you?" Michelle asked.

"Really, I didn't know what his plans were, or how deeply he felt. I feel really bad, but I can't marry someone just because I feel sorry for them," Sue replied.

"You know, everyone expected you two to be together. Even with your talk of college, no one believed that you would go through with it. When your parents gave me the job at the store, I thought that it was because Cal didn't want his wife to work! We all just knew that y'all were gettin' married! We all just thought that you and Cal would make a life here." explained Michelle.

"Everyone but me!" Sue answered quickly. "Besides, I am really looking forward to living on my own. I've been under my parents' roof for eighteen years, and I'm ready to see what else is out there. I'm ready for a little adventure, you know: independence, freedom, no one looking over my shoulder every waking moment. My parents' have taught me right from wrong. I just wish they'd quit hovering over me and trust me to do what's right." Sue really believed that she would be fine on her own, and she was ready to spread her wings and fly.

"Your Daddy obviously trusted you to make the right decision about Cal; I'm sure that college will be plenty excitin'! You'll be a good couple of hours away. They won't be able to look over your shoulder from that far away; I don't care how long your Mom's neck is!" said Michelle with a laugh. "I just hate it for poor Cal, though. He's such a nice guy."

Sue became a little irritated. "If he's so nice, you can marry him!" retorted Sue. And then there was a silence.

Finally Michelle broke through. "Well, I guess the break up was for the best," Michelle said with a sigh.

"What do you mean?" asked Susan.

"He drove a Chevy," Michelle answered.

"What? What does that have to do with the price of eggs?" Sue asked with a small laugh.

"Everybody knows that there ain't nothin' better than a Ford Man! You drive a Ford, I drive a Ford; how did we all ever think that you would have been happy with a man who drove a Chevy? I'm sorry girl! We had you all married off, and you would've been miserable!" she said as both girls erupted in laughter!

"Thanks Michelle, I needed that!" said Sue as she finally felt at ease with the situation. Whatever was in store for her, she knew that it would be more exciting than living in Campbell's Grove; a one dog town, forget the horse! God had something for her. She knew it, and she had plenty of time to figure it out.

Chapter 2

The summer flew by, and before Irene knew it, the day she dreaded had arrived. As she, Max and Sue stood outside the car parked next to the curb of Atlantic Coast University in the small town of Sunset, North Carolina, Irene's eyes began to fill with tears. She was lost for words. She knew that this day was coming, and she thought that she'd be ready for it, but she thought wrong.

Sue had driven her own Ford Focus to the campus with her parents following behind. She tried to persuade them not to bother with seeing her off, but there was no changing her Mama's mind. "Mom, please don't cry! I'm only a few hours away. Michelle will keep you company at the store since y'all gave her my job!" said Sue.

"Somebody's gotta run that register," Max said, "the money will help with her beauty school, and your Mama will need the companionship."

"Only Mama?" asked Sue as she looked at her Daddy, whom she was truly going to miss.

"I'm just gonna miss you!" said Sue's Mama as she threw herself into her daughter's embrace. The tears just kept flowing. Sue looked away as Max took her duffle bag and footlocker from the trunk of their Ford Taurus. Max left the trunk open and turned to the ladies.

"Okay, Irene. We need to go," said Max with urgency in his voice.

"But Max," cried Irene. "We need to..."

"We *need* to catch our plane," interrupted Max, "I don't want to spend all day trying to reschedule a missed flight."

"What?" Irene's reddened eyes looked at him in bewilderment. Sue began to smile, as she had been an accomplice in her Daddy's plans for her mother.

"I'd rather spend it in Hawaii, wouldn't you?!" said Max with a large grin on his face. "Don't worry about a thing. Sue packed your bags, and you have everything you need." Max pointed at the open trunk, revealing the luggage and his brilliant plans. "Now let's go! Getting through security will take hours!"

"Why Max? What have you done?" asked Irene in utter confusion.

"I knew that we would need this time to start our new lives, just as Sue is starting hers. JEGS is throwing a junket in Hawaii, and guess who had the highest sales in the region of JEGS products last month? That's right!" Max said proudly as he pointed to himself. "Our anniversary is next month, so consider this an early anniversary present! Now would you stop blubbering already and get in the car?" Max said as he pried Irene away from Susan and pushed her towards the car.

"Oh Max, you're wonderful!" said a radiant Irene.

"I know!" Max replied with a devilish smile.

"Well," said Irene as she looked up at Sue with all smiles, "I guess I have a prior engagement." She gave Susan one final hug, and then jumped into the front seat.

"Thanks you two, for everything. Have fun! Call me when you get there!" Sue said.

"We will," said Max as he drove off, rather speedily.

"Well, that's done," said Sue as she turned around, picked up her luggage, and walked off to find her new home for the next four years. As she walked across the plush, green lawn, Sue's heart was filled with a barrage of emotions! She felt fiercely independent, but at the same time, a little scared! *'I wonder about my new roommate, new classes, new professors, new guys… Now where did that come from?* Sue thought to herself. *'Now is not the time to be thinking about new guys! I don't want to start this first semester off on the wrong foot! No complications, remember, Sue! Stick with the program!'*

She checked in at the registration tables in front of the main lecture hall. A rather handsome looking blonde guy helped check her in and gave her a card with her dorm room assignment, key, and a map of the campus on the back.

"Miss Haybert, you will be in Hines Hall in room 28. That's on the other side of the campus. Do you need someone to help you find it? We have some volunteers helping freshmen today," the young man offered.

"Thanks! That'd be great!" Sue replied as she took the papers from him.

"Hey, Kim," called the young man to a very petite young brunette who came bouncing towards them. "This is Susan Haybert. She is going to Hines. Can you help her out?"

"Sure! I'd be glad to! I'm Kim Stewart. I'm a sophomore here. How are you?"

"I'm good," Sue answered as she set down her duffle bag to shake Kim's hand. Kim seemed very cheerful, perhaps one of those cheerleader types. Whatever the case was, Sue was awfully glad to have her help.

"Let me help you with your things," offered Kim.

"Thanks, you can have the duffle. I'll heft the trunk." replied Susan as she handed over the duffle bag. The two began to walking towards the girls' dormitory. The walk across the campus was nothing less than exhilarating. The campus was carpeted with lush green lawns and bubbling fountains. The grey cobblestone sidewalks reminded Sue of old European villages, not that she had ever seen any; she had only imagined that they would look that way. The lecture halls all exhibited a turn of the century charm that Sue found very 'collegiate'. Sue marveled at it all, as she and Kim walked along to the building that would be her new home for the next four years. They arrived at a huge, almost gothic designed building with several stairwells. Sue told Kim that she could handle it from there and thanked her for her help. Kim wished her luck and returned to the registration area. Sue walked into the grand building, took a deep breath, and climbed the stairs with her things, finally arriving at room 28, as she began her new chapter of independence.

As she slipped the key into the door, she sighed, "Here we go." She opened the door and almost fell backwards at the smell. She saw a small room, with a mirror-imaged layout. There was a closet immediately to her left, and further down on the left-hand side was an empty twin bed. Next to that on the outside wall was a large desk, and above that was a window. As she looked on at her new 'home,' she immediately became nauseated by the smell of last semester's all-night kegger that had left beer saturating the carpets. Her first step into the room pressed onto a stiffened carpet that appeared shiny. Such were the drawbacks of attending a secular college.

The other side of the room was already inhabited, but her new roommate was nowhere to be found. The mattress cover on what would be Sue's bed caught her eye-some Greek Symbols, no doubt from belonging to some nearby Sorority, were sprayed painted on it.

Not wishing to have beer tracks on her shoes later on, Sue tiptoed towards her closet, dodging the green fumes of odor that she just knew she could see steaming up from the floor. She opened the door to find that it smelled worse in there because the small enclosed space had been shut up for too long. She tiptoed on towards the desk and laid her trunk and bag on the desk. She sat down on the bed, slipped her shoes off, and placed them on top of the trunk. She then balanced herself between the bed and the desk and struggled to get the window open. Finally, it went up and then she reluctantly laid down on the bed and began making a mental list. *'First things first-rent a steam cleaner'* she thought to herself. She was almost discouraged, but she quickly determined to pick herself up and get to work. She had been looking forward to this day forever, and Sue was determined that nothing was going to ruin it. She also realized that she needed to get to the bookstore before all of the good used books were gone. Then, she decided she would rent the steam cleaner. She took a deep breath, and then she realized- the green fumes were beginning to slip away.

Just as Sue was beginning to breathe easier, a young red-head stepped into the door way. "Oh! You must be the new girl. I'm Marissa Estill, your roommate. Everybody calls me Mari," said the girl as she moved towards Susan with an extended hand.

"Hey, Mari, I'm Sue Haybert. I'm glad to meet you," Sue replied as she shook her hand in return. Sue was pleased at the sight of her new roommate, and she confidentially wondered if they would be good friends. She certainly hoped so; she so wanted her college experience to be fulfilling, but even Sue wasn't so naïve as to believe that everything would be cupcakes and lemonade. She knew that there would be storms to weather, but at the moment, the forecast seemed clear.

"Hey, you wanna gimme a hand with this steam cleaner? It's kinda heavy," asked Mari as she stepped outside the door and pointed down the stairs to where the coveted machine rested at the foot of the stairs.

"I love you already," said Sue with a laugh as she slipped her shoes back on and jumped up to help. The girls ran downstairs to lift the carpet cleaner up to their second floor room. They made small talk as they dragged up the machine. Finally, they made it to the room with the cleaner. Sue hated to seem lazy, or like she was putting off the task, but she desperately needed to purchase her books. "Mari, can we do this when we get back? I really want to get my books before the good used ones are all gone," asked Sue.

"Sure. Who do you have this semester?" asked Mari.

"Well let's see," said Sue as she pulled her printout from her pocket. "I have Math 110 with Jamison, English 102 with Roget, Marine Science 210 with Delaney, and Geography 103 with Davis."

"Wow. I don't have any of those classes. Sorry. But I know that we'll be seeing a lot of each other. I do have some others things that I need to take care of, so I'll meet you back here at about two o'clock, and we'll tackle it then," said Marissa. She reached for her backpack and headed towards the door.

"Sounds like a plan," said Sue, and with that, Marissa left.

Sue grabbed her own bag and raced out towards the bookstore. As she stepped out of the doors of Hines Hall, Sue really gained a sense of adventure. She had begun to settle into her new life, and now she was off to purchase her books. She managed to make her way back to the parking lot where she had left her Ford Focus, when she noticed that the red Toyota Yaris parked next to her was parked way too close. She could hardly get the door open. *'Stupid Toyota driver,'* she thought to herself, *'Those little cars look like bugs. Why can't people buy American anymore?'* She walked around and had to crawl in from the passenger side, but she made it to the bookstore without incident. Thankfully, there were some good used textbooks left, and she was able to stay within budget. Sue knew that this was also the providence of God. She had a limited amount of funds for books and supplies, and even though she thought that time had run out, God knew she was right on time. He had provided even the simplest of details to ensure that Sue had exactly what she needed. She drove back to the dorm, parking in the dorm parking lot this time, making sure to avoid parking to close to anyone, after her previous experience with the Toyota.

Sue then made her way back to room 28, ready to knock out that nasty carpet. It wasn't a pleasant job, but she felt 'adult' enough to handle it. After all, she was on her own now. As the girls were cleaning the carpet, Sue tried to find out some information about the town and about her new roommate. "Mari, do you know of a good church around here?" she asked.

"No; I don't really go to church. I can think of a lot better things to do with my time, no offense. But, I'm sure that someone at the student union can help you out with that. They keep all sorts of directories there," Mari replied.

Sue was just a little shocked. This was her first time away from home on her own, and she realized that not everyone went to church, but she didn't expect for her roommate to be one of them. Secretly, she was grieved at Mari's response. "Oh. Okay I'll check with them," replied Sue as she made a mental note not to press the church issue with Mari, but to simply pray for her. She had noticed that Mari's clothes were a little on the immodest side, but she never judged. Sue remembered, '*You can never know what a person is truly like simply by their appearance. 'The Bible says that man looketh on the outward appearance, but the LORD looketh on the heart'*. She decided then and there to continue to pray for her and see what the Lord would do. Perhaps she was here for the simple reason that Mari needed the Lord. Or could God have something else in store...

"But the LORD said unto Samuel, Look not on his countenance, or on the height of his stature; because I have refused him: for the LORD seeth not as man seeth; for man looketh on the outward appearance, but the LORD looketh on the heart."

I Samuel 16:7

Chapter 3

After a restless night, Sue awakened to find Marissa already gone, if she ever came home at all. Mari had left shortly after the girls had the carpet cleaned, and Sue hadn't seen her since. She hoped that Mari hadn't avoided her because she didn't like her or because of the church issues, but then she thought that she was just being paranoid. Sue did have that tendency. When things were going good, Sue often waited for something bad to happen. She decided that maybe she inherited that from her mother. The truth was Sue wanted to change that little quirk about herself. She wanted to have a positive outlook in everything that she did, and with that thought in mind, she grabbed her robe, key, and her bathroom basket complete with everything she would need to get ready and headed down the hall to shower up for her first class, Math 110. This was a new experience. She had heard that some people in Campbell's Grove still had to go outside to go to the bathroom, but she still liked her bathroom at home right next to her room. But, next to an outhouse, going down the hall to a multi-unit bathroom was okay with her.

Sue, determined to be a good steward of God's money that He had provided for her, had decided that she would walk to her classes and conserve her gasoline for other uses. Cantley Hall was not that far, and she was making good time. Her Math class was from eight o'clock until nine fifteen in the morning on Mondays and Wednesdays with Dr. Jamison. Mari had told her that he was an excellent professor and explained things very well. Sue certainly hoped so because Math was not her subject, and she really had to work hard at it to keep her grades up. After all, she was carrying that burden of being the first college grad from her family, and that was no light matter.

Mari's description of the professor proved to be correct. Math seemed like it would be a good class for her, and she felt relieved. She had forty-five minutes until her next class, so she found a cubicle in which to do her homework for Math while she waited. As she finished up her assignment, she thought to herself, *'Well, one class down for this first day, and one class to go.'*

Sue scooted over to the next building across the way, Buchanan Hall, and found the room for her English 102 class with Professor Roget. As she entered the lecture hall, she saw a familiar face sitting in the fifth row up in the center section. Just as she entered, he looked up and smiled when he caught her in his glance. It was Brady Sheffield. Sue remembered him from the youth group at church, but only as a friendly acquaintance. Even more recently than that, Sue remembered how Brady had stepped in to assist her in the Cal-breakup incident. At that recollection, she felt a little embarrassed, but, that was then, and this was now; and right now, Sue was glad to see someone from home, and what a sight to see! Brady was busting at the seams with devastating allure in his white Atlanta Braves T-shirt that stretched nicely across his broad, cut shoulders. He had played baseball in high school and showed a lot of promise on the mound. He was Webster's definition of tall, dark, and handsome. His dark brown hair and Hershey chocolate brown eyes were adored by several girls in the youth group; but he didn't have much of a social life because his ailing grandmother took up most of his time. He came to live with her when he was about eight, as Sue recalled. Brady's parents had died in a boating accident when he was very young, and his grandmother had raised him. When he had turned about fifteen, she became seriously ill, and Brady missed out on a lot to take care of her; he even had to quit the baseball team during his sophomore year, as her health had declined severely, and she passed away about a month before his graduation. Brady smiled and motioned for Sue to come up, pointing at an empty seat next to him. Sue was so glad to see someone from home that she sprang up the steps towards Brady. Brady stood to greet her.

"Hey! What in the world are you doing here? I didn't know you were coming here?" exclaimed Sue as she stood staring at Brady in disbelief.

"Yeah, I didn't either until mid-June," answered Brady. "Please, sit down," Brady sounded like quite the gentleman as he moved his backpack out of the way for Sue to have room. "I hear that Roget is quite the eccentric, and I'm not sure how this class is going to go," Sue sat down and placed her backpack at her feet and began to take out her necessary supplies for the class.

As soon as the words had left Brady's lips, the professor walked in. "Young people, this is an institution of learning and not a pool hall; please take your seats." shouted Professor Roget as made his way toward the podium in front of the room. Sue quickly grabbed a notebook and pen. Brady and Sue both looked at each other in disbelief as they found that Brady's information had been correct.

"English 102 is all about writing. Expressing one's thoughts through written language dates back to early cave drawings in which Cro-Magnon Man left behind his story for future generations to see. We, young people, have changed very little from that time. Surely we have improved our methods, but the written word has proved to be a powerful tool in educating and moving generations in the progression of mankind." said the professor, as he began his walk from side to side of the lecture hall.

Brady cut his eyes at Susan as if to say, *"Can you believe this guy?"* and with that look he turned and wrote a quick note on his paper for Sue that read, *"Do you have a class after this?"*

Sue wrote back on her notebook, *"No- I'm done after this."*

Brady answered in kind on the paper, *"Let's grab some lunch."*

Susan quickly penciled out, *"OK,"* as the professor

was beginning to look their way.

"I hope that everyone's paying attention; I'd hate to have to repeat myself," said the professor as he stared towards Brady and Sue. Sue thought to herself, *'So do I!'* The two quickly sat straight up in their chairs, and 'paid attention' to the lecture.

After class, Brady and Sue walked down towards the Student Union which housed, 'The Greasy Spoon,' the campus grill. On the way Brady stopped for a moment and pulled the Atlanta Braves Baseball Cap out and slung it on it his head. "Whew! That's better! I'm not complete without my hat." Sue gazed at Brady; the baseball cap only added to his charm. She always had a soft spot for baseball players and Cal had been Clover High's premier pitcher. She stood there and just stared at Brady for a moment. "What's wrong? Is it on straight?" Brady asked. She had to quickly remind herself that she came there to earn her degree, a Bachelors of Arts in Independent Studies, her BAIS, not her MRS! She had no time for a boyfriend, even if it was someone as handsome as Brady!

"No-you look really…great!" she answered, and then she figured that she should be quiet, for her own good! She decided to walk and simply think. Sue was perplexed at the very thought of Brady being at her school. As far as she knew, she was one of only a few graduates from Clover High that was going to college anywhere, much less away from home. Most of the seniors that were going to school were either going to the two-year Community College in Rutherford County or to the beauty school in town.

The two freshmen came in and sat down at the table and began checking out the menu. It wasn't long before the waitress walked up and took their orders. Brady ordered the official college cheeseburger and Sue ordered a regular cheeseburger, with an order of barbecue chicken nachos to split. Sue was more than a little curious to find out why Brady had chosen to come to Atlantic, and she decided to pry a little.

"So, what's the story? How'd you end up here?" asked Sue.

"Well, this all began a few weeks after Grandma passed away. I got this letter in the mail from Atlantic saying that I had been awarded a scholarship," replied Brady. "I don't even remember applying."

Sue could believe that. Bless his heart, she didn't know if she could have handled the matters that Brady had been forced to endure. "I know. That was a hard time for you as I remember. Pastor Creighton had put you and your Grandma on the prayer list," said Sue.

"Well, I wasn't quite sure what to do. I'd been praying for a while, asking God for clear direction. Grandma was the only family that I had left, and I thought about just going down to the plant and applying for a job there; but like I said, the letter came, and I just had peace about taking the scholarship. My grades weren't all that bad in school, and I just felt like I needed a change; you know?"

"Well, change we got!" chimed in Sue, as the waitress brought their nachos. Sue tried one right away as she felt like she was starving. "Ooh! These are good!" said Sue as she savored the appetizer. "Wanna bite?" she said as she stretched her arm across the table, lifting the nacho to Brady's lips. Brady opened his mouth, and leaned toward the nacho, but then, coming out of the dream world that he was currently orbiting, he shook his head and politely refused. Brady couldn't believe that Sue was here. He remembered how he had come to her rescue back at Clover High, but back then, he couldn't stop to think about a girlfriend. His Grandmother came first, but now that he was free and away at college, maybe God had brought someone truly special into his life, or so he was now thinking.

As Sue continued rambling on about her room and the mess it was in when she found it, Brady couldn't help but get lost in her eyes, which he noticed were as blue as the sea. *"She is so beautiful-her brown hair looks as soft as silk,"* he thought to himself, as he fought the urge to reach out and touch it to see if he was right! He suddenly snapped out of it when Sue called his name. "Brady, are you okay? You look like you left me there for a second!"

"Oh, sorry, I...just...had something on my mind. You were saying?" he said as he recovered from his daydreaming.

"I've only been here since yesterday. My parents, well my mom mostly, were a little worried about me coming to college, something about running off and going wild. It was so bad that they had to run off to Hawaii to forget about it!" she said with a giggle. Brady also laughed at the thought of Mr. Haybert and "Mrs. Irene," as the youth group called their Sunday School Teacher, screeching off to a Hawaiian getaway after depositing their only child at a four year university! Brady remembered Sue's parents from church, as being a well-respected Christian family, and had he admired Max from afar. Since Brady's parents had died when he was young, he never really had a father figure in his life.

"Well, I've been here since the first of July. I came early to get an apartment and a job. The scholarship was for tuition only, so I had a lot of work to do. But, I came to town and found a good church, and the Lord put me in contact with the right people. The pastor's son, Justin, got me a job at The Bargain Bin, a little discount store on Main Street, as a night stocker. The pastor also knew of a couple in the church that has a grand old Victorian house that they have converted into four apartments, and they rented one to me for very little a month. They said that they consider it a blessing to help out young Christian people who come to school here. The Lord's opened every door for me since, so here I am."

"That's great, Brady. I was glad to see a familiar face from home. I'm so glad to hear that you have found a good church here! I asked my roommate about the churches in the area, but she's not a church-going gal," Sue said with a hint of sadness in her eyes as she thought about Mari.

"I've been going to Sunset Community Church, and I really like it there. It reminds me of our church back home. I know that I didn't get to go there a lot towards the end, you know with Grandma and all, but there was no place like the Lighthouse. Pastor Creighton was a great help to me during those hard times." Brady paused a moment to collect himself. "If you like, you can go with me to Bible Study on Wednesday night. They have so many college students there that they actually split the classes, men's and women's. You would feel comfortable going in class without me, right…" Brady asked.

"Oh, sure. I've made it this far haven't I?" Sue said with a laugh. Just then their burgers arrived. Their conversation changed to their classes, the town, and they wondered about things at home.

Brady thought to himself while he ate. He wondered about Cal and how that relationship had all turned out. He debated on whether or not to ask Sue about it. He certainly didn't want to put a damper on the charming lunch date they were having, but his curiosity got the better of him. "Listen, Sue, do you mind if I ask you something?" began Brady.

Sue wondered where he was going with this. "Sure, I guess."

"Whatever happened with you and Cal after that day in the commons?"

"Oh…" Sue began, as she felt her cheeks go flush. She remembered the day vividly, especially the part about how Brady had come to her rescue; and now here he was, her hero sitting at the same table with her. "Well, he did take it rather hard."

"Has he ever come back to try and work things out? You've not had any more trouble out of him, have you?"

"No, not at all. I hate to say it, but I think that he was not only hurt, but embarrassed. We did make quite a scene there, didn't we?" Sue said as she recalled how the people had begun to stare. She was so grateful that Brady was one of those people. "I never really got to thank you for your help in that little skirmish. I sure am glad that you were there."

"That's no problem. God always does seem to put His people at the right place, at the right time to do His bidding. I'm just glad that I was able to help." Brady paused for a moment and seemed to deliberate on his next words. "Just know that if you ever need anything, I'll be here to help you. Please don't hesitate to call on me, for anything."

"Oh, thank you. That really means a lot to me to have someone here from home. I guess we both have to stick together, right?" Sue asked.

"Right. I'll always be here for you, Sue," Brady answered with a deep conviction that Sue didn't quite pick up on. Brady knew that it couldn't possibly be a coincidence that he and Sue were at the same university. God had placed him in the commons at Clover High to help Sue during a trial, and he was sure that God had some purpose for bringing them together now in this place. He was sure that he'd find the answer through prayer and Bible study, but until then, he decided that he would enjoy the lovely friend that God had sent him.

After they finished their lunch, they parted ways, and Sue returned to her dorm room to complete the first reading assignment for English and prepare for her first essay. *'How strange to find Brady here at Atlantic,'* Sue thought to herself, *'I never really knew him back home. He seemed very distant, but I guess that was because of his ailing grandmother. He seems so spiritual. It's exciting in a way, how everything has happened for him. I'm glad to see that God is still working in people's lives,'* she thought. *'I wonder what He's doing in mine?'*

Chapter 4

The first day of college classes was a success. Sue was so tired that she thought she would surely sleep well, but when her head hit the pillow that night, she could hardly sleep a wink! As the clock's alarm sounded, Sue was ready to get up for day two, but she found herself moving a little slower than she would have liked. She followed her routine and headed for the showers, but, much to her surprise today, she found that all of the showers were taken. She asked one of the girls waiting in line, "Where's the next Bathroom?"

"Every floor has a full bath, but you probably won't have much luck there either." the girl replied.

"Well, I've got to try; I didn't figure on having to wait," answered Sue. She turned with her basket and headed down stairs to find the ground floor showers. She arrived only to find that indeed there was a line for those showers as well. She groaned and headed back up the stairs. Floor three, no luck. On the fourth floor, Sue found the bathroom had a sign, "Out of Order" which explained the lines on the other floors. With dread, Sue headed back down to the second floor bathroom. When she arrived, she found that the line was moving quickly, as the girls realized that others were waiting. Sue knew that she should get up earlier from now on, no matter how well she slept.

Now that she had finally gotten ready, Sue decided to skip breakfast and grab a power bar from her stash in her dorm room desk. If she ran, she could make it to the Bruener Science Building for Marine Science in time. She would hate to start this class off on the wrong foot. Sue absolutely loved the beach, and she could hardly wait to learn more about it! She ran across the campus, looking carefully as she went. As she entered the parking lot, she heard screeching brakes, only to look as a Red Toyota Yaris almost ran her over as it was pulling into a parking space.

"YOU!" thought Sue to herself as she stepped back onto the curb, remembering how this same car had blocked her in yesterday.

"Sorry!" yelled the guy that jumped out of his car and ran towards the Science building.

"I can't believe he just said that! He didn't even wait to see if I was okay!" Sue thought out loud as she ran after him towards the Science building. Sue found her classroom in the nick of time. The professor was just starting to lecture. Sue quickly found a seat and took a deep breath. She took a quick scan around the classroom to see if she recognized anyone, remembering what she learned yesterday, *'you never know who might be there.'* As she panned to the right, she saw Mr. Toyota himself sitting two rows up. Sue snapped her head around quickly, and her jaw dropped in disgust. *'How dare he be in my class? This was the one subject that I was really looking forward to learning about, and now he has cast his red Toyota shadow on it!'* Sue thought to herself. *'He definitely better keep his distance from me.'*

The class proved to be very interesting. Sue loved science, and she loved the ocean-so how could she lose with Marine Science? That was one reason that she wanted to come to Atlantic Coast University; it was only about thirty minutes away from the beach. As the professor ended class, Sue waited for the run-a-way stranger to leave first, to be sure that she wouldn't be mowed down like road kill.

Sue's next class was Geography and was just across the courtyard from the Science building, so thank the Lord, there was no rush. She again found a cubicle in the Social Arts building to complete her first reading assignment from Marine Science. Upon completion of her reading, she quickly found her lecture hall and found a seat. When Professor Davis entered, she was taken by something familiar about him. She knew that she had never seen him before, but something made him special. As he began to speak, the feeling became stronger. Professor Davis talked about God's World as a special place that should be explored and treated with respect and responsibility. He quickly told the class that he was not a 'psycho environmentalist,' but he did believe in taking care of the Earth that God gave us. He worshipped the Creator and not the creation. That was the connection. Sue remembered reading in her Bible in Romans and I John about the Spirit bearing witness with believers. Sue had detected the professor's kindred spirit. At the end of class, Professor Davis extended an open door invitation to all of the students, if they ever needed any help or needed to talk. It was evident that he was a professor that cared about his students and was willing to help them in any way that he could. Sue knew that Professor Davis's class would be great.

Sue was a little tired now, especially after the morning's events, so she went back to her dorm room and laid down for a quick nap before beginning her homework from Geography. As soon as she no more than closed her eyes, her cell phone rang. Sue checked the caller ID and it was Michelle.

"Hello,..." Sue moaned out.

"Girl, what's wrong with you, you sick or somethin'?" quickly asked Michelle.

"No..." Sue answered, "...just tired. Long story. What's going on with you? How's beauty school, and how's working at the store?"

"Well, everything's going great at the store. I can't wait for your parents to come back. Do you think they'll bring me a present?" Michelle asked in childish expectation.

"Yes, I'm sure they will! Now, how's beauty school?" Sue asked with an inquisitive spirit.

"It's okay. It's a lot harder than I thought it would be," replied Michelle, with a voice of disappointment.

"Well, don't be a '*Beauty School Drop-out,*' Sue sang through the phone.

"Very funny! But really, how's life over there,

college-girl?" Michelle asked, as if she secretly desired to be there with her friend, feeling what it was like to be free.

"It's good so far! Hey, did you know that Brady Sheffield is here?" asked Sue in a sudden change of thought.

"Get out-he is not! Girl, we all thought he just dropped off the face of the earth. No one's seen him at church in months, and there was a rumor going around that he joined the Army! I'm glad to hear that he didn't join the Army, with such a shortage of good-looking men around. So, he's over there with you?" said Michelle excitedly.

"Well he's not *with me;* he's just here. I was shocked too! He said that he got a scholarship, and couldn't turn it down. I gotta tell you; it was a relief to see a familiar face here, especially one as good-looking as his," said Sue.

"I don't really remember much about him, just that he was fine as frog hair, and that he'd spent a lot of time taking care of his grandmother. What's he have to say?" asked Michelle.

"Well, he's really deep, spiritually that is. He told me all about what the Lord had done for him since he left Campbell's Grove, and he seems…nice," Sue answered, as she searched for the right words.

"Nice?" Michelle fished.

"Nice, like friend-nice. You know that I'm not looking for anything right now. I have to concentrate on my studies," Sue answered quickly.

"I smell a hook-up!" said Michelle in her teasing tone.

"Didn't you hear me? I am not looking for a man right now. I just came off of a relationship with Cal. I'm not ready. Plus, things here are a bit different. I like having the freedom to come and go as I please-I don't need another 'man' to answer to. Brady Sheffield is a friend, that's all-now drop it."

"What's he drive?" asked Michelle, as she refused to let it be.

"Oh, Lord, not that again. I don't know; I haven't seen his car," answered Sue, in disbelief at her friend's current source of wisdom when it came to guys.

"Well, you know what I told you; there ain't nothin' like a Ford Man," Michelle supplied, stating the law as she saw it.

"Well, do you have a Ford Man?" asked Sue in her defense.

"Girl, I ain't got no man at all, but if I did, you know he'd be riding me around in a Ford," she replied, very matter-of-factly.

"Pick-up or car? Ohhh! Now you've got me doing it" groaned Sue as Michelle laughed.

"Atta-girl!" sneered Michelle.

"Well, I'll tell you one thing, I 'ain't got no man' either, and I don't need one right now. If I was to get a man, I can certainly tell you who it wouldn't be." exclaimed Sue.

"Do tell..." answered Michelle with intense curiosity.

"Well, I don't know his name, but first he parked so close to my car that I couldn't get in the driver's side door; I had to crawl through the passenger side."

"Uh-uh" chimed Michelle.

"Uh-Huh!" Sue returned. "And then, when I was running to class today because the shower situation..."

"OOOO! What shower situation?" asked Michelle in a juicy sort of way.

"Michelle, come back to me, the guy almost ran me over trying to park his car because he was running late too. All he said was, 'Sorry,' and ran inside the building. He didn't ask if I was okay or anything."

"Is that right?" said Michelle in her mocking tone, which at this point Sue missed, as she was telling her story with such enthusiasm.

"Yes, that's right," answered Sue as she felt her anger level rising. "And then, he had the audacity to be in my

Marine Science Class."

"Uh-Uh! Your two favorite subjects?! The beach and science? Just who does he think he is?" Michelle paused for a breath. "Let me ask you something,..."

"What?" replied Sue.

"What does he drive?" said Michelle, in all seriousness.

Sue sighed and then answered, "A Toyota Yaris"

"And my case is closed."

Chapter 5

The next day was Wednesday, and Sue thought about how she looked forward to going to church with Brady. Well, not with Brady, but to the same church, she reminded herself. She was eager to meet some of God's people. Brady had asked her in English if she could drive tonight because he was low on gas. Since Sue had been saving her gas, this was no problem. They agreed that they would meet at the Greasy Spoon for supper, and they would ride to church from there. Brady had ridden to school with his neighbor, and Justin had agreed to take him home after church. She suddenly found herself amazed at how much she and Brady ate at the Greasy Spoon and at how much she enjoyed his company. They ate there for breakfast, lunch, and dinner just about every day! She wondered how closely related independence was to loneliness. She thanked God right then and there for the friend that He had sent her way. Sue still felt independent, but now, she couldn't really see her life without Brady. He had become a regular fixture in her world, and she was glad that he was!

Brady navigated Sue as she drove, and they arrived at the Sunset Community Church at about ten minutes after seven, for the seven-thirty service. Brady introduced Sue to Pastor Rhodes, his wife Patricia, and their son, Justin, Brady's friend. The service was great. Pastor Rhodes brought the message as sort of a welcoming to all of the new college students there that night. Sue was surprised at the number of people that she recognized from the campus. Pastor Rhodes took his message from II Corinthians 5:17, *"Therefore if any man be in Christ, he is a new creature: old things are passed away; behold, all things are become new."* He preached this firstly to sinners, so that they would see their need to accept Jesus as their Saviour. Jesus is able to make all things new. Then he talked about New Beginnings from I John 1:9, *"If we confess our sins, he is faithful and just to forgive us our sins, and to cleanse us from all unrighteousness."* He reminded them that Jesus is there every day, ready to forgive their sins and re-make them, like a broken piece of pottery. He can re-shape them when we've sinned and become broken. He challenged all of the new college students to see this new school year as an opportunity for Jesus to remake them-spiritually, academically, and personally. Sue then remembered Cal. She silently prayed in her heart that Jesus would re-make him and help him move on. She also thought about Brady, her new-found friend. She thanked God for placing him here to be a constant reminder of how He will also take care of us, just as He said in His Word, *"...I will never leave thee, nor forsake thee."*

After the service, Sue thanked the Pastor for the message and told Brady that she'd see him tomorrow. She drove back to the dorm and climbed the stairs to her room. As she opened the door, she noticed that Marissa was not there, as usual. She took a moment right then and there to pray for her. "Lord," Sue prayed, "I don't know what her need is, but Lord, I know that You can fill it. Please have Your Will done. Amen"

Sue then dressed for bed and laid down. She tried to sleep, but God kept bringing someone else to her mind- the Yaris guy. Maybe Sue was being too harsh. Maybe he was having a bad day. Maybe he needed Jesus too. As much as she didn't want to, she knew that she needed to ask God's forgiveness for being so judgmental, and that she needed to pray for him too. These were Sue's last thoughts as she drifted off to sleep.

*****

As Brady entered his small apartment, he felt his cell phone vibrate. He checked the ID that saw that it was his friend, Justin, Pastor Rhodes' son. "Hey, J! What's up?"

answered Brady.

"Hey, Bro." began Justin. "I was just wondering..." he began.

"Yeah?" asked Brady, as he pretty much had an idea about what Justin was asking about.

"The girl you brought to church tonight. Are y'all like exclusive, or what? What's the deal?" asked Justin.

"I knew that you'd be calling me tonight: I noticed how you were sooo friendly at church," retorted Brady.

"Now, you know, I'm friendly to everyone! It's just my nature!" rebounded Justin with a laugh. "Now, back to the matter at hand. Is she spoken for?"

"Her name is Sue, as opposed to 'she', remember? She's really focused on her education right now. She's going to be the first graduate from her family, and I don't think that she's looking for anything right now. Plus, she's just gotten out of a serious relationship from back home, and she's probably not ready to move on yet. The education is probably a good distraction for her," answered Brady, as if he was trying to convince himself.

"Bro, if you've called dibs, that's all you had to say!" said Justin with a laugh.

"That's not what I said at all!" replied a defensive Brady.

"Well, it sounds to me like you've gotten pretty cozy with her. You know all about her break-up and what-not."

"Look, the only reason that I happen to know about that is because I walked up on it in the commons garden at our high school. The guy looked like he was about to get rough, and I stepped in-that's all."

"So, you're already her knight in shining armor!" teased Justin.

"Please! A girl like that wouldn't give me the time of day. She's..." Brady paused.

"Oh, I totally get it. But what I need to know from you is, is she off limits?" asked Justin as he cut to the chase.

Brady sat in silence, carefully deliberating his response. How could he say that she was off limits? "Look, she's her own woman. Who am I to speak for her?"

"Off limits it is, my friend. That's all you had to say. There's no need to get all philosophical on me!" Justin scoffed.

"What do you mean? I didn't say…" Brady began.

"Oh, you don't know how loud you did say it, brother! Don't worry! From here on out, I will consider Sue spoken for," said Justin as he hung up, rather abruptly.

Brady wondered. *'Have I alluded to anyone that I might be attracted to Sue? I wonder if she thinks so? And if I have, I wonder if she might feel the same way? Dear Lord, she is so beautiful- on the inside and out-and I know that there are no coincidences with You. Did you bring Sue here for me?'*

*****

The weeks passed on, and Sue was adjusting well to her new found freedom and independence. Brady had turned out to be a great new friend, even though she found it strange-having a friend that was a boy, but not having a 'boyfriend'. Maybe she was growing a little. Whatever the case, Sue was enjoying being on her own and her new college life.

It was time for the Marine Science class to begin their first lab project. The class would meet at the lab today and select partners for the project. Sue found a lab table in the front of the class, a place that everyone else seemed to avoid. This made Sue very happy, since Marine Science was her favorite subject, and she really didn't want to work with anyone else. Then she was immediately smitten in her heart. *'How selfish of me.'* she thought. *'Forgive me, Lord.'*

Just as she had uttered the words to herself, 'Mr. Yaris' came rushing in, late as usual, at the last minute. Professor Delaney was just about to close the door. "Mr. Dolen," the professor began, "Your tardiness has earned you a seat right here in the front. Enjoy." Sue's eyes widened as Professor Delaney pointed to her lab table, which had the only empty seat in the room. *'Oh, dear Lord'*, Sue thought to herself, *'What are You doing to me?'* She again felt smitten. *'I'm sorry, Lord. I'm such a mess, please help me,'* she silently prayed.

The class went on, and Sue and 'Mr. Yaris' got their project assignments. At the end of class, the man turned to Sue. "Hi, I'm Jason Dolen. Sorry to have to be your partner like this. I couldn't find the lab. Look, we should probably exchange numbers or something so that we can work on this project. I really don't need to foul this up. I'm graduating this year, and I was only missing this one science credit that I needed. I figured that this one would be easy." Jason seemed to ramble worse than Sue did!

Sue's head reeled at what he was asking for; her disdain for him was beginning to grow. She didn't want him sitting in that chair, and she definitely didn't want to give him her number, but she did. "It seems to me like you might need to plan a little better," she replied as she handed him the slip of paper with her number written on it.

"Excuse me?" Jason said, as he raised his eyebrows.

"You're late just about everywhere you go. I can tell by the way you park, and you didn't plan your courses very well or else you wouldn't be here in this lower level science class," Sue explained. She recalled how silly she must have looked, crawling through the passenger side of her own car because of the way he had parked.

"For your information, I took all of the higher level courses that I needed for my engineering degree, and I thought that I'd actually enjoy this 'lower level' class. I was hoping that it'd be easier so that I could focus on finding a job, and why am I telling you this...like you matter..." Jason said as he stood and went to Professor Delaney. "Hey Prof, can't I switch partners or something, I can't work with her."

Sue stood and came right behind him. "And I can't

work with him!" she exclaimed.

"Well, now, it seems we have a predicament on our hands, don't we. I'm sorry, but there are no changes. You'll just have to learn to 'swim together in this school!'" said Professor Delaney as he walked out, laughing at his fishy Marine pun.

Jason dropped his head, and then turned and looked at Sue. "Okay, look-I don't like this anymore than you do, but it looks like we're in this for the long haul. We'll just try to grin and bear it because we both need this grade. Deal?"

"Deal. When do you want to get together to work on this? Here's the lab schedule sheet," said Sue as she walked toward the clipboard hanging on the wall.

"It looks like tomorrow at seven o'clock is free; how about that?" Jason asked.

"That's fine with me," Sue replied.

"Fine," said Jason as he turned and walked out of the lab.

"I can't believe it," Sue said in repulsion. "He did it again! He didn't say 'Goodbye,' 'kiss my grits,' or anything! Lord, be merciful!" and with that she grabbed her backpack and headed out of the door.

*****

Every step seemed heavier, and the day crept along as Sue dreaded the evening that she would spend tonight in the Science Lab. She couldn't believe that she would have to pass up a Youth activity at church for the lab project, and especially with him, Jason Dolen- 'Mr. Rude.' She really needed grace today. Finally, seven o'clock came. Sue was there in the lab, but no Jason. *'Shocker!'* Sue thought to herself as she checked the time on her cell phone. Jason finally moseyed in at about ten minutes past seven.

"Don't even say it!" Jason blurted out as he threw his backpack down on the ground.

"Wasn't gonna..." replied Sue as she turned to the handouts about their project.

"Well, I've been reading over this material..." Jason began.

"*You've been reading*?" prodded Sue.

"Yes, I've been reading. Someone told me that I should plan a little better, as I recall. I thought I might try it." Jason answered.

Sue was taken by surprise, and even felt a little bit embarrassed at her comments yesterday. "...okay...well let's start here, with the Brine Shrimp. The handouts say that they exhibit bioluminescent properties."

"So, they glow in the dark." said Jason.

"Yes, but I think that they have to be crushed to release the bacteria that causes the bioluminescence," Sue stated as she continued to peruse the handouts.

"How do we do that?" asked Jason.

"Well, we can add a little distilled water and mash them out. Hand me that mortar and pestle from over on that counter, if you don't mind," said Sue.

"The what?" he asked.

"The little porcelain bowl and stick over there?" she answered in obvious irritation.

"Okay," said Jason as he walked over and brought Sue the porcelain bowl and crushing tool. "Do you need this bottle of water too?"

"Yes, please," answered Sue as she began to grind the shrimp.

"Here you go," said Jason, as he poured some of the distilled water into the bowl. "Well, if they're glowing, I can't see it."

"Well, I know that's what I read?!" answered Sue disappointedly.

"Hey, I'll go turn the lights off, and we'll really see if it worked," Jason suggested as he jumped up to turn off the lights.

The darkness did the trick! The shrimp were emitting a very fluorescent blue glow. As Jason was walking back to the lab table, he suddenly tripped over his backpack and fell right on top of Sue, nearly missing the porcelain bowl.

"OW!" shouted Sue as she struggled beneath the weight of Jason; he wasn't a weakling!

"Oh, cool! They are glowing," said Jason, as he stared at the bowl. Sue was still struggling to get up from underneath him. Suddenly the lights came back on; it was Professor Delaney.

"What's going on here? What's all this ruckus?" he asked with a stern look on his face.

"OH! This is not what it looks like!" pleaded Jason, as he regained himself and stood up.

"It certainly isn't!" added Sue as she quickly stood up herself.

"I expected you two to make things work, and it looks like you didn't waste any time." chuckled the professor as he walked off.

Jason turned and looked at Sue. "I'm so sorry!"

"That's all you ever take time to say to me is, 'you're sorry'!" Sue erupted.

"What are you talking about?" asked Jason in an exasperated tone.

"First you blocked me in with your stupid little Toyota when you parked on the first day that I arrived here…I had to crawl through the passenger side of my car to even go anywhere…" Sue said as she began to move towards him wagging her finger in his face. "Then, you almost ran me over while you were parking to come to the first day of this class because you were running late as usual…" she lectured.

"You should've moved out of the way…" interrupted Jason as he began moving closer to Sue.

"Oh, and then you have the gall to end up sitting at

my lab table because you were late again? Late, late, late-don't you even care about the class? Don't you care about anything but yourself?" she continued.

"I can't stand you..." Jason yelled at her, almost directly in her face.

"And I absolutely loathe you..." Sue shouted, but was cut off when Jason grabbed her by the arms and kissed her quickly and forcefully.

Sue pulled away in shock. The two of them backed away from one another. Sue grabbed her backpack and ran out of the lab, leaving Jason standing there, in bewilderment. Sue stormed back towards her dorm, reeling from what had just happened. *'Who does he think he is?'* she muttered to herself. *'He can clean up that mess-there's no way that I'm going back there to clean it up. The sheer nerve of him, just up and kissing me like that when I absolutely hate him! I hate his blonde hair. I detest his blue eyes and I really don't care for how... his shoulders are...broad... and cut.'* Then it occurred to her. When had she taken the time to notice these things? Sue dismissed those thoughts promptly and felt more than a little disgusted at herself for thinking them. Then she thought, *'I'll wait about ten more minutes and then go back to the lab. If that mess isn't cleaned up in the lab, Delaney will have our hides for sure. I know he hasn't stayed around to do any actual work!'*

So, Sue waited ten more minutes at the fountain in the courtyard in front of her dorm, and then she returned to the science lab. As she was approaching the door, she noticed that the light was turned off. She quickly flipped the switch on and saw that the lab table was indeed clean; everything had been returned to its place. "Oh, great," Sue thought out loud. "Delaney's already cleaned it up and, boy, are we in for it on Thursday."

"Cease from anger, and forsake wrath: fret not thyself in any wise to do evil."

Psalm 37:8

Chapter 6

Sue dreaded the next Marine Science class, even more than she had dreaded the lab session. This was her favorite class, and now Jason had proficiently succeeded in getting her into trouble with the professor. Sue walked in and took her seat on the front row of the lecture hall. She kept her head down, hoping not to exchange glances with Jason when he came in, but she had no such luck. Jason came in and they locked glances. Sue didn't show any expression at all, and Jason continued on up the stairs to the fifth row. Why should she give him the benefit of a smile? She had nothing to smile about. She was about to get raked over the coals, and it was all his fault; then he had the nerve to kiss her? Oh, Sue could feel the anger rising, and she could feel her cheeks becoming flushed. Then, her heart fell into her stomach-Professor Delaney walked in. He cast a glance at Sue, and then scanned the room for Jason and cast a glance at him. He simply raised his eyebrows under his black-rimmed glasses and turned back to the dry-erase board. Sue was bewildered, and then she realized, he's waiting until after class. Oh! An hour and fifteen minutes more of torture before he would drop the bomb. *'Why, Lord, Why?'* Sue thought to herself.

Finally, the class was over, and Sue prepared herself for the worst. Then, Professor Delaney simply picked up his briefcase and walked out of class. Sue sat there in her seat and waited a few seconds, to see if he was coming back. After the entire class had exited the room, she realized that he wasn't coming back, but Jason had walked up to her seat. She immediately stood up, as she was not going to be vulnerable to him again.

"Sue, about last night in the lab…well, you're welcome." said Jason sheepishly.

" 'You're welcome?' That's all you have to say to me is 'you're welcome?'" shouted Sue as she stormed out of the door.

Jason followed her. "Well, it's a change from 'I'm sorry'!"

"What should I be so welcomed for? My ruined reputation with my science professor or for that wonderful little gift you gave me?"

"Ruined reputation? I had no idea that I was such a sorry catch!" shouted Jason.

"Well, for starters, I haven't caught you. 'Hello'!-I wasn't even fishing! And secondly, you caused Professor Delaney to have to clean up our mess in the lab."

"What are you talking about? I cleaned up the lab! Delaney was long gone, but I knew better than to leave it! You know what, never mind. I don't need this!" said Jason as he stormed off.

Sue suddenly felt about two inches high. Why couldn't she have a civilized conversation with this man, and why did he get under her skin so? She suddenly remembered what he had said to her last night in the lab-'someone told me that I should plan a little better.' He had listened to her comments and actually took them to heart. He was also on time for class today. Maybe he was trying, and maybe she was shooting him down like a mallard in January.

Just then, her cell phone rang. It was Brady. "Hey-where are you?"

"Huh? Oh! Brady, I totally forgot. I'm on the way." answered Sue as she took off running for the Greasy Spoon. She had forgotten during her heated discussion that she was supposed to meet Brady for lunch. She arrived at their usual table, sliding into her seat.

"Wow, I've never seen you so rushed, Sue. Is everything okay?" asked Brady.

"No-I mean Yes; everything's fine." answered an out of breath Sue.

"I ordered for you. Barbecue Chicken Nachos,

right?" Brady asked.

"How'd you know?" asked Sue.

"I pay attention. Like to this guy over there that has followed you in here; and it looks like he's waiting outside for you. You wanna talk about it?" asked Brady, as he hoped she'd explain.

"Well, he's my lab partner, and, well, we've got some things to work out," answered Sue. She wished Brady wouldn't ask for any more details, but she had no such luck.

"Are you sure that's all?" Brady probed. For his own peace of mind, he really needed to know more about the situation.

"Yes, I'm sure. Thanks though," replied Sue, as the waiter brought their plates. "I really appreciate your being there and looking out for me and all."

"It's my honor and privilege to do so, Miss Haybert," answered Brady as he bowed his head in a chivalrous acknowledgment. Brady cast another glance outside and noticed that the guy, Jason, was still there. He then returned his attention to Sue as she smiled. They bowed their heads for the blessing, which Brady prayed, and then they enjoyed their lunch.

They carried on small talk while they ate, but Brady kept wondering in the back of his mind, *'What is going on with these two? And why is it bothering me so much? Is it You, Lord? What are You showing me?'* He simply shook it off and tried to change the subject.

"Let's shoot some pool over at the rec room. Are you game?" asked Brady.

"Oh, I got game! You're on!" said Sue cheerfully as she finished her drink. "Let's go."

Brady and Sue walked over to the recreational area in the Student Union building and started their game of billiards. Brady noticed that Jason had followed them there as well. He was sitting in a chair, reading from his Marine Science book. Jason kept glancing towards Sue, and Sue kept catching those glances. Finally, Brady couldn't stand it anymore. "Look, Sue, it's obvious that your lab partner wants to talk to you. Would you please go over there and talk to him? I can't take much more of the googley eyes between you AND him." Sue quickly filled Brady in on the situation, leaving out the fact that Jason had kissed her.

After a moment of honest deliberation, Brady began, "Well, maybe you're not giving him a fair shake, Sue. You remember how Pastor preached about new beginnings? It seems an awful shame that Jesus gives us new beginnings every day, and you won't even give this guy one. Maybe he's a part of God's Plan for you, Sue. Maybe he needs Jesus. You'll never know until you go talk to him!"

Sue knew deep down that Brady was right. "Brady, how do you always do this? You always have the most spiritual advice! Okay, I'll go talk to him. Thanks for the game." Sue placed her cue back on the rack and headed toward Jason.

As Sue walked away from Brady, he felt a strange sensation in the pit of his stomach. He didn't like what he was seeing. But why? He knew what he was telling Susan was the truth, but why did he resent it so much? Was he being selfish? Did he actually want Sue for himself? *'No,'* thought Brady, *'I have to see this through Your Eyes, Lord. Please help me,'* With that thought, Brady grabbed his backpack and left the building.

Jason, seeing Sue's approach, sat up at full attention. "Sue, I..." started Jason, as he was interrupted by Sue.

"Let's start over. Hi, I'm Susan Haybert, and you are?" asked Sue with a smile.

"I'm Jason Dolen, and I am very pleased to meet you," Jason said as he extended his hand to her with a smile. "I would like to get to know you a little better, Miss Haybert. Could I accompany you somewhere?"

Sue, playing along with this formal game answered, "Why, yes, Mr. Dolen. I have the perfect place for you to accompany me. Please do me the honor of accompanying me to church this Sunday."

The request seemed to take Jason by surprise, and he temporarily dropped the formalities. "Church? I haven't been to church since I was a little kid! Sure, I'll go to church with you."

"Very well, then Mr. Dolen, you may pick me up at nine-thirty Sunday morning-Hines Hall-I'll be waiting in the foyer for you," responded Sue. She shook his hand and left for her dorm.

Sue felt like a burden had lifted. She was beginning to see this 'thing' with Jason in a new light, and it was all thanks to Brady. *'Where was Brady?'* Sue thought, as she took a quick look around. *'He must have gone on to work,'* she decided as she continued walking towards her dorm. Her thoughts were interrupted by her cell phone.

"Hi, Michelle. How's it going?" Sue answered.

"Girl, how'd you know it was me?" Michelle asked, temporarily forgetting about the caller ID. "Listen, I can't decide what dress to buy for the church Christmas Banquet. Can you help me pick it out?"

"Now how can I do that when I am three hours away?" exclaimed Sue.

"You might be three hours away, but I'm not!" shouted Michelle.

Sue turned around quickly, and saw Michelle standing in the courtyard in front of the dorm. "AHH!" they both yelled, as they ran towards each other in a girlfriends' hug! "What are you doing here?"

"Daddy had to make a quick run for his logistics company. Some package had to be delivered 'today,'" she said as she used her air quotation marks and rolled her eyes. "So he said that I could ride along. He's taking a nap in the truck, so I only have a little while. Let's go do something!"

"Great, I'll show you around!" said Sue. She grabbed her friend by the arm and led her towards the student union building.

"Where's Brady?" Michelle inquired.

"Oh, I think he had to go to work. But listen, I've got something to tell you. Please don't laugh or scream or anything..."

"Oh, girl, whatcha done went and done?" said Michelle with a grimace.

"I asked 'Yaris' man on, sort of, well, a date," said Sue, as she threw her arms over her head to shield herself from Michelle's swats.

"Girl, what I done tole' you! You messin' up! An ole' 'Yota man. That ain't even American!" said Michelle in her attitude tone.

"I know, I know, but look, Brady and I talked about it, and we decided that it would be the Christian thing to do. It's only a date to go to church on Sunday. I'm only trying to give him a fair chance you know, not judging him and all..."

"Um-Hum. Brady said! Brady done become your new BFF?" said Michelle with a little neck-roll.

"No, now you know! It's different with Brady. You know you my girl!" said Sue as she grabbed Michelle's neck in a hug!

"Um-Hum-You know that's right! Just lemme know how it goes, alright?" begged Michelle with genuine concern in her eyes. Michelle had known Sue since they were little. They both went to church together and had been saved at an early age. Michelle played around, a lot, but when push came to shove, Jesus always came first. Michelle could sense something uneasy about the situation, and she was almost worried. "You promise?"

"Alright, I promise," said Sue as the two girls walked off arm in arm.

"Now, where is Brady, again?" Michelle asked.

"I told you, I think that he's already left for work. We had lunch together and then played a round of billiards..." explained Sue.

"Um. Billiards. Listen atcha usin' all those big college words now. My little pea brain just cain't process all that," answered Michelle in her countrified tone.

"Now-would you just stop that! You are just as smart as the next girl! Why, I don't ever think that I've heard you speak properly!" teased Sue.

"But, if I did speak 'properly', would I still be Michelle?" she asked.

"No, I guess not. Anyways, we 'shot a game of pool' is that better?"

"Much betta, thank ya!" answered Michelle with a laugh. "Now, how could you go and ask Mr. Rude 'Yota man on a date, and not ask fine-looking Brady out?"

"Chelly-girl! I've already told you; Brady and I are just friends. I'm not looking for a relationship right now."

"Well, aren't you going on a date with this terrible guy?" rebutted Michelle.

"It's just church. I'm just doing the right thing, you know. Don't worry! I'm not gonna fall for him."

"Famous last words. So please tell me that this guy is ugly?!" begged Michelle.

"No, actually he's kinda cute. He's blonde, great build, deep blue eyes..."

"But he drives a Toyota! Girl, he ain't nothin' but trouble!"

"Look he's just a senior who's taking Marine Science with me and ended up being my partner. I'm not interested, really."

"Um-hum. We'll see. Just please promise me you won't do anything stupid," asked Michelle.

"Did Mama send you up here to spy on me?" asked a suspicious Sue.

"No! I ain't no rat! You oughta know me better than that. I'm just worried about ya, that's all. I don't trust no Toyota driver, I don't care what he looks like. You'd better behave!" admonished Michelle as she and Sue arrived at

Sue's Ford Focus. "Now-show me the place that always makes me feel better-the mall!"

Chapter 7

Sunday rolled around, and Sue found herself ready bright and early with a strange sort of anticipation. She had no idea where this new 'relationship' was going, and she didn't quite know if she wanted it to go anywhere.

"Mari, how do I look in this?" asked Sue.

"Rather, stiff! Just kidding! Look, you've gotta learn to loosen up a little. Have a little fun! Life is too short to be so boring, no offense," answered Mari in her usual tone. "Listen, I just completed my sports trainer courses, and I'm not going to be here as much. I will be traveling with the basketball team taking care of the injuries and whatever else they need. I just wanted to give you a heads up."

"Thanks. That will be great experience and credit towards your physical therapy degree!"

"And, I'll get to go to all of the games for free! You can't beat that! Hey listen, since you'll have an extra bed in here, you ought to see if the dorm mom would let your friend come up and spend a weekend here. You guys could chalk it up to recruitment." suggested Mari.

"That's not a bad idea. I'll talk to her soon. Just let me know you're schedule!" said Sue as she picked up her Bible and purse. "Thanks! Well, I've gotta run. Jason will be here soon. Are you sure you don't want to come too?" asked Sue.

"No, you go ahead. I've got plenty to do here. Have a great day!" said Mari as Sue left for the foyer.

"You too," called Sue from the stairwell.

Sue ran downstairs, afraid that Jason would beat her there. That absolutely could not happen; he was the one that was always late not her. But today, he'd show up an hour early just for spite. Why did she even care, and why did she feel like she was about to be sick?

Just then there was a knock at the door. It was Jason. Not early, but right on time. The two exchanged 'hellos' and

Jason showed her to the car. It was silence until Jason pulled out onto the highway. "You look nice today, Sue."

"Thanks," Sue said with a smile. "I'm glad you decided to come with me today."

"I'm glad you gave me a second chance. I really am a nice guy; I've just been under a lot of stress lately. I appreciate your understanding. Besides, I haven't been in church since I was smaller. I used to ride a bus to this church; I don't even remember the name of it, but the people there were really nice." Jason recalled.

"Well, the people here are really nice too; there are a lot of people from campus that go here. The Sunday school classes are split, male and female though; you can go with Brady if that's that okay?"

"Your watchdog? That's no problem. He seems pretty harmless," Jason joked.

"My watchdog? What do you mean by that?" Sue asked.

"You're always eatin' lunch with the guy, and this past Friday, when I followed you to the Greasy Spoon, he looked like he wanted to hurt me," Jason replied with a laugh.

"You're imagining things. Brady is a good friend of mine from my church back home. That's all. We spend time together because we have those things in common. How do you know that we eat lunch together all of the time?"

"Well, you know, I've seen you around that's all. So, there's no one else that I need to worry about?" Jason asked.

Sue realized where he was going with that question. "No. There's no one else." This put a new spin on the entire day. How could he have been so rude, but yet be interested in her? They were pretty heated, but in anger, she thought when he grabbed her and kissed her in the lab that night. Was this a purely physical attraction? Sue guessed that time would tell and until then she would just enjoy the ride. But at the same time, Sue was disappointed that she couldn't stick to her plan of avoiding men at all costs. But who could tell when Mr. Right would appear? She couldn't foresee the future! So, Sue decided that she would take everything one day at a time.

The couple arrived at church, where Brady was waiting for Sue and was quite shocked to see that she had arrived there with Jason. He didn't really expect Jason to accept Sue's invitation to church. Jason just looked like trouble to him. As soon as he thought it, he immediately felt guilty again. *"Lord, if this is your plan for Sue, please help me to step out of the way,"* he thought to himself as they approached him on the church steps. Brady extended his hand to Jason. "Good morning. It's good to see you here ..."

"Jason. Jason Dolen," he answered.

"Jason. It's good to put a name to a face," answered Brady.

"I'll bet it is," Jason said sarcastically.

Sue cleared her throat in order to break the growing tension. "Brady, can you show Jason to class, it being his first time and all?"

"Sure. Right this way. We'll see you in a little while," said Brady as he turned toward the church building.

"See you later," Jason told Susan with a million dollar smile, which Sue returned as she turned away to go to her class.

Brady led Jason through the hallway down to a small classroom just off of the sanctuary. "So, have you ever been to church before, Jason?"

"Yes, just when I was a child though," he responded, as if only to satisfy Brady. He really hoped that he wouldn't ask him too many more questions.

"Have you ever asked Jesus to save you?" Brady asked.

"Actually, I did. There was a youth meeting one time. I guess I was about twelve. The bus came around to pick us up, and I had nothing better to do, so I went. The speaker told about me about Jesus and the cross. At the end of the meeting, he asked that if there was anyone that wanted to go to Heaven and be with Jesus when we died that we should come down front, and so I did. Someone came by and prayed with me, and I signed a card. That's all I remember. My parents divorced, and my mom and I moved away, and I haven't been back to church since."

"Wow. Hopefully, you can grow in the Lord while you're here. You've made the best decision that anyone could ever make," said Brady.

"Yes, I believe that I have." Jason replied.

Brady sensed that Jason was referring to Susan. "You know, Jason, Sue is a really special girl."

Jason became a little cautious. "I know she is."

"I would hate it if anyone hurt her," Brady admonished.

"Well, I have no intention of doing that-are we agreed?" he offered.

"Agreed," said Brady as nodded his head.

*****

Meanwhile, in Sue's Sunday School class, her teacher Miss Christmas, was beginning to start the lesson when she had a special announcement. "Every fall, our class seems to grow with new college students from ACU. We welcome you, and we would like to invite you to our first class activity." Miss Christmas paused, as if to muster courage and strength for the somewhat uncomfortable subject on which she was about to speak. "Today's society is saturated with immoral behavior. It is more difficult for young people to maintain their purity today as there are pressures on every hand. Every fall, any member of this class who wishes to, can go with us to the Christian bookstore where we will purchase Purity Rings. There are several styles to choose from. Those who already have them are welcome to come along and enjoy the fellowship. After a luncheon we all meet back here, and pray, making a vow to God to save our purity for the mate that God has intended for us."

"Miss Christmas, I thought that couples gave each other purity rings?" asked one of the new college girls.

"Well, some couples do, but you don't have to be in a relationship with someone to make this commitment. And ladies it is important. This is a vow to the Lord God Almighty. It is a serious thing, and is not to be taken lightly. But I can tell you this, if you sincerely make this vow to God, he will give you the strength to help you keep your vow. You ladies pray about it, and if you are serious about this, meet us here at the church this Saturday at ten in the morning."

Sue thought to herself, *"This is a no brainer. I've always intended to save myself for my husband, and a ring would be a beautiful reminder of that, so, I'm in."* She was actually excited about the outing and looked forward to the coming weekend.

*****

After church, Jason and Sue went to the ACU cafeteria for lunch. "So, Jason, how did you like church?" asked Sue.

"It was pretty good. I enjoyed hearing you sing in the choir."

"How could you hear just me? Everyone was singing!" she asked with a laugh.

"You just really stand out. There could be a whole a crowd of people in a room, but I only see you," answered Jason with an inviting look on his face.

Sue blushed. She could tell that he was trying so hard, and it was working.

"Sue, would you please go out with me on Friday? Say, the basketball game and some dinner?" he asked.

"Sure. That sounds nice," Sue answered as the butterflies began to flutter in her stomach. She couldn't believe that she said, 'yes'. She had tried so hard to avoid getting involved with a man, but she just couldn't help herself.

The couple finished their meal, and Jason walked her back to the dorm. "I had a good day today," he said as he fidgeted with his keys.

"Me, too. I'm looking forward to Friday. I'll see you in class on Tuesday," Sue answered. She turned to go into the dorm.

"Tuesday," Jason said as he watched her every move back into the dorm.

Susan closed the door and lingered there for a few minutes. She peeked out of the sidelight and watched Jason drive away. "Hm," she thought to herself, "I wonder what Tuesday will be like."

*****

Before Sue knew it, Tuesday had come. She had made it to class before Jason, as usual. When he got there, their eyes locked, and he gave her that million dollar smile again, but then he took his normal place on the third row. Now, she was puzzled. There was an empty seat right there beside her, why didn't he take that one? She dared not turn around and let him know that she even noticed, or worse than that, she even cared that he didn't sit beside her; *"Oh, this is getting ridiculous,"* Sue thought to herself, *"We barely even know each other, and he's got me twisted all up inside!"* Class ended almost as quickly as it came. When the professor dismissed, Jason bounded down the steps as usual, giving Sue that million dollar smile again, and a quick head nod, and then simply left. Sue had returned the smile, but was somewhat perplexed. What kind of game was he playing with her? Was she really the kind of girl that was going to take the bait? She could say that she was smarter than that, but then she'd just be fooling herself.

Wednesday passed, and Thursday's class came around, but Jason was not there. Surely he didn't ditch a class just to play mind games?! Whatever the reason was, a mind game was definitely the result. Jason hadn't called or so much as said one word to her since their luncheon on Sunday, and Sue was becoming inclined to not make their Friday night game at all!

Friday rolled around, and Sue had spent most of the day studying. She watched the clock and wondered if she should stop to get ready. *"But get ready for what? To be stood up! No thanks!"* thought Sue as she put her books away. Just then the phone rang, and it was Jason, of course. "Hello," Sue answered, with just a hint of irritation in her voice.

"Hey, you! Are we still on for tonight?" asked Jason.

"I don't know? Are we?" Sue replied with her fury rising.

"Well, I can't imagine why we wouldn't be going? Can you?" he replied with a sickingly sweet tone.

"Well, considering we haven't spoken since Sunday, I wasn't sure what you had planned, sir."

"Nothing's changed for me. I'm still coming to pick you up at five o'clock to grab some dinner and then on to the game."

Sue felt her temper getting the best of her, and before she could stop herself, she replied, "Well, I think I'm busy tonight. We'll have to do it again later." No sooner than the words had left her mouth, she regretted them.

"No, you're not. I'll be by at five o'clock. See ya then," he replied, and with that he hung up.

"I know you did not just hang up on me?!" Sue thought out loud as she snapped her cell phone shut and threw it down on the bed. *'Does he really think that I'll be ready and waiting for him? Boy, does he have another think coming! I'll show him. It'll take the FBI to find me this afternoon.'*

Sue thought as she grabbed her purse and headed downstairs. She yanked the front door opened in her rage, and screamed, as Jason stood only inches from her face.

"Hello, beautiful!" he said, "Going somewhere?" he asked.

"Well, I did tell you that I had plans!" she quickly responded, with a bit of pride at her own quick wittiness.

"I know," he said, condescendingly, "You're plans are with me tonight."

"Oh, are they?" she replied as she tried to pass by him.

Jason blocked her every move. "Well, if they're not, that would certainly be a shame. I just happened to find this horse-drawn carriage, and, well, it sure would be a shame not to put it to good use. Besides, I love to see you angry. It just does something to me right here," he said, pointing to his heart.

Sue realized she had played right into the palm of his hand. Every mind game, the empty seat, all of the lack of communication was to draw out her rage. Inwardly, she was fuming, but at the same time, she wanted to cry! "How did you..."

"I know a guy! C'mon!" he said as he helped her into the buggy.

Jason had the driver take them on a tour of the historic district, and then let them off at a small bistro, not too many blocks from the arena where the game was to be played. They had a wonderful dinner-the best food that Sue had ever eaten.

When the two had finished eating, they had plenty of time to walk to the arena. Jason helped Sue with her jacket, and then placed his hand at the small of her back to guide her out of the door. She shuttered as she sensed the closeness between them; it was something she hadn't felt in a while, and something that she longed for again. As they walked down towards the arena, Jason told her about his father and how they became closer when he had gone to college. His father was an engineer and had several influential friends, hence the buggy ride. He also alluded to the enormous pressure of living up to his father's expectations and joining the family business. Sue listened intently, and she found herself gaining great respect for him as well as admiration.

Just before the arena, there was a small park with a gazebo and several trees. Jason took Sue by the hand and guided her into the garden. He found a cozy weeping willow tree and brought her beneath the cascading branches that were pruned specially, creating a private nook for such an occasion. Sue leaned against the tree as Jason moved in nearer. He took his hand and gently caressed her face. "The game will be so loud. Do we really wanna go?" he asked. Sue simply shook her head *'no'*. Jason's lips gently pressing against hers felt like warm velvet. The butterflies ran across her shoulders, and she felt herself shudder, only to be stilled by his strong arms. The moon was just beginning to rise, and a gentle breeze blew. The light shone against his sandy blonde hair and chiseled face as he continued to gingerly shower her with kisses. Then Sue let out a small giggle as it occurred to her-*"What would she tell Michelle?"*

*****

The next morning, Sue was at the church at ten a.m. to meet with the other members of her Sunday school class. After last night's date with Jason, Sue was more determined than ever that she would make her vow of purity to God. The young ladies all loaded the church van, and Miss Christmas drove them down to the Christian Bookstore. Sue was one of ten college girls who had decided to take this step for Christ.

Upon arriving at the store, Miss Christmas asked the girls to all bow their heads. She began to pray, "Dear Lord, thank you for being such a wonderful Lord and Saviour to us. Thank you for each one of these girls that has come out this morning to take a stand for right in today's world. Please guide them as they select the ring that would be the most honoring to you, Dear Lord. It is in Your Name we pray, Amen."

After a hearty 'amen' from Sue and the other nine ladies on the van, they began to file out of the van and into the store. After browsing through the Southern Gospel CD's, Sue finally found the rack with the purity rings. There were several beautiful designs that caught Sue's eye. After much browsing, Sue decided on the Gold Un-blossomed rose design. It was a thin band of gold, with an unopened rose that came 'growing' out of the band. The words 'love waits' were inscribed inside the band.

After purchasing her ring along with Whisnant's CD and a McKamey's CD, Sue joined the other young ladies for a luncheon at McCallister's Deli. Sue selected a super spud, a loaded baked potato complete with turkey, ham, cheese and black olives; no meal at McCallister's would be complete without their famous sweet tea and a Heath Bar Cookie! The young ladies spent more than an hour enjoying their meal and fellowshipping. After they became afraid that the servers were going to run them out, they decided to go back to the church for a time of prayer.

The young ladies filed in to the sanctuary with Miss Christmas taking her place at the front near the altar. "Ladies, we've had a wonderful time of fun and fellowship today around God's people, and we are so thankful for that. Now it's time to get serious with God. We know the pressures that face us on every hand in regards to our purity…" As she spoke, Sue remembered the date that she and Jason shared the night before, and she was quickly awakened to how difficult keeping this vow could be. Jason had in no way pressured her towards that end, but she realized how powerless she felt in his arms, and even though she enjoyed being there, she knew that she would have to keep her guard up, to keep her Bible read, and stay 'prayed up' for the strength of the Lord.

Miss Christmas continued. "Ladies, if you are determined to make this vow before God, you may come forward at any time and kneel down here to pray." At the very ending of her words, several ladies got up and made their way down to the altar. Sue placed the gold ring on her finger and fell right in line. She knew that she would have no strength when it came down to it. She needed the Lord to sustain her, and she knew that He was faithful to do just that.

"Flee fornication. Every sin that a man doeth is without the body; but he that committeth fornication sinneth against his own body. What? know ye not that your body is the temple of the Holy Ghost which is in you, which ye have of God, and ye are not your own? For ye are bought with a price: therefore glorify God in your body, and in your spirit, which are God's."

1 Corinthians 6:18-20

Chapter 8

The weeks passed on, and Jason and Sue were inseparable. They went everywhere together, including church. This made Brady a little jealous and resentful, even though he didn't show his feelings to Sue.

Before Sue knew it, exams were upon them. She didn't know what to expect, and was literally spazzing out about it! Jason invited Sue out on a study date to go over the study guide for their Marine Science class. They went over the paperwork once or twice, but since Jason had taken her to the park to study, where their favorite weeping willow tree stood, they didn't get much studying done at all.

The night before the English exam, Sue felt herself drawing a blank about her composition for Professor Roget's class. He had allowed Sue to re-read a book that she had read in high school. She had explained that it was her favorite book, and even though she had read the book her Freshman year in Mrs. Eargle's English I class, she really wanted to take another look at it through more experienced eyes. The professor thought that her request had showed maturity and a quality that 'so may young people were lacking these days.' He agreed with the utmost excitement. But now, Sue felt like she was going to end up disappointing him on the exam. Brady had also read this same book in high school, just in another one of Mrs. Eargle's classes, so she opted to call Brady for some help.

"Hey, Brady. I hope that I'm not waking you up, am I?" asked Sue as she noticed that she was calling a little late.

"No, not really. I think that I fell asleep under this book I was reading. How can I help you tonight?" he asked.

"You know how Roget said that I could do my exam composition on that book from Mrs. Eargle's class, right? Do you remember much about the book?" Sue began.

"Yeah, I do remember it pretty good, but I can do even better than that. My grandma had a copy of the old black and white movie that Alfred Hitchcock produced, she was a big Hitchcock fan! You wanna watch it?" Brady offered.

"It's so late! What do you have in mind?" she asked.

"Well, the library has extended its hours to midnight this week for those 'last minute' crammers who need to study for exams. I can meet you over there with the movie, and we can watch it together. How does that sound?"

"You're a life saver! Thanks, Brady! I'll meet you there in thirty minutes."

"Why so long? Your dorm is only a couple of minutes walk away from the library?" Brady asked.

"Because; I was already dressed for bed. I've can't go out looking like this!" answered Sue as she looked down at her Hello Kitty pajamas and bunny slippers.

"Oh, you look good in anything. Just come on! I'm sure that there won't be that many people there. We'll grab one of the study rooms, and a TV; just come on! We don't have that much time to spare!"

"Okay, but I am changing my bunny slippers."

"No, keep the bunnies. That will make the evening just right!" said Brady through a hearty dose of laughter.

"Okay, Mr. Smartie-pants! Just for that, I'll keep the bunnies, and then you can be the one who's embarrassed!"

"I'd never be embarrassed to be seen with you-not even in a brown flour sack!" Brady replied as he began to regain his composure.

"Alright, country boy. Let me go, so that I can meet you there, or otherwise we're never gonna make it! Bye!" Sue said as she flipped her phone shut and grabbed her backpack. She bounded down the stairs, and almost slipped, as the bunny slippers didn't have good grip! She peeked her head out of the door of Hines Hall and took a good look around. It was about 9:45, and there were not many people about. So out of the door she crept and made her way to the library. *'I'd better not have to wait on him. I don't want anyone to see me like this!'* She thought to herself. Just as the thoughts left her, Brady rounded the corner. "How'd you get here so quickly?" she asked.

"Well, when you called, I just grabbed the movie and started walking this way. I knew you needed my help, so off I went! I figured the worst thing that could happen was that you wouldn't want to come out this late, and then I figured that I would enjoy the walk back to my apartment. I really love to walk. The fresh air's good for the soul," Brady explained as he opened the doors for Sue. "And by the way, the bunnies are so…YOU!"

"Yeah, yeah, yeah," Sue answered sarcastically. "Thanks for meeting me here, Brady. I really appreciate it."

"Like I told you, anytime you need me for anything, you only need to call. Now, there's an empty study room over there; you 'scurry' over there little bunny, and I'll get the TV stand." Sue rolled her eyes, but did just as Brady had told her, desperately looking around, making sure that no one was looking at her.

It didn't take long for Brady to bring in the TV cart with the VHS player. He checked his watch-10:00 dead on. So he knew that they would have enough time to watch the entire movie, and then they'd have plenty of time to talk about it. He popped in the tape and switched off the light. The small room glowed with the fluorescent blues that the TV emitted as they watched the movie together.

Brady wished that this was a real date and not an exam-cramming study meeting. He knew that Sue was really into Jason, and he had tried praying and talking to God about his feelings, but when it came to Sue, Brady was all heart. He wished that he had not been so hesitant, and that he would've asked her out first, but their friendship was going so good that he really didn't feel like it was the right time to ask. He wasn't even sure if it was God's will that he date Sue. He knew that he couldn't always trust his own feelings; but right now, he knew that there was nowhere else that he'd rather be than sitting right there with her.

As Sue leaned back in the chair while she sat and watched the movie, she could feel his eyes watching her, and a few times, she thought that she caught him, but he quickly turned away. *'He must be very bored-poor Brady. I do wish he could find someone like I've found my Jason,'* Sue thought to herself. *'He is such a good friend to me. He's always there when I need him.'* Quickly then, Sue turned her thoughts back to the video, so as not to waste the good deed that her friend had bestowed upon her.

The movie ended, and Sue was delighted. The story was one that she had enjoyed in high school, and Hitchcock's rendition of this tale had proved to be one of her new favorite classic videos. Brady reached up and turned off the TV and began rewinding the tape. Sue gazed down at her notes that she had been scribbling on a legal pad. The only final detail that Sue needed some help developing was that of the villainess of the story. She had burned down the English estate of the hero and heroine of the story, a rich Englishman and his new bride; *'But why?'* Sue wondered. Brady saw the perplexing look on her face, and inquired of it.

"What don't you understand?" he asked.

"Well, why did the housekeeper burn down the estate? She lost her life in the fire! She could have just left and never have come back. Surely, it wasn't worth her dying over?" replied Sue as she thought on the matter.

"It's simple, Sue. She didn't want them to be happy together. She went 'over the edge'. She had served the first lady of the house and was so endeared to her that she could not accept anyone else in that role. If her dear Mistress couldn't be there in that palace of a house enjoying the power and prestige that went along with it, then no one would enjoy it at all," answered Brady. "Some people always want what they can't have…" he said as he stopped and marveled at his own statement. Here he was pining over a girl that he couldn't have, and he wondered if that was indeed the main reason that he was pining over her-simply because she belonged to someone else, Jason.

"But, why not lash out at the new Mistress alone? Why not just take her life?" asked Sue.

"Well, because then the Master of the estate would still have his lovely English estate and all of the luxury that it held. She was attacking him personally by taking away the home that he loved, and in the same token taking away any future that he could have afforded any new wife that might have come along. No, the housekeeper attacked his heart-by taking out the one thing that would hurt the most people involved."

"But, she didn't kill the love. The master and his new bride simply went to another town and started over. She lost," rebutted Sue.

"But, it was never the same between them. They always shared the tragedy. They always had the dark cloud of memory looming over them."

"Wow, Brady. That's so…sad. Maybe the tragedy made them stronger! Made their love stronger?" Sue asked changing the tone.

"Maybe," Brady answered as he thought about the love that he felt for Sue. He realized that his emotions were more than just a man pining after forbidden fruit. He loved her for who she was, a beautiful, smart, Christian girl who always tried to look on the bright side and who was absolutely wonderful…bunny slippers and all.

*****

All of Sue's exams went well, and with their passing brought Christmas break and an opportunity for Sue and some others to go back home and visit with family and friends. But what Sue looked most forward to was introducing Jason to her parents; but to Michelle…not so much! Michelle had finally confessed that she had confidence in Sue's ability to select a good man, no matter what he drove!

Sue talked with Jason, and he agreed that they would offer to let Brady ride home with them, to help on his finances. Brady worked very hard for everything that he had, not that he ever complained. Sue admired that in her friend. He was a living epistle of the verse, *"I have learned, in whatsoever state I am, therewith to be content."* Brady was reluctant at first, but with a little coaxing from Sue, he finally agreed. There was nothing he wouldn't do for Sue, even if it meant torture for him. He had fallen hard, and dealing with his unrequited love was proving to be difficult. Brady placed a call to Brother Connery, his old youth pastor from the home church, and he gladly invited Brady to stay with him and family for Christmas Break. He was dealing with Sue and Jason's relationship, and he couldn't bring himself to stay in his Grandmother's house all alone at Christmas; that would be a little too much to handle. He opted for the Connery's and some good Christian fellowship.

The three-hour ride home was almost too much for Brady to stand. The display between Sue and Jason was almost sickening. The looks, the air-kisses, and the hand-holding were slowly gnawing away at his soul. He wondered if Jason was laying it on thick just in spite. He remained silent, reading his Bible, searching for strength just to make it through, with only the occasional comment here and there.

The car finally arrived in Campbell's Grove just before lunchtime. Jason followed Brady's directions and dropped him off at Brother Connery's home. Brady had never been so glad to get out of a car. He thanked them for the ride and told the two that he'd see them at church on Sunday.

The couple then drove on to the Haybert's residence. Sue could tell that Jason was nervous. She took his hand in hers before they left the car. "It's gonna be alright. They'll love you, just like I do."

"I hope so." Jason said as he let out a sigh. The two of them walked up the steps, bags in hand. The door opened. It was Max.

"Hey, kiddo!" he yelled as he grabbed Susan up in a big bear hug. "I sure have missed you!" He then turned his attention to Jason and extended a hearty handshake. "And Mr. Jason-We sure have heard a lot about you!"

"It's an honor, sir," replied Jason, as Max patted his arm. The couple entered the house to a wonderful lunch and a promising start to the next two weeks. The first week was filled with family dinners and get-togethers. Sue was all too pleased to introduce her new beau to all of her friends and family. All the country folks of Campbell's Grove were so excited and impressed with Jason's promising career in Engineering, following in his father's lucrative path. She and Jason were the talk of the town. When Sunday arrived, the entire Haybert household left for the morning worship service. As they parked their car, Max and Irene hurried into the doors, so they wouldn't be late. As Jason and Sue were getting out of the car, a familiar face approached them from across the way. It was Cal.

"I guess you think you're something, bringing him here like this," said Cal with anger in his voice.

"Hey, pal do we have a problem?" asked Jason, stepping in front of Sue.

"Please-not here, not now," Sue said as she stepped out in front of Jason. "Cal, please-not here at the Lord's House. I've been praying for you. I know that I hurt you, and I'm sorry. Please, you have to move on." Sue pleaded.

"You have no idea what I've been going through for the past three months. Don't talk to me about prayer. God hasn't answered any of my prayers. I haven't heard anything from you, and now you show up with…him!" said Cal as he fought back the tears that his anger brought up.

"Maybe He has answered them, but you've just not listened to the answer," Sue replied as she took Jason by the arm. The two of them walked towards the doors of the church.

"I wondered would he be a problem when you invited me home," remarked Jason. Sue had told Jason about Cal. She wanted their relationship to be open and honest; she had nothing to hide.

"I'm sorry, but I didn't think that he would confront us like that. I really have been praying for him." Sue worried herself when she told Jason all about Cal, and how she had come to college with some 'extra baggage.' Jason assured her that nothing would stand in their way, and that everything would be alright.

The church service was wonderful, and since Sue was home, Pastor Creighton asked Sue to sing a solo, as the choir had lost one of their most favorite singers when she left for college. Sue, being placed on the spot, asked the pianist to please play *'Sheltered in the Arms of God,'* an old, trusty favorite. There were several hearty 'Amens' both during and after the song. The pastor thanked her and began introducing his sermon.

The pastor preached on Joseph, being a type of Christ. Joseph's brothers had sold him into slavery because of their jealousy and hatred; but God had kept his hand on Joseph and raised him up in favor with his master, Potiphar. The Pastor preached that there was nothing wrong with enjoying God's blessings and being a success, but, when you're on top of the mountain, you'd better be looking for those wolves that will be coming up behind you to try and push you off. He then read the portion of Scripture telling about Joseph being alone in the house, and Potiphar's wife trying to seduce him. He ran literally out of his clothes and out of the house. Potiphar's wife, of course, then lied on him and had him imprisoned. Because Joseph was innocent, and he had still honored God throughout his entire ordeal, God promoted him to the second most powerful position in all of Egypt. Pastor Creighton explained, "Even though God took this event and used it for His Glory, Joseph should have never been in that compromising position. Potiphar's wife had made several attempts to seduce him in the past. As soon as he noticed that they were alone, he should have fled then. There are times that we as Christians put ourselves into bad situations, and then pray for God to get us out. We need to be 'sober and be vigilant' because the devil is out to get each and every believer and destroy their lives." He then reminded the congregation, in spite of our failures, God will hear the prayer of the repentant soul. He reminded everyone of his favorite verse in the Bible, I John 1:9: 'If we confess our sins, He is able and just to forgive us our sins, and cleanse us from all unrighteousness." He also preached that this was not a license to sin, but that because all Christians still fight the flesh, we need daily forgiveness, because no one is perfect.

With that, he opened the altar for prayer time, and several people went forward. After everyone was finished praying, Pastor Creighton dismissed the services.

After church, Brady came by to check in with Sue. "Hey-I really enjoyed that song. It's one of my favorites, and you really did a great job."

"Thank you so much, Brady; that means a lot coming from you," Sue replied. "Wouldn't you like to come with us for dinner?"

"No, I'm afraid that I can't. Pastor Creighton has invited the Connery's and me over for dinner, but thank you, just the same," Brady replied as he bid her goodbye. There was nothing in the world that he wanted more than to spend time with Sue and her family, but not with Jason around.

*****

Later on at the Creighton's as the men sat in the den for conversation while the ladies cleaned up, Brother Connery asked Brady why he hadn't spent any time at Sue's. "Well, Brother Connery, I think that they have a full house, and I'd just be in the way."

"Surely, you don't mean that? The Haybert's have always had 'room in the inn'" joked Pastor Creighton, as he punched Brady on the arm.

"Yeah, Brady. Are you a little jealous of that fella she's brought home?" asked Brother Connery.

"Sirs, I know that I speak in confidence. I *am* jealous. I never really got to know Sue at all when we were here because I spent so much time taking care of Grandma; but over at the college, we spend a lot of time together, and well, I keep praying for God's will to be done, but I'm really having a hard time," confessed Brady.

"Well, Brady, part of any relationship, friendship or other, is sacrifice. Sometimes we have to set aside our desires for His will, which is the greater good," answered Pastor Creighton.

"I've been praying that way but…" started Brady.

"I know, it doesn't make it any easier," answered Brother Connery. "You're on the right track, though. We'll be praying for you also."

*****

Meanwhile, back at the Haybert home, Sue was able to steal a few moments with her mother, Irene, alone in the kitchen. "Mom, what do you think about Jason?"

"Well, honey, I just don't really know yet," she replied.

"What do you mean? Isn't he just a dream?" Sue asked, with no hint of apprehension.

"Well, that's just it. Doesn't he seem just a little too good to be true? You don't seem to see any fault in him. That can be very dangerous you know."

"Well, I did tell you how he got under my skin at first, but he's changed a little. Now, I don't seem to mind. I really didn't understand him at first, but now, we get along perfectly!"

Irene stood and thought for a moment. "Did he change, or did you?" asked Irene, as she walked out of the kitchen. Sue wondered what her mother meant by that, and she lingered there for a moment, staring at the floor in thought. Just then, Jason walked in and grabbed Sue in a bear hug. "Hey, there's my girl! Are you ready to watch some football?" Jason then noticed that Sue wasn't smiling. "What's wrong?"

"Oh, it's nothing." Sue said as she quickly dismissed her mother's thoughts. She gave Jason a quick peck on the cheek. "Let's go watch the game." She led him into the living room with a smile on her face, but with questions in her heart.

Sue sat beside Jason and tried to watch the game, but her mind could not escape the words that he mother had put to her so bluntly. *'Have I changed?'* thought Sue to herself. *'She may be right. I've never been so enchanted with someone before in my life. I never felt this way with Cal; but the way Mama said it, I think she means that I've changed in a bad way."* Sue went on torturing herself with these thoughts. *"The truth is, I don't think that I'm any different than any other adult in love. I love Jason, and he loves me. It's only natural that I want to spend every waking moment with him-in his arms.'* The more that she thought about Jason, the more that she wanted to steal away to a dark, quiet place alone with him-and then it occurred to her, *'Maybe this is what Mama was talking about. Maybe I am a little too eager to crawl into his arms. What's wrong with me? Is this normal?'* Sue desperately tried to put the matter out of her mind, and when Jason and Max yelled over their team's touchdown, Sue came immediately back to earth.

*****

Days passed, and Christmas Eve had finally arrived. Max and Jason stole away to get in some last minute shopping, and Michelle and Sue took off to the mall in River City for some girl time. The two girls had not really had a chance to hang out since she had been home.

"I'm kinda nervous, with my Dad and Jason being all alone," said Sue.

"Why? Don't they get along?" asked Michelle.

"Mom mentioned to me the other day that she wasn't so sure about Jason. Daddy hasn't said anything to me about him. He hasn't been rude or acted like there was anything wrong, but I don't know. Mom's talk gave me the willies."

"Why's that?" asked Michelle, as she stuffed in another piece of gum.

"...Because I love him. I really love him. There's nothing that I wouldn't do for him, no place that I wouldn't go..."

"Hey, whoa, now you just slow down there little one, and let's talk about this," said Michelle, as she just about choked on her gum. "What do you mean, 'nothing that you wouldn't do?' Exactly what *have you been doing*?" Michelle asked with a very stern look on her face.

"Not *THAT,*" Sue replied most emphatically, "But it sure isn't because I haven't wanted to," Sue confessed.

"Now, it's only natural to have the 'urge to merge', but girl, you gotta put a hold on that. You know better. You wasn't raised that way!" Michelle admonished in her countrified tone.

"I know, I know. I got this purity ring with my Sunday school class the day after our first date," said Sue as she held up her hand and twiddled the ring. "I made a vow to the Lord that I would wait until my wedding night, and I will. I just had no idea that it would be this difficult."

"I know," said Michelle with a long pause. Then, in an attempt to change the subject, she spoke up. "Well guess what, I've decided to quit Beauty School. I really don't think that it's for me,"

"*Beauty School Drop-Out...*" Sue began singing.

Michelle slapped her arm, "You just stop that right now. You know how you said that you'd have a free bed on the weekends, well, I think that I might just take you up on that. I gotta make sure that my girl's not filling that empty bed with the wrong person."

"Michelle!" Sue objected.

"Well, it's the truth. Brady's the only one up there to watch out for you, and he can't be there all the time, so I guess the duty falls on me," Michelle said nobly as she lifted her head towards the sky.

The two girls had a wonderful day of shopping, and then returned to Campbell's Grove. Sue wondered how her Dad and Jason had made out that day-what was discussed, what they had bought. She'd just have to wait and find out.

*****

Christmas morning came, and everyone assembled in the Haybert den for the opening of gifts. Sue's parents gave her a new dress, some earrings, and some other clothes for school. Max gave Irene a gold watch, which she cried over. The Haybert's also gave Jason a very nice watch, for which he thanked them politely. Sue gave Jason a leather day planner, with his name embroidered on it. He appreciated it, and more than that, he appreciated the inside joke.

Max and Irene held their breath as Jason presented a small box to Sue. "Merry Christmas," Jason simply said as he placed the box in her hand's.

"Thank you," Sue said as she began to open it. As Sue got the wrapping paper off, and exposed a velvet box, Irene leaned over so far to see that she almost fell out of her chair! Sue opened the box and inside was a beautiful golden heart locket. "I love it. Thank you so much!" she said as she kissed Jason on his cheek, and Max breathed a sigh of relief.

Chapter 9

The remaining days of Christmas break flew by, and Sue and Jason has kissed in the New Year, so it was time to be getting back to ACU. Brady managed to survive the ride back-by sleeping the entire trip. Sue and Jason simply talked about what they needed to do to get ready for the next semester. They had already registered for her classes online, so they only had to shop for their books when they arrived on campus. Upon entering Sunset, Sue and Jason dropped Brady off at his apartment, and then headed to the campus bookstore. Brady unlocked his door and walked into the apartment only to find it just as he had left it-dark and lonely. Brady prayed, *'Lord, please help me get through this semester. I know you have a plan for me, and I'm trying to be patient. Please show me something-please give me some direction.'*

*****

The trip to the bookstore was a successful one. Sue had decided on purchasing used books to save money; but Jason insisted on buying all new books, even though they were astronomically priced! He declared that the Dolen men always had nothing but the best; that's what his father had always taught him. Jason also offered to purchase a laptop for Sue. She couldn't believe that he was willing to fork out that kind of dough for her, but according to Jason, the sky was the limit when it came to his girl. Even though the laptop would've made her life so much easier, she declined. Sue decided that the computer lab at the library and her memory stick were doing the job just fine.

After purchasing their books, Jason dropped Sue off at the dorm, so that he could go back to his apartment and get settled. Sue entered her room to find Mari back. She had a great rest from Christmas Break, but was still running ragged as the athletic trainer for the basketball team! "I'll be glad when baseball season comes! Maybe I'll get some rest!" she relented.

"Well, I'm glad that you had a good rest over the break. Jason and I had a great trip home," said Sue as she began to unpack her bags.

"You two seem to have a good thing going. You know, the only boys that I've dated have been from the basketball team, and those guys just really haven't worked out for me." Mari paused with a very thoughtful look on her face. "You know that there's a home game on Friday, right?"

"Yeah..." answered Sue, not sure where she was heading.

"Well, how about your friend Brady? I've noticed that he's not dating anyone; do you think that you could hook us up after the game, or does he have a girl back home or something?"

"No, he's not dating anyone." Sue paused to think about the situation, and she noticed that it didn't sit too well with her. "I don't know, Mari, he's probably not your type..." she answered as she tried to discourage Mari. Mari's request had stirred something in Sue that she had not felt before. But what should it matter to her if Brady goes out with Mari?

"Well, why don't you let him decide that? I'll even stay at my cousin's house this weekend so your friend Michelle can come up and stay with you. Please, Sue, I need a change of company!" begged Mari.

Sue thought to herself, *'I've been praying for Mari for some time-praying that she would come to the Lord. Maybe God is working in her heart. This could be His answer.'* "Okay, I'll set it up with Brady," Sue finally answered.

"Thanks. I really appreciate it. I've gotta run; gotta take care of some things downtown. Thanks again," she said as she grabbed her backpack and ran out of the door.

'Sure,' Sue thought, *'maybe this is a good thing, but why*

do I feel so strange about this? The thought of Mari and Brady just makes me feel...I'm not sure how it makes me feel...but I don't think I like it. But why should I care...I have Jason!' Sue tried to convince herself that there was nothing to this feeling that she was having, but it was becoming something that she couldn't shake. Sue abruptly changed her thoughts to Michelle's first weekend on campus and quickly gave her a call to explain the date. Michelle was overjoyed and promised that she'd be there. Then came the dreaded task of calling Brady.

As Sue dialed his number, she hoped that Brady wouldn't answer so that she could call the whole date off, but he did answer.

"Hey, Sue, what's up?" Brady answered.

"Hey, Brady, I've got something to ask you," started Sue.

Brady remembered his prayer earlier in the morning, and his heart raced in anticipation, "Yes..." he replied hesitantly. Brady's thoughts ran wild through his mind. He wanted to hear some sort of encouraging words from Sue-*'You're wonderful-You're so fine-You smell nice-I dumped Jason-Will you marry me-I love you'-SOMETHING* that would let him know that she felt the same way about him as he did about her.

"Mari asked about you this morning," Sue said in barely more than a mumble.

"What do you mean asked about me?" Brady asked as his spirit fell.

"Well, she wants to go out with you, and she offered kind of a double date after the basketball game this weekend. I told her that I didn't think that she was your type, but she seemed insistent." Sue really sounded down as she retold the tale from this morning's reunion with her roommate.

"She did?" said a surprised Brady. He was extremely disappointed, but, more than that he was confused. He didn't know how the Lord was answering his prayer from this morning. Maybe he had it all wrong. Maybe he and Sue weren't meant to be. Maybe this was a sign. Maybe Brady was supposed to move on.

"She even told me that she would stay at her cousin's house in town for the weekend so that Michelle could come up too," Sue explained in an exasperated tone. She was trying as hard as she could to paint a negative picture for Brady so that he would decline the invitation.

"Well, then I accept." Brady answered.

"YOU DO?" yelled Sue as she couldn't believe her ears.

"Sure. I'll go out with her, and I think that I'll bring Justin along too, so that Michelle won't feel like a third wheel," Brady suggested. Brady was a little surprised at his own words, but he also realized that he'd never know what God had in store for him if he didn't step out there in faith and see. As devastated as he was that Sue was not the person he would be going out with this Friday, he had to show the Lord that he was willing to seek His absolute and perfect will for his life, whether that meant Sue or someone else.

"Well...I guess...that settles it," said Sue sadly. She could not believe that Brady had agreed to this pairing. Sue could feel the heat of anger rising up in her, as she thought about the whole situation.

"Okay, then. I'll see you tomorrow sometime," said Brady as he hung up.

Sue closed her cell phone and sat there in unbelief. *'Who knows what's going to happen this weekend! Why did he have to say 'yes'? What's wrong with me? Shouldn't I be happy for my friend? That's what I wished for in the study room at the library! Maybe God is bringing someone to Brady, like He brought Jason to me! But why do I feel like I'm about to be sick?!'* she thought to herself, and with that she sat down at her desk to do some early reading for her first class; she needed something to take her mind off of the Friday to come.

*****

Sue's new classes were all great. Brady wasn't in any of her classes this semester, but Jason decided to take Music Appreciation with Sue, just to share a class. It was different for Sue, and somehow she found herself missing having Brady with her to joke around with. Jason seemed to only want to distract Sue in class, and she rarely found herself paying any attention to the lectures. It seemed like her favorite part of the class was stealing away to a study room at the library to listen to the required classical CD's with Jason-alone and in his arms-what he liked to call, 'quality time'.

The week flew by, and Friday brought butterflies to Sue's stomach, as well as Michelle's. Sue had told Michelle earlier in the week about Justin coming along, and she was very nervous. When Michelle pulled up in her Ford Escort, she almost tripped getting out of the car because she was running to Sue's so quickly.

"I can't believe I'm gonna be a real college girl for the weekend. I'm so excited!" said Michelle. She hugged her friend and showed her upstairs to their dorm room.

"Sue, I'm so nervous. I haven't been on a date in a while," confessed Michelle. "Wait, does this Justin know that this is a date?"

"Yes; Brady did touch base with me this week, and Justin is really looking forward to it."

"Okay, now I'm *really* nervous. I don't even know what he drives? Do you know?" Michelle asked.

"Oh, for crying out loud, does it really matter?" asked Sue with a whine. Michelle put her hands on her hips and tapped her foot waiting for the answer. Sue reluctantly replied, "It's a Mercury Marquis-his parents' hand-me-down."

"Okay-that will do- Mercury and Ford are basically

the same company. I can deal with that," Michelle reasoned. She turned to her duffle bag and began unpacking some clothes. "Come and check out my outfit for the game; do you think it's okay?" She began laying clothes all over the bed, pairing up tops and bottoms here and there. "Oh, no! Where's the black shirt? Where is it?" she began to yell!

"Michelle, calm down; this is going to be fine. Stop obsessing."

"Okay, I'm sorry, I just gotta breathe…we just gotta breathe," said Michelle as she flopped down on Mari's bed, right on top of her black shirt!

"Don't worry. I'll bring paper bags tonight in case you start to hyper-ventilate, you nut-job!" said Sue as she threw her pillow at her to distract her from the evening at hand.

*****

Game time rolled around, and Jason, Brady, and Justin met the two girls in the courtyard in front of the dorm. Brady introduced Justin to Michelle. Justin was captivated by Michelle's bubbly personality. He was immediately head over heels, and it was evident that the feeling was mutual. The couples paired off, with Brady driving alone, and went on down to the arena, where Mari was already on the courtside with the home team.

The game got off to a good start, with ACU leading Clemson 30 to 24. Sue and Brady were somewhat concerned, as they discussed the game, about Clemson's reputation for being a come-back team. The second half would prove to be very interesting.

During half-time the two girls made a run to the restroom while the guys held their seats. Sue was glad to get a moment away, to see how things were going with Michelle. The two friends turned walking quickly to the restroom into nearly a sprint, as Michelle could hardly control her emotions. Michelle could hardly contain her excitement. "Girl, he is so fine!" began Michelle.

"Yeah, he is kinda cute," replied Sue.

"Kinda? Girl, he's my dream! Mercury must be the Ford Elite, because he is awesome!" exclaimed Michelle, "It's like we've known each other forever. I feel so comfortable with him. I hope that he feels the same way."

"Michelle, I never figured you to be one who believed in love at first sight, but you sound absolutely smitten!" Sue marveled at her friend.

"I just never thought that I would meet another Christian guy out of town like this. It can't be a coincidence. I just know that I'm having the time of my life. Thanks so much for setting this up!" Michelle was absolutely beaming!

"Well, it was Brady's idea actually. You can thank him later. Let's get back," said Sue. She grabbed Michelle by the arm and headed back to their seats.

While the girls had taken their trip, Brady got a few words in with Justin. Jason barely spoke with Brady at all that night, but Brady did notice that Jason sat there intently watching the cheerleaders' half-time show.

"So… how 'bout it, Justin? How do you like our Michelle?" asked Brady with a smile, as if he didn't already know the answer.

"She's definitely one of a kind. You know, when I confided in you the other night that I was looking and praying for a wife, I had no idea you'd bring me one by the weekend," Justin said with a laugh.

"Are you for real?" replied Brady with a huge grin.

"I've never been more serious in my life. When she walked down those stairs at the dorm, the Lord whispered to me, '*go up there and meet your wife.*' I've really been praying for a wife for so long; when you told me that she was a Christian girl when you called me about tonight, I really spent a lot of time in prayer that God would show me right away if she was the one, or if I should keep looking. He confirmed that with me tonight." Justin paused as he checked over Brady's shoulder to see if Jason was listening; but he was safe, as Jason was casting lustful glances at one of the red-headed cheerleaders, or so Justin thought. *'Hum, remind me to ask you about that later, Brady'* he thought to himself. He lowered his voice just in case, and he recalled the first time that Sue came to church. "I remember wondering when I first saw Sue at church with you, if she could be the one, but there was doubt-that's why I called you. I felt like there might be something between the two of you; but not with Michelle. There's no doubt in my mind. She is God's pick for me."

"I am so envious of you. I wish that I had such clear direction," said Brady as his countenance changed. Justin knew that he couldn't say much because of the company they were keeping.

"Maybe you'll get some direction this evening after the game, with this Mari person," suggested Justin.

"We'll see," answered Brady just in time, as the girls had made it back to their seats.

The game ended with ACU 62 and Clemson 77. It was a tough loss for the Vikings, but at least there weren't any injuries, and Mari was free to keep the date. Mari approached the group at the end of the game.

"Mari, this is my best friend Michelle Brolin, and I believe that you know everyone else," introduced Sue.

"It's good to meet you, Michelle. Whattya say we all go down to the Greasy Spoon for some burgers?" suggested Mari.

Everyone seemed fine with that, so the crew went off to enjoy their new found company. Brady and Mari seemed to hit it off. Sue noticed that Brady kept Mari in stitches with his little jokes. That was something that Sue admitted she really loved about him. And then she realized…did she say love?

The group laughed, talked, and carried on for about

an hour, and then the couples decided to break off for a while. Brady and Mari were the first to leave, Mari leading Brady by the hand. Sue's eyes followed them all of the way out of the door. There was still something unsettling about seeing Brady and Mari together-especially with Mari holding Brady's hand like that! Sue didn't really know how she felt about the notion of the two of them possibly being a couple. *'Could I be jealous? I've got Jason, and not one thing to be jealous of! What's wrong with me? Snap out of it Haybert!'* Sue thought to herself.

"You okay, babe?" asked Jason, who had noticed that she seemed a little distant.

"Yes, I'm fine. It's nothing," she answered as her mind joined the conversation again. Justin suggested to Michelle that they go for a walk.

"Miss Haybert, at what time do I need to have Miss Brolin home?" he asked jokingly.

"By midnight of course, before this princess turns back into the maid," said Sue with a laugh.

"Somehow I doubt that that could ever happen," said Justin, as he cast a loving glance at Michelle, who received it with blushing cheeks. Sue remarked to herself, *'I don't believe that I've ever seen Michelle blush.'*

So the new couple left for their walk, and that left Sue and Jason to themselves, as they realized that they too should be making their way out of the Greasy Spoon. "How 'bout it, Sue? Do you mind spending the rest of this evening with an old man like me?" Jason joked, as he stood up with his coat, letting Sue know that he was ready to go. He was the only senior in the group, and he felt strange about it sometimes, but he wouldn't neglect his Sue for anything.

Sue looked at Jason and decided to channel all of her frustration in a familiar direction. "I'd be delighted. How 'bout we go find us a weeping willow?" she asked, as Jason noticed the desire in her eyes.

Jason returned that same look with a simple, "Yes, Ma'am."

Chapter 10

The following day, Brady and Justin had a night shift of stocking at the Bargain Bin. Justin couldn't wait to tell Brady his news. He nearly came running into the stock room, as Brady was grabbing a cart filled with tissue boxes to fill the shelves with.

"Brady, I had the most wonderful time of my life last night," said Justin as he was grinning from ear to ear. Justin grabbed the cart from Brady, who in turn grabbed another cart filled with twenty-pound bags of dog food.

Brady looked at him in shock. "How wonderful did you say?" implying that Justin and Michelle had better have behaved themselves.

"A very *respectable* and wonderful evening," corrected Jason.

"Thank You!" said Brady with a smile, as the two of them headed out to the sales floor to work the back stock.

"Well, I'll tell ya, I'm gonna give it about a month and a half, if I can stand it that long. Gotta keep everything respectable you know, and then I'm talking to her daddy."

"The talk?" said Brady with eyes open wide.

"Yep-that's the one. There's no question in my mind," answered Justin with a serious resolve.

"I'm really happy for you, 'J'," answered Brady as he picked up a box of tissues. "Your evening went a lot better than mine!"

"What happened? Did you do something to make her mad?" asked Justin as he hefted a large bag of dog food to the bottom shelf.

"No, it's what I *wouldn't do* that made her mad," answered Brady.

"Are you serious, man?" Justin stopped and looked at Brady in disbelief.

"I couldn't BE more serious. I had to peel her off of me in the truck on the way back to the dorm," Brady said as he turned his attention back to the tissues. He found the recollection of the night to be a little embarrassing! "Sue said that she has been praying for her for some time, and she confided to me earlier in the week that she thought that this date request might have been a step in the right direction. Mari had told her that, 'she needed to be around different people'. Knowing what I know now, I guess that's probably because she has already worked her way through the whole basketball team. I don't know; maybe that sounds cruel, but, from what I could tell, she's very 'experienced.'"

"Dude-I wonder what she's gonna tell Sue?" asked Justin.

"I've been worried about that. I don't know what she'll tell her, but I think that I'm gonna let Sue mention it to me first. If she doesn't say anything, then I'm not gonna say anything," decided Brady.

"I think that is very wise," answered Justin, as he also picked up a case of canned dog food.

*****

And nothing is exactly what Mari told Sue. When Mari came by the dorm to pick up some more clothes for Sunday, Sue asked her how the rest of her evening went. Mari simply told her, "Fine, but I don't think we'll be going out anymore though. You were right. I don't think he's my type." Relieved, Sue left it at that, and never brought it up again.

*****

The next eight weeks flew by. Justin and Michelle had been running the road ragged sharing every weekend, one at ACU and one at Campbell's Grove. Sue had never seen, or heard, her best friend so happy. Michelle was like a whole new person. Sue wondered, '*was I ever that happy over*

Jason?' She found herself actually jealous of Michelle, in that she was not as happy with Jason as Michelle seemed to be with Justin. Maybe Sue was just ready for Jason to make some decisions. His graduation was almost here, and all she had thought about for the past eight weeks was what her life would be without Jason. She nearly perished at the thought! Spring break was here, and it was time to make a quick trip home. This week home would prove to be life-changing for everyone.

This trip consisted of a caravan from ACU to Campbell's Grove. Jason and Sue led the way, and Justin and Brady followed. Justin could hardly wait to get there. He had already asked Michelle's father for her hand in marriage two weeks prior, and he had given them his blessing. Justin then proposed to Michelle on a lovely moonlit night at the Campbell's Grove Rose Garden. She most excitedly accepted and had been walking on air since that night! He couldn't wait to see what wedding plans she had made this week!

Both cars made their way to the Haybert residence where Michelle was waiting to be picked up by Brady and Justin. Michelle just about got run over as she charged the Grand Marquis pulling into the driveway. She then persuaded Sue and Mrs. Haybert to ride with her and Justin to look at wedding flowers. So, they all piled up in Justin's car, with Brady who was riding along for 'male support', and headed to the local florist. Jason had declined, as he said that he was a bit tired from the drive.

As Jason entered the house with their bags, he seized the opportunity to speak with Max, alone. "Mr. Haybert, I've been dating Sue for a while now, and I don't mind telling you that I'm crazy about her."

"Go on..." answered Max, as he motioned for Jason to have a seat.

"Well, sir, I am a senior this year, and I have a very promising job waiting for me when I graduate. It is in

Virginia, but it's not too far over the border. I can't imagine trying to live without Sue. I guess what I'm asking, sir, is, may I please marry your daughter?" asked Jason, as he rubbed the back of his neck, in a fidgety, nervous display.

"I must say, I rather enjoyed that," answered Max.

"What's that sir?" asked Jason in bewilderment.

"Watching you squirm! It was refreshing to see all that confidence dwindle," said Max with a laugh. "What about Susan's schooling?" asked Max.

"If she wants to finish college, I'll wait for her and we can marry after she graduates. However she wants it, that's what I'll do," he replied.

"Jason, all that I require of a man that asks for Susan's hand in marriage is that he be a Christian. You declare that you have asked Jesus to be you personal Lord and Saviour, correct?" asked Max.

"Yes, sir, I have." answered Jason.

"Then I suppose you may have permission to marry my daughter. Please remember that marriage is about give and take. You will have problems-everyone does. If Christ is not the center of your home, you won't make it. There will be things that she will do that will really get under your skin, and vice versa. You must remember that Christ is the glue that sticks you together, and once you say 'I do,' that's exactly what you are-you're stuck! The Bible says *"Husbands, love your wives, even as Christ also loved the church, and gave himself for it;"*

"I appreciate the advice, sir, and I won't forget it," Jason answered as he stood up and shook Max's hand. Then he took a velvet box from his pocket, opening it to Max.

"I've had this for a week now, and it's been burning a hole in my pocket." The ring was beautiful in a marquis cut; it looked to Max to be about a half-carat.

"Well, I am certainly glad that you waited for our little talk," Max confessed. He wondered what God had in store for his daughter.

"I wouldn't have had it any other way, sir," answered Jason. He then thanked Max and took their bags upstairs.

*****

Meanwhile, as the motley wedding crew was walking out of the florist, Sue noticed someone sitting, as if they were waiting for someone on the bench across the street. It was Cal. When he noticed Sue and her friends leaving the florist, he jogged across the street. "Sue, can I please have a minute?" he asked.

Sue look at her mother with fear. After her last encounter with Cal, she was very concerned about what he might say or do. Irene looked at her daughter peacefully and said, "It'll be okay."

Reluctantly, Sue agreed and followed Cal to the Alice's Diner.

"Sue, I really appreciate you giving me this opportunity to speak with you," said Cal as he offered her a seat at the window table. "Can I get you something to drink?"

"No, thanks. What's on your mind, Cal?" asked Sue quickly, as she still wasn't sure where this conversation was going. Something was different about Cal this time; Sue was unsure of what it was, but she was glad that she no longer saw the anger and resentment in his eyes, like she had at Christmas.

"Well, I wanted to apologize from the bottom of my heart for my behavior towards you and Jason back at Christmas. I had hit rock bottom then. Sometimes that's where we have to be before we look up to God-where we should all look to begin with. Anyways, after that day, I realized that I had nowhere else to go. I cried out to God for help and I crawled into His Word. I started reading my Bible day and night, looking for direction. It took a couple of weeks, but I finally got to where I could actually go to church again. God really started to work in my life," extolled Cal with such fervor. "I felt a peace like I'd never known. I began going to youth meetings again, and that's where I met Bethany."

It suddenly became clear to Sue that God had brought someone else into Cal's life. He had moved on with God's help. "Oh, Cal, that's wonderful! I've been praying for you for a while!"

"And that's not the half of it Sue. We're getting married in two months," Cal reported, with a huge smile on his face.

"What? Mama didn't tell me anything, or Michelle either for that matter!"

"I asked them not to. I wanted you to hear it from me; and there's more Sue," said Cal as he paused cautiously. "I'd always planned on just working there at the plant and just living a life here, but God has other plans for me Sue. He's called me to be a missionary to the American West. Bethany and I will be going on deputation right after our honeymoon to raise support, and then Lord willing, we will be going on to the mission field of Montana."

"Montana?" asked a surprised Sue.

" Do you know that you can ride for over a hundred miles before you can find a good Bible-believing church?" informed Cal.

"I had no idea!" Sue couldn't believe what she was hearing! Cal had a renewed faith in God, and also now such energy, a genuine zeal, to go out and do the work of the Lord! She had no doubt from the witness that she was seeing in him that he most assuredly had a call from God.

"I went out on a survey trip with some other missionaries and went to visiting, you know door to door, and one teenager thought Jesus was someone running for political office! And that's right here in America!"

"I'd of never believed that!" Sue marveled.

"Well, I tell you all of this to simply thank you," Cal said with a smile.

"Thank me? For what?" asked Sue.

"For breaking my heart so that Jesus could put it back together," said Cal as tears filled his eyes. "If you hadn't broken up with me, I might have missed Bethany, and more importantly, I might have missed God's call on my life. Thank you for being obedient to the Lord's will for your life."

Sue felt tears welling up in her own eyes, as she thought about the last time that she had really prayed for God's will to be done in her own life, or the last time that she had even read her Bible. She wondered, *'When was the last time that I even considered where God is leading me?'*

As she brushed back the tears and her thoughts, she answered, "Glad I could help!" The two hugged and wished each other well as they returned to their homes. As Sue walked back home, she thought about her own spiritual life. She knew that she hadn't been reading her Bible like she should've been. *'I can't remember the last time that I really spent any time in prayer. I'm always so busy. I've only prayed for people as they've entered my thoughts, which is good to a point, but I've just got to make time to do right-even if that means putting off Jason at times, I must do right. I'm gonna miss it if I don't,'* Sue determined as she walked up the steps of her home.

*****

Later that night, as Max and Irene prepared for bed, Max told her about Jason asking for Sue's hand in marriage.

"Max, I know that you didn't tell him 'yes'?! Please tell me that you didn't tell him 'yes,'" said a frantic Irene in an extremely loud whisper.

"I did tell him 'yes'." Max answered with an odd peace about him.

"Are you nuts? We've talked about this, how we

didn't feel that he was right for her! What are you doing?" asked Irene in a frenzy.

"Irene, trust me; it will never happen," answered Max.

"What do you mean, 'it'll never happen'? You just gave him your blessing!" said Irene, getting louder by the minute.

"Shh," Max said as reminded her that Jason and Sue were there in the house, and it was very quiet. "I didn't give him my blessing. I gave him *permission* to ask her. That's all. It'll never happen."

"Max, in case you haven't noticed, Sue thinks about nothing else but him. I think I'm going to have a heart attack!" Irene threatened, as her breaths got shorter. "I can't believe what you've done!"

"Irene, please! Calm down. I've prayed about this, and I have perfect peace in my heart that everything is going to be okay. Something will happen, I don't know what, but they will never marry; now please, just take a pill if you gotta and go to bed. Everything will be fine; I tell you, they will never marry," and with that, Max turned out the light.

*****

The rest of the week was filled with relaxing in the back yard by the pool and barbecues. The church youth group had planned a softball game at the community park for that Friday evening. Sue loved softball and baseball too, for that matter. She couldn't pass up that activity, and she actually drafted Jason for the team.

Friday came, and Sue was dressed in her old faded gauchos and her Atlanta Braves T-shirt; she had her hair up in a pony tail, and she was ready to rumble on the softball diamond! Jason and Sue pulled out of the driveway and headed down towards the park. He stopped at the end of the street and just sat there.

"What's wrong? Hurry up, we're gonna be late!" said Sue as she began working on her glove.

"I think that you're missing something." Jason said, with a frown, as he began 'looking around' for a lost object.

"I've got everything that I need. I've got my glove, my bat, my visor, my water bottle. What else is there?" Sue asked as she was beginning to become frantic. She loved the game, and she was ready to get going.

"Well," Jason said as he pulled the box out from his pocket, "I don't think that Campbell's Grove's softball diamond's is what you need. You need a diamond of your own," he said as he slowly presented the marquis cut diamond ring. "You wouldn't mind marrying me, would ya?" he asked.

"Oh, Jason, are you for real?" she asked in shock.

"I think so..." he said with a smile. "I've got a good job lined up, Sue, a really good job. It's in Virginia. When I realized that I'd be away from you, I couldn't stand the thought of it. I love you, Sue. You can finish school, or do whatever you want to do, just please, be my wife."

"I will." she answered as she kissed him. He quickly took the ring from the box and placed it on her left ring finger. Sue's tears began to fall.

A swift beeping was heard from behind their car as Sue's neighbors impatiently sounded their horn for the couple to proceed from the stop sign. They both laughed! Jason and a tearful, but cheerful, Sue drove on to the ballpark. As they both got out of the car, Michelle ran up and yelled at them, "What took y'all so long? We've been waiting forever!"

Jason and Sue both got out of the car. Jason took the initiative to mark his territory, "Oh, sorry! I was just asking Sue to marry me, that's all!" he said as he smiled in Brady's direction.

Sue held up her hand and displayed her new pride and joy. Michelle ran over, jumping up and down in glee with her best friend. Justin and Brady hung back at the dugout. Justin leaned on Brady's shoulder- "Just breathe, brother, just breathe."

Chapter 11

The ride back to ACU was heaven in one car, and silence in the other. Jason and Sue were all abuzz talking over their wedding plans, while Justin and Brady rode in silence for most of the journey, until Brady broke down.

"You know, I thought that I was over her. I was really praying for God's will to be done, and then Mari asked me out. I thought that maybe that was God's plan, and then that was a bust. I'm trying to be patient and wait, but deep down, I really thought that we would be together. My heart is past broken-it's shattered," Brady said as he dropped his head into his hands, propped on his knees.

"Bro, I don't even know what to say except, that the Lord knows all about it, and he makes no mistakes. I know that doesn't sound very comforting, right now..." offered Justin.

"I know, I know. His ways are Perfect. I've just gotta trust Him.... *'Trust in the LORD with all thine heart; and lean not unto thine own understanding. In all thy ways acknowledge him, and he shall direct thy paths.'* I've learned that verse as a child, but I need to claim it now more than ever."

"Just please Brady, don't get bitter. I know that you're hurting right now, but God does have a plan. There is light at the end of the tunnel, just don't turn your back on Him, or you'll miss it," begged Justin.

"I won't. I just need some time to sleep," Brady said as he flipped the seat back and closed his eyes. "Do you have any music to put on?"

"Sure, bro." said Justin as he slid in a CD. The Crabb Family's 'Through the Fire' was first on the list. Brady tried to just treat it as noise to sleep by, but he couldn't help but listen to the words: *'He never promised that the cross would not get heavy, and the hill would not be hard to climb...'* Brady knew that this trial paled in comparison to those that others were going through at the time, but to him, Sue's engagement had turned his world upside down. Satan was telling him to, *'give in,'* but Brady knew that God had something better in store for him; he just had to stand still and wait for the Lord to show him what to do next. *'For right now, I'll just have to endure the fire-but I'm glad I'm not alone. Thank you, Lord,'* he prayed as he drifted off to sleep.

*****

Meanwhile, Jason and Sue had made some decisions on their drive back to ACU. Sue did want to finish college with at least a two-year Associates degree. She could transfer that anywhere that she needed to go when she married Jason. She would still be the first college graduate from her family, and she would finish her four-year Bachelor's degree later on. Jason would graduate in the spring, and Sue would stay at ACU to pick up all of the extra summer courses that she could. Any extra credits would always be helpful in a transfer. She would also try to find a part-time job, to save some extra money for their wedding. Her mother and father had given her so much; they had totally paid for her college tuition, room and board. Even though she knew that they would offer, she and Jason wanted to pay for the wedding themselves.

*****

A few more weeks went by, and everyone was back into their normal routines. Justin and Michelle's wedding was planned for June, a week after graduation, and there were a few fittings to be done, but other than that, it was business as usual. ACU's baseball team had done rather well that season, and the gang had become pretty big fans. Sue really wanted to travel to one of their away games, just to do something different. Since Mari had never mentioned her date with Brady, and Brady hadn't breathed it to Sue,

Sue had no qualms about asking Mari to book them some extra rooms along with the baseball team for the next away game. Mari thought that she would have a break during baseball season, but there was an orthopedic practice that was interested in hiring her as a Medical Assistant, and the extra training was now required, so Mari had gone back to traveling with the teams. This made Sue, and ultimately Justin, happy, as Michelle got to come over more to fill the empty bed in Sue's dorm room.

Mari was more than happy to help out her roommate, and so there were three extra rooms booked, one for Jason, as he insisted on staying by himself, one for Justin and Brady, and one for Michelle and Sue. The weekend finally came and Sue was extremely excited. She had always loved the game, and now she would actually get to know some of the college players.

Everyone arrived at the inn and got settled. Sue and her crew all decided to go out for pizza that night, and then back to the hotel for some fun and games. The baseball team and Mari, had just come back in from their practice and were cleaning up to go out, as Sue and her friends were trying to find something fun to do.

"Hey guys, I brought my PS3 from home and a NASCAR game-anybody wanna play?" asked Jason.

"Sure!" said Sue, and Michelle agreed to go with her.

"I think I'll just go hang out by the pool, while you two girls have fun. Wanna join me Brady?" asked Justin.

"Yeah, that sounds good," said Brady, as he turned and followed Justin down to the pool.

Sue and Michelle walked with Jason to his room, and propped the door open to let in the summer breeze. Jason fixed up the system, and they were off! Michelle raced Sue first, in a Ford of course, and was winning. The television volume was turned up so loud, that the NASCAR three were drawing a crowd! Some of the baseball players had stepped into Jason's room to watch the race and take rise for the next rounds!

Jason stood up and stepped out of the room, unnoticed by the girls who were really into their game. They were both so competitive! As he stepped out, he nudged one of the baseball players to follow him. After walking down to the vending machines at the end of the outdoor stairwell, Jason asked for a little assistance.

"Hey, buddy…" he began.

"It's Kirt." replied the young man.

"Thanks, Kirt, for coming out. I could use a hand. You see, I need some 'quality time' alone with my girl, and I'm gonna need some help clearing the room, do you understand?"

"I think so; some things just can't be done in crowds. You need a little privacy, right?" said Kirt with a very devious smile.

"So, we understand each other; I've put in a lot of time, and effort for it, and it's rather over due. You get my drift?" explained Jason with that same devious smile.

"No problem bro, I've gotcha covered. Just give me a few minutes," answered Kirt, as he turned around and walked downstairs.

Jason quickly returned to the room with two cans of soda for an alibi if questioned. The crowd was still growing. By this time, about eight of the baseball players and Mari had come in to watch the video game. Michelle beat Sue in their race, and then Jason tagged in. Sue was leading Jason, and then he bumped her in the video game.

"Hey, that's not fair!" she yelled.

"I'm not going down like you!" he returned, as they both turned their remotes wildly in desperation to win the race!

At that moment, Kirt came bursting in the door, "Hey guys! Michael's got the football in the pool, and he's rounding up a team! Let's go!" With that, everyone, including Mari and Michelle, who got caught up in the excitement, ran out of the room, and then Kirt closed the door, shooting a glance at Jason.

Sue didn't even notice that they were alone, as she was still really into the race. As she crossed the finish line, she yelled, "Hah! I won!"

"You sure did," answered Jason he moved in for the kiss. Sue was somewhat caught by surprise, but enjoyed it nevertheless. She enjoyed it so much, that she didn't feel Jason laying her back on the bed where they had been sitting playing the game. She laid there for a moment, caught in a haze, as he kissed her relentlessly. She caressed his face with her hand, and then when she opened her eyes, she saw her sparkling diamond ring. "Susan," he whispered hungrily in her ear, as she pulled his face to her and kissed him again, running her fingers through his hair. She felt his hair get wrapped around her diamond, and opened her eyes to free it. It was then she noticed her purity ring, peeking out from under her diamond.

*****

Meanwhile, back at the pool, Brady and Justin had been talking about the weather, the Bargain Bin, and this and that, and then all of a sudden a stampede of baseball players, Michelle and Mari came running onto the patio. Michelle ran up to where Justin was sitting, and plopped into his lap. "Hey, babe! Guess what? I beat Sue!"

"In a Ford, no doubt!" teased Justin.

"You know it!" Michelle answered.

"Hey, where's Sue now?" asked Brady.

"She's still up there, I guess. We all left so fast, I think she and Jason were still playing," she answered.

Brady looked up at the room through the second floor balcony bars and he noticed that the door was closed. "Yeah, but what are they playing?" he said as he jumped up and bolted up the outdoor stairs towards the closed door.

*****

Sue stared at her purity ring, and realized where all of this was headed. She pushed on Jason to stop. He ignored her. "Jason, please…" said Sue as she pushed against him again, a little harder this time. "Jason, stop. I can't…We can't…" said Sue as she was finally able to push Jason off of her. She couldn't believe that he hadn't stopped when she first asked, and the two stared at each other, panting. Sue's eyes began to well up with tears, as she quickly turned and pulled open the door, only to see Brady standing there, about to knock. Sue never even stopped to acknowledge him, but ran straight to her room.

"Sue, are you okay?" Brady asked as he ran behind her.

"I'm fine, I'm fine," she called back through her tears, as she made it into her room and slammed the door.

Brady knew that she was not alright; this episode had been no little deal. Bent with anger, Brady ran back to Jason's room, in a blaze of fury. By that time, a few more baseball players had heard about the PS3, and had stopped in to play. Brady stepped into the doorway, which was now propped open again. Brady's eyes seared through Jason's, as he let him know that he was on to him. There was no way that the episode had happened by chance, and Brady knew it.

*****

Sue threw herself on the bed and sobbed. She knew that she had come way too close to breaking her vow to God. She stared at her ring. She had no idea that when she made this vow, how difficult it would be to keep it. She prayed, "God, please help me." Immediately, God reminded her of the sermon she had heard regarding Joseph and Potiphar's wife. She then realized that she had put herself into a bad situation. She should have never been in his room, for any reason. The temptation would not have been so great there. God reminded her that she had to do her part, and then He would give her strength. She determined then and there, that she would make all attempts to *'abstain from all appearance of evil.'*

Brady paced back and forth along the balcony and decided to go and check on Sue. He knocked at her door. She didn't answer. "Sue, it's Brady. Please open the door." he pleaded.

"No! Please. I just want to be alone," she answered without opening the door. Deep down she knew that Brady was just trying to help, but she really didn't want to see anyone. Brady walked back down to the pool where Justin and Michelle sat. He looked at Michelle in desperation. She knew immediately that something wasn't right.

"Michelle, would you please go check on Sue? She won't let me in to talk to her," Brady pleaded.

"What happened? What's wrong?" Michelle asked with a look of concern on her face.

"That's what I want to find out! Please go help her," he continued to beg.

Michelle bounded up the stairs and used her key card to get in the room. From the look on Brady's face, this was no time for knocking and asking for permission to come in. As she came inside, Sue's tear-stained face looked up at her in surprise. "What's going on Sue? Why are you so upset? Brady said that something was wrong!" Michelle walked over and sat down on the bed beside her friend.

"Oh, Michelle!" she cried as she leaned her head on Michelle's shoulder and began sobbing again. Reliving the moment was just about a painful as when it occurred. "We started kissing, and…well…it was going too far…and…"

"Sue, you didn't?" asked Michelle.

"No-we didn't. But, he didn't want to stop. I begged

him, and I had to fight him off," said Sue as she began to cry again.

"Sue! Why didn't you tell Brady? He and Justin could be taking care of bid'ness right now! How dare he?" began Michelle as she put her 'gangsta' on.

"No, it was my fault, Michelle," Sue replied. She lifted her head up and looked at her friend, who could not believe what she was hearing.

"YOUR FAULT? Are you kidding me?" Michelle was really getting steamed.

"I should've never been in there in the first place. I should have never been in his room. I put myself in a bad situation," explained Sue.

"Well, the last time I checked, it takes two to tango, honey, and he is just as guilty; and even I'm guilty. I shouldn't have run out of there down to the pool. I wasn't thinking about the fact that I left you alone with him. Oh! I can't believe him! He knows how important waiting is to you!"

"Yes, he does; but we are both human, I guess. I won't make that mistake again. You've got to help me, Chelly. Help me think about things before I do them."

"You can count on me, Sue," Michelle said as she hugged her friend. "You know, you two have got to talk about this. You can't just let it go. It has to be dealt with."

"I know-but just not tonight. We'll talk at breakfast. I don't want to see him anymore tonight," replied Sue. As the words left her mouth, the phone rang. Sue shook her head, indicating that she wasn't going to answer it. Michelle moved over and picked up the phone. It was Justin.

"Oh, hey baby cakes," answered Michelle in a bubbly tone, masking the current crisis at hand. "No, I don't think that I'm coming back down. Me and ole' Sue are pretty tired, and we want to get our necessary beauty sleep for tomorrow. Even though some of us need it more than others…" Michelle said as she poked Sue, "…I will also turn in early!" she said with a laugh! "I love you too, honey. Sweet dreams," she said as she hung up the phone.

"I know I must look a sight…" said Sue as she walked over to the vanity sink and began to wash her face.

"Oh, girl, those are only tears and mascara. They can be washed away. You're beautiful-inside and out, and that's what really matters," Michelle said as she made her way over to Sue, looking into the vanity mirror by the sink. She put her arm around her and gave her a squeeze. She really loved her friend, and she'd be there with her every step of the way, no matter which path she chose. She just knew that she had to do her best to help steer her back on the right path. Michelle looked very somberly at her friend, as to impart some great nugget of wisdom, "Just remember what they say, *'beauty is only skin deep; but ugly is to the bone!'*" she said as the two girls erupted in laughter!

*****

The next day at breakfast, Sue and Jason took their muffins and doughnuts out to the patio by the pool to talk. As they sat at the patio table to eat their continental breakfast, the silence between them was so thick it could be cut with a knife. Sue wondered who would be the first to speak, until she could take it no longer. "Jason, last night was too close," began Sue.

"Sue, you know, we are engaged now. We'll be married in about a year. What's the big deal?" retorted Jason.

"What's the big deal?" Sue caught herself yelling, and she quickly hushed her tones, so as not to make a scene. "You know that I've made a vow. Not only to myself, but to God! You're supposed to be a Christian, too. Doesn't that mean anything to you?"

"I'm a Christian, but I'm also a man. All I know is that I can't keep going on so far, and then just stopping...it's not fair."

"Listen to yourself... I... I... I. This is about more than me and you, Jason. It's about the Lord and doing right by Him. I'm as much to blame here as you are. I shouldn't have been in your room. I'm not going to let that happen again."

"You're not going to let what happen again?" asked Jason in puzzlement.

"I'm not going to compromise myself alone with you again," Sue answered.

"Why, you don't trust me now, is that it? What do you think I am, Sue, a rapist? You can't tell me that you didn't want it to happen just as much as I did!" Jason rebutted.

"No. I did want you, and that's why I have to take extra precautions not to be totally alone with you in that situation again. I don't trust myself," Sue admitted.

"Okay, look, graduation is only two weeks away. I guess that it'll be a little easier to do that, as I'll be moving to Virginia and only seeing you on the weekends. Are you gonna make me bring a chaperone on all of our dates now?" Jason asked sarcastically.

"Do I need to?" asked Sue as she looked at him earnestly.

"No." he answered. He looked around in guilt as he knew that he had stepped out of line. "I do know what's right, Sue. I just also know what feels right," Jason answered.

"I know that it feels right, and it's supposed to. It's only natural to want to be together like that. It's only a little while longer, and then we'll be married, and it will *all* be right. It will be right by God. Please just hang in there with me."

"Alright, Sue. I won't pressure you like that again. I promise," Jason said as he changed the subject to the game that day. Sue wondered in the back of her mind, *'why has*

Jason only now made this such an issue? I can't let this diamond ring be a license to sin and break my vow. I wonder if things will ever be the same?'

"But every man is tempted, when he is drawn away of his own lust, and enticed. Then when lust hath conceived, it bringeth forth sin: and sin, when it is finished, bringeth forth death."

James 1:14-15

Chapter 12

Two weeks passed, and so did graduation. The dreaded day had arrived for Sue and Jason-his moving day. The engineering firm of J. Watson and Beasley was providing an apartment for Jason completely paid along with all of his utilities. The salary was below entry level for his position, but the benefits more than made up for it. He would be able to save up more money to buy a small starter house for Sue and him.

It was indeed a bittersweet day. Sue drove Jason's Yaris behind the U-Haul truck to his new apartment in Ridgeway, Virginia. Michelle and Justin followed Sue in Justin's Grand Marquis to help with the unloading and to bring Sue home. Sue had made sure to surround herself with her friends, to ensure that she would not be alone with Jason like she had been on the baseball trip. Justin had become store manager of the Bargain Bin, and he scheduled Brady to work that day, so that he would have an escape when Sue asked him to ride along too.

Ridgeway was a small town, but it had easy access to interstate 95, which would allow Jason to commute to work in Richmond. As they entered the small townhouse apartment, Sue became excited. She envisioned where some of her things would go in less than twelve months now, and her heart floated for just a moment, until it came time to actually move Jason's things in. She never realized that he had so much junk! In the recesses of Sue's mind, she thought, *YARD SALE!!!*

The U-haul truck was backed against the small porch, and the crew began unloading the larger items. Justin and Jason hefted the heavy furniture and set up the bed. Sue came behind them and dressed it the sheets and comforter. Sue decided that Jason could unpack all of his clothes himself after she had gone. Jason had to set up all of his stereo and television equipment himself. He was so obsessive about his expensive toys.

Sue and Michelle made their way to the kitchen and began to unpack his few dishes into the kitchen cabinets. Sue took a look around at the small kitchen. It was just big enough for two, and in less than twelve months, it would be two-she and Jason. She looked around and thought about where she would like to hang her country décor, and what would be the best place for storing her spices, and *'does this Buffalo Bills mug really have to stay?'* She had a million thoughts racing through her mind! She only knew one thing-it was going to be very hard to leave this place today, knowing that they would be apart and that he would be living in their future home alone. She wanted to be there! She wished that they would have decided to marry right away, but then she thought about her Daddy, he had worked so hard to put her through school. *'No,'* she thought, *'I need to at least graduate with a two-year degree. I owe him that much.'*

At the end of the day, Michelle and Justin did give Jason and Sue a few moments together on the front porch of the apartment. Sue then presented Jason with a gift bag. Jason smiled in surprise, "For me? As if I didn't have enough junk!"

"Hey! This isn't junk!" said Sue as she watched Jason pull out the set of picture frames. The frames were identical, but one housed a photo of Jason and the other a picture of Sue. She took the frame with her picture and handed it to Jason. "This goes on your nightstand. Now, when we go to sleep at night, our faces will be the last things that we see; it's just a reminder of the good days that are on the way."

"It will definitely be sweet dreams then. Susan, I'm gonna miss you so much, that it hurts to breathe." Jason said as he wrapped his arms around her in a soft embrace. I'll be home every weekend… I love you."

"I love you," Sue managed to get out as her voice

began cracking and the tears began to flow.

"Please don't-it kills me to see you cry. I'll be home soon, I promise!" Jason said as he nodded for Michelle to give him a hand. He knew that Sue would've stayed on that porch until next June when they planned to marry.

Michelle came and touched Sue on the back. "Come on, Sue. It's time to go," she said as she put her arm around her friend, in compassion and understanding. Michelle knew what it was like to only be able to see her fiancé on the weekends, and she also knew about the episode on the baseball trip and felt the apprehension that Sue had about being away from Jason. She would be praying for her, and she would always be there for her when Sue needed her.

The ride back to ACU was quiet. Sue slept a good portion of the way, and Justin and Michelle were very careful about their conversation, as they didn't know what Sue was hearing and what she wasn't. Both Justin and Michelle knew that Brady loved her, but they also knew that he was a praying man that wanted God's will above anything, and he would never do anything to jeopardize that. They ached for him and Sue, but they had accepted the situation. When the three got back to ACU, Justin took them to the Western Sizzlin' Steakhouse; he insisted it was his treat. Justin tried to lighten the mood a little. "Well, Sue, you mentioned that you wanted to find a part-time job to save some money for next June, right?" asked Justin, carefully choosing his words, so as not to mention 'Jason' or 'wedding'.

"Yeah," replied Sue, woefully.

"Well, I am the store manager now at the Bargain Bin, and we can always use another good cashier. Didn't you used to work for your Dad's automotive store?" offered Justin.

"Yes, I did, and you know, I did like running the register. I think I'll take you up on that. I really appreciate it. Registration for the summer courses does not begin for another two days; I can come by and get started right away, if that's alright." Sue asked.

"That would be great. It's all settled then. You're an official Bargain Bin employee!"

"Great! I think I'll be needing to fill all of my extra moments on Monday through Friday!" she said with her mood picking up a bit.

They finished their meal and drove Sue back to the dorm. Sue brought in her bag with her picture of Jason. She sat is beside her bed, and then kissed it. *'Only a few more months,'* she thought to herself as she drifted off to sleep.

*****

The next day Sue was at the Bargain Bin, bright and early. Brady met her at the glass doors with the key. "I'm sorry, Miss. We don't open for another hour," teased Brady as he opened the door for Sue to come in. "What are you doing here?" he asked.

"Justin didn't tell you? You're looking at the newest Bargain Bin employee! 'Cashier Extraordinaire'!" replied Sue.

"No, Justin didn't tell me anything about it," said a very confused Brady as his eyes searched the store for Justin, "Nothing at all…But here-let me take you to the office, and I'm sure he'll be along soon to get started on your paperwork," Brady said as he led Sue to the stock room, and up the staircase to the office and training room. The store was located on Main Street, in an updated storefront. The entire ground floor was reserved for product and store room, and the upstairs that was originally used as the storekeepers quarters was remodeled into the offices and training rooms. Sue and Brady climbed the stairs and found that Justin was there to welcome them.

"Good morning, Sue! I'm glad you're here so early. You'll have plenty of time to train on the register today. Let me get your forms straight," said Justin as fiddled through some papers on his desk.

"It shouldn't take me long to learn your system. I took a good look at the register coming in, and it looks like the basic scanner system that Daddy has back home. It shouldn't be hard at all to pick up."

"Great! Just fill these out for me, and I'll be right with you okay? I'm going to go down and create your sign-on number on the register," Justin said as he headed for the door.

"And I'll go down and work the back stock from the last truck. See you in a bit," said Brady as he followed Justin down the stairs. As soon as the two of them were out of earshot, Brady grabbed Justin by the arm. "Just what are you trying to do? Are you trying to kill me?" he asked in an almost angry voice. "You know how I feel about her, and that she'll never be mine. You expect me to work with her everyday? What is going on in that mind of yours?"

"Well, Brady, first of all, Sue is my friend too, and she needed a part-time job. Since I was in a position to help her, I did; second of all, the fact that you love her is irrelevant to the Bargain Bin; and finally, as to your comments of 'she'll never be mine' all I have to say about that is, 'it ain't done 'til you say 'I do.'' Now, would you please get over yourself and go ahead with that back stock," exclaimed Justin in a good dose of tough love.

Brady stood there in shock for a moment, and then he realized that Justin was right. He was putting his personal feelings aside to be her friend at school and at church, and he would also be able to do it at work; and besides, it was only part-time, so maybe he'll just make the most of it. After all, it was some time that she would be there, with him, and Jason wouldn't be there; not that Brady was trying to interfere with their relationship, but he would actually feel unencumbered when he spent time with her. *'This might be a good thing after all'* he thought.

*****

Sue worked her shift and went straight back to the dorm. It had been a long time since she had spent that much time on her feet, and she was aching to just lie down. Mari was there, backing a duffle bag again. "Hey Sue! What's up?"

"Oh, hey, Mari. I started a part-time job today, and I'm just not used to standing for long periods of time. I gotta get back into the groove. Where you going now, you gotta game?" asked Sue.

"No, the Orthopedics Practice that has hired me is sending me to some of their area clinics in some of the hospitals in the neighboring counties. I'll be working some forty-eight hours shifts, so you won't be seeing much of me for a while. Just consider my side of the room as vacant, and when I need it, I'll call you! ACU is still counting all of this extra work as clinical credit; so, I can't pass it up!"

"I don't blame you! I really appreciate your letting Michelle stay here like that. I know that she does too," Sue said as she dressed for bed. She picked up her picture of Jason from her night stand.

"A little love memento?" asked Mari, "I'll bet yesterday was tough for you!"

She sat there and stared at his picture. "Yeah, it was a little, but we'll get through it. I'm tired. I think I'll turn in early tonight," Sue said with a yawn. She kissed the photo and placed it back on the night stand.

It caught Mari's eye, and she let out a little giggle! "You got it bad, sista! Goodnight, chick-see ya soon!" said Mari as she shut the door and headed for her car.

"Goodnight Mari!" Sue yelled as Mari was leaving, "and Goodnight, Jason," she said as she rolled over with thoughts of Saturday playing in her mind-Michelle and Justin's wedding. How fitting that Jason's first weekend back home would be to attend Justin and Michelle's wedding!

*****

Tuesday rolled around and the dress shop called Sue to say that her dress was in. She needed to stop by and try it on to make sure that there were no last minute alterations needed. Sue stopped by on her way to work her shift at the Bargain Bin. The dress fit perfectly! Sue was so glad that she hadn't gained too much weight in between fittings-the Greasy Spoon wasn't exactly the healthiest place to eat, and those late night dates left little time for exercise! Thankfully, Sue had tried to walk all over the campus to her classes, to get a little exercise in, as well as to save gas.

Sue paid the tailor the balance owed on the dress, and then drove on to the Bargain Bin to begin her shift. She hated to let the dress wrinkle in the car, so she brought it in to the stock room and hung the black garment bag up near the break table. Just as soon as she had hung the bag up, Brady walked in to punch the time clock to begin his shift. The large black bag caught his eye. "Hey, girl! What's in the bag?" he asked.

"It's my dress for the wedding. By the way, have you picked up your tuxedo?"

"No, we don't pick them up until Thursday. Can I have a peek?" asked Brady as he walked towards the black bag.

"No, you may not!" said Sue as she blocked his way.

"Hey! There's no rule about seeing the bridesmaids' dress before the wedding-only about seeing the bride! What gives?" Brady rebutted.

"I'm sure Michelle doesn't want anyone to see her bridesmaids' dresses before the ceremony! Not you guys anyways!"

"I guess I'll just have to wait and be surprised like everyone else, huh?" said Brady as he played along with

Sue. He was so glad to be able to talk with Sue without worrying about Jason walking in and thinking that he was trying to steal his girl. Just then, Sue's cell phone rang. It was Jason.

"Hey babe, what's up?" answered Sue, as she mouthed the words, *'It's Jason'* to Brady.

Brady turned around and acted like he was checking out the back stock carts so that Sue wouldn't see him rolling his eyes. *'Speak of the devil'* Brady thought to himself.

"Oh, you're kidding me? This weekend?" Sue said in disappointment.

Brady's ears perked up. He noticed Sue's disappointed tone, and he knew that something was up.

"Well, then I guess then I'll see you the next Friday. At least there will be enough festivities going on that I will be distracted from missing you!" Sue replied.

Brady was glad that his back will still turned to Sue as he made a gagging face! It was at that moment that Justin walked in. Justin caught Brady's little gagging episode, and he was mortified! "Brady, are you okay?" he asked.

"Just...fine..." Brady said as he rolled his eyes towards Sue, who was still whispering sweet nothings to her Jason on the other end of the line. Justin caught on and helped Brady play it off.

Finally, Sue flipped her phone shut. Justin caught a glimpse of the large black bag hanging near the break area. "Hey! Is that your dress? Michelle asked me to make sure that you picked it up today." Justin walked up to the bag and began to unzip it.

"Stop! She also gave me instructions that you were not to see it!" ordered Sue, as she began to zip it back up.

"Oh, come on! You girls kill everything!" said Justin.

"Us girls? You guys are the ones! Like Jason-he can't come home this weekend because of some company thing! I can't believe it-his first weekend home!"

"Well, that's just a shame, aint' it?" said Brady, still

with his back turned sorting boxes of product to stock. He was so glad that Sue couldn't see his sarcastic, smirky, mocking faces.

"Now, does that raise a problem? I'm driving home, and you were going to ride with Jason, so now what's the plan?" asked Justin.

"Well, I guess now I can drive down, and..." Sue turned and looked at Brady, "hey, Brady? Would you ride with me so that I don't have to drive alone?" Sue asked.

Brady stopped dead in his tracks and smiled-a genuine smile-"Sure! I'd love to ride with you!"

"Thou art the God that doest wonders: thou hast declared thy strength among the people."

Psalm 77:14

Chapter 13

After a week of working in the Bargain Bin, the store had to close up for the weekend because Justin's and Michelle's big day had arrived. Sue drove Brady down in her Ford Focus, and Justin followed behind them in his Grand Marquis. Justin quickly passed them on the interstate! Sue had a hard time keeping up with him this time, as he seemed to have a lead foot! Friday night was rehearsal night, and everyone was all in a tizzy. Jason had called in his regrets on Tuesday; he would not be able to attend the wedding due to a mandatory conference on a special project that his firm was working on. He would be traveling to Richmond for the weekend. Sue was still somewhat ill that Jason was missing this wedding, and she thought about her own upcoming wedding, which would be only eleven months away now. Sue counted down the days constantly!

Brady, on the other hand, was elated that Jason was nowhere to be found. He and Sue were relatively quiet on the ride home, and at one point, Brady thought that he saw Sue nodding. He immediately ordered Sue to pull over, and he drove the rest of the way home. Only a few minutes after switching seats, Sue was asleep.

Brady tried to concentrate on the road, but was having great difficulty doing so, as he was really enjoying watching Sue sleep. She looked so peaceful. She was so beautiful with the sunset casting a golden beam on her brown hair, bringing out the red highlights. He wanted to reach over and stroke her fair skin. *'I'll bet it feels like satin'* he thought to himself. Then he remembered; he wouldn't be the one that would get to wake up every morning and see this beautiful sleeping face; to feel the warmth of her breath on his face-it would be Jason. *'Oh, how I hate him.'* And then, that quickly, God seized his heart. He knew that the hatred was wrong. *'Please God, please help me to accept whatever You have for me. I know that I can't get prayers up with hatred in my heart. Please forgive me, Lord.'*

*****

At the rehearsal, the wedding director lined up all of the bridesmaids and groomsmen according to their height to make the best possible matches. There were three bridesmaids and groomsmen, and Michelle's little cousin, Jillian, age three, made the sweetest little flower girl! Michelle had a rather large family, and had included her two brothers, Matt and Joe, and her sister, Leah, in the wedding party, as well as Justin's sister Gwendolyn. The director summed up the group of young people before her and came up with the couples of Matt and Leah, Sue and Brady, and Gwendolyn and Joe.

The church sanctuary had one single aisle, and Michelle decided that she would like for each attendant to enter by themselves and then exit together. Justin did point out that it would just make the wedding a little longer, but he detected the 'bride-zilla' beginning to come out in Michelle, so he decided that whatever she wanted was fine.

The rehearsal party practiced entering and exiting twice, and Pastor Creighton ran over most of the vows that required responses from the very nervous bride and groom. Irene, Sue's mother, helped out by being the stand-in bride. Stan, Michelle's father, really enjoyed giving her away; he shoved her into Justin's hands saying, "Please take her! Please!" The crowd laughed, and Michelle and Justin both appreciated Stan's tension-breaking jokes! Pastor Rhodes would also take part in his son's wedding, although, he was not sure if he could get through it without getting emotional-neither was Justin.

After a sumptuous dinner in the fellowship hall provided by Justin's family, who had all caravanned down for the occasion, Sue and Brady stayed and helped put the final touches on the decorations. Sue made mental notes about some of the things that she did like and some of the things that she didn't quite like. Sue gave Brady a bag of bird seed and some small squares of cut tulle, and she schooled him on how to make the little bundles for the bride and groom's exit. As she was helping Michelle drape some white tulle bunting along the banister of the baptistery, she took a long look at her friend. By this time tomorrow, she would be on her honeymoon. Their friendship would change somehow, and she was unsure what it would be like. *'Every life has many chapters, and one of Michelle's chapters was coming to an end, and another beautiful chapter is beginning for her.'* Sue thought to herself. She was happy for Michelle, but then she was also sad that their friendship would be moving into a different chapter. She didn't know how she would handle having to share her with Justin. She also found herself a tad jealous that this wasn't her wedding that she was preparing for. She longed for the months to pass by quickly.

Brady finished the bundles and reported to Sue for additional instructions. She couldn't think of anything else that needed to be done, so Brady offered to escort her home. Sue only lived two blocks from the church, and she had walked there that evening, and Brady loved to walk.

Brady and Sue left the church fellowship hall and began walking down Main Street towards Sue's house. Brady noticed that Sue was a little pre-occupied. "What's on your mind, Sue?"

"Nothing, really." she answered.

"No, now I know better. What's going on in those 'wide open spaces' up there?" joked Brady.

Sue punched him on the arm. "Hey! Watch it! Well, if you must know, I was just thinking about Michelle. She's stepping out there and starting that next chapter, you know."

"Yeah. I know you've been thinking about it. Are

you a little jealous?" he asked.

"Yes, I am in a way. Don't get me wrong; I am so happy for Michelle."

"I know you are." Brady wanted to tell her how jealous he was of Jason and Justin, and how he wanted to take her down that aisle himself tomorrow! "And I know that you probably have so many emotions rolling around in those 'wide open spaces'…" he paused as Sue stopped and reared her fist back to punch him again, "…of your heart..." he finished as a smiling Sue nodded her head in gratitude and lowered her fist. "…that you're probably a mess inside."

"I don't know. Maybe," said a puzzled Sue, as they arrived at her front doorsteps.

"And you miss him." continued Brady.

"Hum?" a distant-minded Sue asked.

"You miss him," repeated Brady.

"I miss who?" asked Sue.

A glimpse of hope shone into Brady's heart, even though he knew he shouldn't take it seriously. "Jason-you miss him; don't you?"

"Oh! Yeah! Jason. I've just been so busy…I kinda forgot about him for a while there," she answered.

Brady just stood there nodding and looking at Sue. "Well, we've both got a big day tomorrow, so I guess I should let you go…" he said. *'…Let you go…'* The words stung his mind with a larger implication to his pining for her. But deep inside, he knew he could never let Sue go.

"Yeah. Good night, friend," said Sue as she reached out and surprised Brady with a hug, one that she so desperately needed. Brady basked in the moment and held her tight. *'Oh, Lord, if she only knew…'*

"Good night, Susan." Brady said softly as he released her. He walked away as Sue turned to open her front door, and then he turned back to her, "Hey…" Sue looked back at him, "See ya at the altar!" he said as he watched her smile and walk inside. Then he turned, and made his way back to the Connery's, knowing, what a bittersweet day lay ahead of him tomorrow.

*****

The next morning came-the big day-and Michelle was a nervous wreck. The wedding was at three o'clock, and everyone was to be there for pictures by one-thirty. It was already one-fifteen, and Michelle had not heard from Justin yet. She was determined not to see him before the wedding, but yet she had to make sure that he was there, and he had cut it very close! Justin rolled into the church parking lot at one-twenty, with his tuxedo in hand! Leah came and calmed her nerves, letting her know that Justin was indeed on the premises, and that everything would be okay.

The girls had their pictures made and were then were whisked away to another room while the guys had their turn. After all of that, it was time to get everyone lined up and begin the processional, if the bride was to enter at exactly three o'clock. As Sue and the other girls grabbed their French-knot bouquets, she crept over beside her friend and gave her a quick hug and peck on the check. "I love you, Chelly-girl! See ya at the altar!" said Sue as she turned around to take her place in the processional. As soon as the words left her lips, she remembered Brady speaking those exact same words to her last night. She couldn't help but be just a little bit curious to see Brady all decked out on the stage!

When she stepped to the door of the foyer, she peeked through the doors, which were closed in order to conceal the bride. The last groomsman, Matt, was making his way down the aisle. It would be Sue's turn next, and then Gwendolyn, and then Leah, who was Michelle's maid of honor. Sue had not seen any of the guys in their tuxedos, and she panned the stage for Brady. He was already in place, waiting beside Michelle's brothers, who were smiling incessantly.

The director motioned for Sue to begin her walk. She began her walk slowly in her royal blue strapless floor length formal, which shone in the glimmer of the dimmed sanctuary lights and candelabras. She wore her hair long, but the sides were swept back with two rhinestone combs that glistened like stars in the sky-or at least that was the way that Brady saw it. He watched her every move as she slowly glided down the aisle. When she made it to the platform, she lifted the skirt of her dress ever so slightly, so as not to trip going up the steps and revealed the silver strappy heels that she and all of the bridesmaids wore. She made her way to her place on the stage, opposite of Brady, and turned to watch the rest of the procession. Brady also turned to watch the remaining girls entering the sanctuary, but he felt his head turning right back to Sue. His concentration was broken when the pianist sounded the chimes that signaled the entrance of the bride.

At that moment, everyone's attention turned to Michelle, as her father, Stan, ushered her down the aisle to Justin, who was grinning from ear to ear. Justin's father, Pastor Rhodes, made the opening remarks with a tear-stained face and joined Justin's and Michelle's hands when her father gave her away. With that, he also took his place by his wife to enjoy the rest of the ceremony, performed by Pastor Creighton.

When the ceremony got underway, Brady felt his eyes wandering across the way to Sue. This time, their eyes met, and Brady mouthed the words, "You look beautiful," to Sue. Much to his surprise, Sue blushed, and then she quickly turned her attention back to the ceremony. Brady determined to try and pay attention. He looked at Justin and Michelle and remembered what Justin had told him at the Bargain Bin. He had taken the 'tough-love' advice to heart, and had been reading his Bible and praying at every waking minute, seeking God's will and not his own. He knew that he couldn't deny his feelings, and he came to the point that he was just going to have to let go. He wouldn't interfere with Sue's relationship with Jason, after all they were engaged, but he was done holding his head down and trying to keep away from Sue. They were friends first, and to Sue, obviously that's where it ended; and she never needed to know that it was any different for him. He again remembered the verse, Philippians 4:11, *"for I have learned, in whatsoever state I am, therewith to be content."* Brady had decided that he would be content for the rest of his life to simply be her friend, if that's what God wanted-he still wasn't exactly sure; he did know this, he was done sticking his head in the sand. If he wanted to say something, he would say it and not be afraid.

*****

Sue couldn't believe that she felt her cheeks blushing! Brady had told her that she was beautiful! What was stranger was the fact that she found herself feeling honored to have those words coming from Brady. She took a good look at him from her side of the stage. He was dashing in the black tails tuxedo, with royal blue tie and cummerbund. His white rose boutonniere seemed to be the perfect accent to his regal look. He was, in Michelle's words, 'fine as frog hair'! She giggled to herself and attempted to concentrate on the ceremony.

*****

Soon, Pastor Creighton pronounced Justin and Michelle husband and wife, and Justin kissed his bride. He then introduced to the congregation, Mr. and Mrs. Justin Rhodes. Michelle and Justin led the party out, followed by the flower girl. Brady and Sue walked towards each other, and as he offered his arm in escort, he noticed that Sue was blushing again, remembering his comment from earlier. He wondered why *his* compliments made her blush! Again, he reckoned, wishful thinking! As she locked arms with Brady, he felt a sensation run through him that almost made him weak. *'Get it together, man,'* he thought to himself, as he helped Sue down the steps. They both smiled, and Brady walked Sue down the aisle to the back of the church; all the while he pictured himself escorting Sue out of this same church, only she was in white, but then he remembered, that Jason would be her escort then and not him. He turned and looked at Sue and noticed that she looked distant. They had reached the back of the sanctuary and were instructed to continue on to the foyer. "I'll bet you're glad that's over," Brady said to her as they reached the foyer.

"No," Sue replied, "it was actually nice to have an escort, especially one who looks as handsome as you! I must say, I've never seen you so decked out, Brady! You are really workin' that tux! You'll have your pick of all the single girls at the reception!"

Brady felt his cheeks go flushed, and his heart melted. He couldn't believe what he was hearing, but he knew that he couldn't take it too seriously. But, oh, how he wanted to! Nevertheless, it gave him a new-found confidence. "You think?" he asked, wishing that he could "pick" her. "Hm, let's go see!" He replied as he offered Sue his arm again, but this time in jest, as they headed toward the fellowship hall. "I know one thing, if I was Jason, I wouldn't have left you here alone at a wedding-not looking like this."

'I know he's just being polite. He's only trying to make me feel pretty since my beau isn't here to do it himself. Boy, what a good friend I have.' Sue thought to herself. "Yeah, but everyone knows that we're engaged!" Sue replied.

"Yeah, but as we just saw, it ain't over until you say,

'I do,'" Brady replied as he opened the glass door of the fellowship hall for Sue as she looked at him in bewilderment. She wondered what he meant by that. They walked in, and Brady took a good look around, and then he looked at Sue, "Now, I believe I'll go and see about all those ***single*** girls!" And with that, he turned and left Sue's side, which was quickly turning green with envy; for a fleeting moment, Sue wished that she were single again.

"Open thou mine eyes, that I may behold wondrous things..."

Psalm 119:18

Chapter 14

The wedding was now over and done, and Justin and Sue were already back from their honeymoon to Niagara Falls. Justin had turned out to be a real romantic, as he had concealed the honeymoon plans from Michelle. It was upon arrival on Canadian soil that Michelle realized that her new life would be nothing short of miraculous. When they arrived back at Sunset at their new apartment, Justin got his paperwork ready for his first day back on the job, and Michelle immediately wanted to call Sue to tell her where Justin had taken her, but it was late. Michelle was tired from all of the traveling, so she just turned in for the night and decided that she would catch up with Sue the next day.

When Justin was finally able to tear himself away from Michelle's 'goodbye' kiss at the front door, he jumped into his Grand Marquis and raced off to the Bargain Bin, so that he would not be late! Michelle then picked up her cell phone and called her friend.

"Hey, Michelle! I'm been afraid to call you! I didn't want to catch you at a bad time, you know!" Sue teased.

"Oh, girl let me tell you! The Falls were beautiful! We took the boat ride on the Maid of the Mist, and we got to go behind the falls on another tour!" Michelle was just overflowing with joy, and she had to talk to somebody!

Sue was ready to listen! Her honeymoon trip did indeed sound so romantic. After Jason's horse and buggy ride on their first date, he seemed to run all out of romantic ideas! "Did you stay on the Canadian side or the American side?"

"We stayed in Canada, and boy, was it beautiful! We had a room that had floor to ceiling windows so that you could see the falls, and at night, they turned the colored lights on them, and girl, you talkin' about somethin' to see! Um-hum!"

"Well, I'm glad that you enjoyed the sights! But, I'm even more glad that you're home now!" confessed Sue.

"Have you started your summer courses yet?" Michelle asked.

"Yes, and in fact, I have a class in about thirty minutes, so…"

"Oh, girl! Why didn't you tell me to shut-up ten minutes ago?" said a flustered Michelle.

"Because I love you, and I really did want to hear all about it-well not *all* about it-but you know!" said an embarrassed Sue.

"Alright, girl! Go get that edu-ma-cation!" laughed Michelle as she hung up.

Since Sue had already began her summer courses, the weeks started rolling by. She had a standing all-day date every Saturday with Jason, as he drove in on Friday nights, and they spent all day together. On most Sundays, he made it to church with her for the morning worship service, but he always drove back to Ridgeway on Sunday evenings, which came all too soon.

It was right after the week of the Fourth of July when Sunset hosted their county fair. Sue absolutely loved the fair. Back home in Campbell's Grove, their fair was always small, but her Mama never ceased to win first prize with her homemade strawberry preserves. Sue had nothing to enter, but she was eager to go and see what it was all about. This particular week, Jason had to represent the firm at an engineering trade show in Washington, D.C. He and Sue both considered it an honor that the firm would place that much trust in him to go alone and present the new innovations that they had to offer. He wasn't sure when he would be able to come to Sunset to see Sue, or if he would get to come home at all. There was no way that Jason could pass up this opportunity, and Sue would not have dared to ask him to do so.

Sue worked all week at the Bargain Bin after class, and she checked out so many families who were on their way to the fair. She wanted to go so bad! But, she knew that she would feel a little silly going by herself! As the last family left the store on Friday evening, Sue hadn't noticed that Brady had walked up to the register with a candy bar and a drink. He got very still and waited until he knew that Sue was totally distracted.

"Boo!" he shouted.

Sue almost wet her pants, and Brady was laughing his head off! "Brady Sheffield!" she hollered as she slapped his arm. "Don't you ever do that again!" Sue said as she scanned his candy and drink.

"Oh, come on! I was just having a little fun! Lighten up! Besides, I know what you've been wanting to do all week, and it's only thirty minutes until closing time, so get happy!" Brady said as he paid Sue for his snack.

"Well, I'm not going. Jason can't come in this weekend, and I'm not going alone. You know, I've never missed a fair yet, and I've never missed a year going without a date either-not since sixth grade."

"Sixth grade? I know Mrs. Irene didn't let you date in the sixth grade?"

"Not really, but it was always sort of a status thing, you know; all of the girls had a boy that would meet them at the fair-sort of a riding partner. I've had one every year since the sixth grade. I know it seems silly, but I'd feel so foolish going alone!"

"Well, you won't be." said Justin. "Because we will all go together. I was planning on taking Michelle tonight, and it would be a big help to me if we all went together."

"Help? What do you mean?" asked Sue.

"Yeah; I only like to go to the fair to eat, but Michelle, you know, she likes looking at all of the those crafts, and jams, and jellies, and stuff like that! Boring! But, you two could do all of that, and Brady and I could eat!" replied

Justin with a huge smile.

"I could definitely eat!" said Brady with a weak laugh.

"So, whattya say, Sue? Will you come with us?" asked Justin, "please?"

"Oh, okay. I guess! For once, I just won't have one date, I'll have three!" Sue said with a laugh!

Justin, Brady and Sue closed down the store and had it ready for the morning before leaving. Sue wanted to go back to the dorm and change before going to the fair, so they all agreed to meet her at the gate in an hour.

Brady watched her drive away, as he and Justin walked to their vehicles. Brady looked at Justin with a determined look on his face. "What's wrong with you Brady?" Justin asked.

"Oh, nothing. I just really enjoy these times when Jason isn't here. I feel like I don't have anyone watching me, or looking over my shoulder."

"Well, what does it matter? You're not 'interfering' in their relationship anyways, so what's there to see?" Justin poked.

"Well, I just feel free to be myself. Sue and I didn't see much of each other this past semester, and we haven't talked as much as we used to. I thought we had kind of a break through at the wedding. I actually told her that she was beautiful, can you believe that?"

"No, actually, not from you. How'd she take it?"

"She blushed; twice! Once on the stage, and then when I escorted her out. Wonder why she would do that?"

"No, clue, bro! Sorry I wasn't more aware of what was going on between you and Sue. I was a little distracted-getting married!" said Justin in a sarcastic tone.

"And then, she told me I looked good, and that I could have my pick of any of the single girls there! I tried making her a jealous, by leaving her at the door in search of the 'single girls'! I doubt that it worked though. She's still with him," Brady said with a singe of disappointment.

"You never know though. You never know how your actions affect others-good and bad," replied Justin.

"I know. That's why I'm trying to be so careful. I'm not going to interfere, but I have decided that I am done hiding in a corner. It may not be God's will that she be with me or him; I'm still not sure. She doesn't need to know that I love her, but I'm not holding my tongue about Jason anymore. He doesn't deserve her."

"Tell me something I don't know."

"Well, I'm going home to get a shower and a shave. She might not be ordering right now, but there's no harm in letting her see what else is on the menu, right?" said Brady with a laugh.

"Right. I'll meet you at the gate in forty-five minutes. Don't be late!" admonished Justin.

Brady climbed into his truck and drove to his apartment. *'I've really got to make sure that tonight is very platonic-friends only. That will be no problem on Sue's part; I've just got to keep myself in check. No staring, no accidental brushing of the hands or anything. Be good, Brady, be good.'* Brady thought to himself as he drove up to his small apartment.

As promised, everyone met at the gate within the hour. Sue was so excited she could hardly contain herself. They walked in through the gate, and the boys immediately wanted to stop for food. Sue and Michelle helped themselves to the crafts display. Michelle really enjoyed looking at the quilts.

"You know, Sue, I've always wanted to learn how to quilt," Michelle confessed.

"Well, why haven't you? You've always been good at whatever you wanted to do?" replied Sue.

"Well, not beauty school, remember?! I don't know; I might give it a try! Uh oh-don't look now, but here come the garbage disposals!" laughed Michelle as she directed their attentions to Justin and Brady who were coming up the walkway, with snacks just dripping off of them! They both had bags of cotton candy tied to their belt buckles. Brady carried two sausage dogs, and Justin carried two Styrofoam trays filled with funnel cakes. Justin scouted a table and chairs and nodded to the girls for them to meet them there, which they did. "Boy, I'm glad y'all are here, 'cause I'm starving," said Michelle.

"Oh, did you want something to eat?" Brady asked with a laugh. "Well, I guess I'll have to go back!" If looks could kill, the girls would have been calling the undertaker. "Just kidding! Here;" Brady said as he pulled a plastic knife out of his shirt pocket. "We thought we'd share," he said as he began to cut the sausage dogs in half.

"Yeah, really-this is so much for anyone to eat alone." Justin said as he tried to fold back the lid of the funnel cake. The group ate their food, and then they decided to take themselves for a walk on the midway. Michelle and Justin walked along, hand in hand, with Brady walking alone on Justin's side, and Sue walking on Michelle's. Suddenly, Michelle stopped in front of the Ferris Wheel.

"Oh! Justin, please-let's ride." she begged.

"Oh, yes! Justin, please, let's go!" chimed in Sue.

"Okay, I guess that's okay with me," Justin answered as he looked at Brady. Then he and Michelle bounded up the ramp to get in line for the ride.

Brady and Sue hung back as she looked at him sheepishly. Brady knew that she wanted him to ride with her, but he thought about it for a moment, and then decided that it would not be a good idea for he and Sue to ride together. Not only would it mean personal torture for him because every guy knew what girls expected at the top of the Ferris Wheel, and that definitely wasn't going to happen; besides, if anyone noticed the two of them riding together on the wheel, they might misconstrue their friends' outing as a date which would make it look like Sue was cheating on

Jason. Brady could not take that chance of ruining their relationship, and Sue's reputation.

Brady followed Sue up to the line for the Ferris wheel. "Um, okay, so, I'll meet you when you get off of this, okay?"

"You're not riding with me? Brady Sheffield! Are you afraid of heights?" Sue chided.

Brady knew he couldn't tell Sue the real reasons for not riding. "NO, I am not afraid of heights. I am afraid of rickety old Ferris Wheels that are thrown together basically overnight and then taken down just as fast to go to another town!"

"You know they have these things inspected before they allow folks to ride them?" Sue rebutted. She really thought she would look silly riding a Ferris Wheel all by herself, and she knew she would have to beg.

"Yeah, but..."

"Oh, come on! Please?" she pleaded.

Brady rolled his eyes, as Sue grabbed him by the hand and led him up the ramp to the Ferris wheel, where they waited in the rather lengthy line.

"I really don't feel right about this." Brady began.

"Well, it seems that once again you've come to my rescue!" Sue admitted. "I didn't have another soul here to ride it with me!" Sue said, and then she suddenly screamed as someone came up from behind her and grabbed her around the waist. She quickly turned around.

"Well, I wouldn't say that!" Jason said with a huge smile and he gave her a quick, but forceful kiss.

Brady looked away; he was sure that the kiss was for his account.

"Hey, Baby!" said Sue with a smile, and then she looked at Brady, who returned the best mock smile that he could give.

"Thanks for stepping in for me Brady, but I think I can take it from here," said Jason, and he moved into the line.

"No problem. Tell Justin and Michelle that I'll be waiting for them when they get off the ride. You and Jason have a good night."

"You're not coming with us?" Sue asked.

"Well, wouldn't you rather you and me take a little stroll on our own?" Jason offered. Again, Brady was sure that Jason was simply marking his territory again.

"Oh, yes," Sue answered as she looked at Brady sadly. It was so strange. Part of her was actually sad that Brady was not riding with her. She knew that he was now feeling like a fifth wheel, and for some reason, that just didn't sit well. "Thanks for being such a good sport and being willing to help me out," she offered in retribution.

"It was my pleasure," Brady answered as he walked away sadly. He had one destination in mind-the shooting gallery.

As he put his money down for the pellet rifle, he looked at the duck targets swimming lazily by. He took a shot and missed. Then he took another look as all the ducks little faces turned into bobble heads of Jason as they rolled by. He took another shot, and-direct hit! And then another, and another, and another! Brady was beginning to enjoy his task a little too much as Justin and Michelle approached. The attendant handed Brady the giant teddy bear that he had won on his venting session.

"Dude!" You're a crack shot!" exclaimed Justin.

"I guess, when you have the proper motivation, anything's possible," answered Brady glumly. Then he caught sight of Sue and Jason still riding the Ferris Wheel. He was so disgusted. "Just look at them," he said under his breath, but not so softly that Justin didn't hear.

"I'm sorry. I guess that this turned out to be a pretty miserable night for you, bro."

"Naw, it's alright. It's just how it is," Brady answered solemnly. "Here you go, Chelly," he said as he handed Michelle the giant teddy bear. "Do me a favor and take this little critter home with you, okay?"

Michelle, realizing what had horrid reminder of the evening that the bear would be, took it. "I would be honored to do so!" she answered, trying to boost his spirits.

"Well, I'm just gonna run on home now. I don't really feel like eating anything else now," said Brady as he extended his hand to Justin.

Justin shook his hand in complete understanding. "Go get some sleep, Brady. I'll see you tomorrow at work."

Brady simply nodded and headed for the gate. Inside, he prayed. *'Dear Lord, I don't know what you have in store for us, but I know that these feelings inside can't be for naught. I can't stand the sight of the two of them together. Please let me know, Lord. Please. I love her so much. If the answer is 'no', then please help me to let her go.'*

*****

After the fair had passed, Sue looked forward to the weekends more than ever. She was always so ready to see her Jason that she could hardly stand it. Sue lived from Saturday to Saturday, and before she knew it, her summer courses where done, and she was well into her next fall semester. Brady had also returned to classes at ACU, which meant he was able to meet Sue for lunches at the Greasy Spoon again. Sue was glad that she and Brady had their old routine back. Ever since the County Fair, Sue felt like their relationship was a bit strained. Brady had really been keeping his distance from her, and she didn't know why. Sue kept her part-time job at the Bargain Bin since Jason was not here this fall; it helped pass the time, and the extra money was going to the wedding fund, after all.

Thanksgiving break was approaching, and Sue had met Brady at the Greasy Spoon for lunch again. Sue had a distant look, and it bothered Brady.

"What's going on, Sue?" he asked.

"Well, I just talked to Jason about Thanksgiving."

"And?"

"Well, I think that I'm going to stay here and spend it with him and his mom. He drives all the way from Ridgeway to here, and I just don't think I should ask him to drive me all the way home."

"Or, did he tell you that he wasn't going to drive you?" Brady asked as he read her expressions. Brady always watched her. He could tell when something was bothering Sue. Her eyes didn't lie.

"No, he didn't say that, but he didn't offer it either; I know things are tight right now, and we'll eventually be rotating holidays between both of our families soon, so I might as well get used to it," said Sue as she tried to rationalize it to herself.

"He ought to be willing to do whatever he has to; he ought to be thinking of you," said Brady in a very condescending voice.

"Well, he is thinking of me-we're trying to save as much money as we can for the wedding; that's thinking of me!" said Sue as she twirled her french fry.

"Is he coming home this weekend?" asked Brady.

"Yeah, he said that he'd been in late, as usual, so he'll just call me on Saturday."

"He doesn't call and talk to you from the road? It seems like he'd a least like to hear your voice to help keep himself awake!" scolded Brady.

"You'd think so, wouldn't you?" said Sue, as she actually thought about it, but she dismissed the thought as trivial, just as fast as it entered her mind.

"Well, on a brighter note, I spoke to the lawyer who is handling my grandmother's estate, and I think I'm gonna sell the house," said Brady, changing the subject.

"WHAT? Brady, you are not going to do that!"

replied an angry Sue.

"And what makes you think that you have a 'say-so' in this? The house is getting older and there's no one living there, which makes it a target for vandalism, and only Lord knows what else. I never stayed there when I came home because I didn't have any extra money to pay utilities, and it's just too emotional. It's time to let it go."

"Well, I can understand that part, but you really should pray a little longer about that," Sue replied.

Something went off in Brady's head that almost made him explode. If Sue only knew the agonizing hours that he had spent in prayer-over her. "You have no idea what I've been under, and what I've been praying about, and the things that I've had to deal with so just…" he began, and then he noticed that Sue's eyes were about as big as golf balls, so he stopped. "Sue, you're not the only one with things going on in your life. Wake up to the world-there's more than just Jason in it."

"WOW! What's gotten into you?" Sue asked.

"I'm not sure, but I know this-selling the house is the right decision, end of story." Brady replied.

"I'm sorry, Brady. I didn't mean to upset you. I guess that I really haven't been there for you like I used to. Jason did take up a lot of my time." Brady rolled his eyes as Sue continued. "Like this-I've missed this, us eating lunch together here. We used to talk about everything, and now I feel so distant from you-especially since that night at the County Fair." Sue confessed.

"And…" asked Brady.

"And I don't like it," Sue said as she looked at Brady.

"Well, I don't like it either. Let's not let that happen again. I'll always be here for you, no matter what Sue. You know that right?" Brady asked with confidence.

"I do." answered Sue, as they finished their lunch and headed to the Bargain Bin for the night shift. She wondered to herself as she ate, *'What's gotten into Brady? I've never seen this side of him before! It really bothered me to know that there was something wrong between us, and I knew that there was something wrong. I hate it when we're not in sync. I need to pray for him more. Evidently, there's a lot on his plate that I didn't know about. I know that I have Michelle right down the street basically, and Jason comes home every weekend, but there's just no one like Brady!'* she concluded.

*****

Thanksgiving came, and as promised, Sue spent it with Jason and his mom, Ms. Collette Dolen. The day started out good, with the Macy's Parade and Sue helping Ms. Dolen in the kitchen. Ms. Dolen had never remarried after she and Jason's dad had divorced. She simply trudged along from day to day, in what seemed to be such an unhappy life. Jason's father had given her everything she wanted in the settlement, and then paid her a generous alimony every month. But still, it was easy to see that money couldn't buy happiness, which was definitely lacking her home. Mr. Dolen had called to speak to Jason, and Ms. Collette intercepted the call, which became nothing less than a shouting match. By the time that she handed the phone over to Jason, she was in tears, and Jason really didn't want to speak with his father. Sue felt so out of place. Every holiday that she had ever known had been overflowing with love and fellowship. Sue felt so sorry for her Jason and determined that she would do whatever it took to make their home a haven of love.

******

Thanksgiving came and went, and Christmas was upon them. The Christmas rush made long hours at the Bargain Bin for Justin and Brady. Since Brady had decided not to go back to Campbell's Grove for Christmas this year, Justin scheduled Brady and himself to handle the Christmas

Eve shift. Finally, the last present was sold, and Justin locked the door. Brady counted down the till, and Justin completed the paperwork.

"I'm glad that you'll be coming over for Christmas dinner, Brady. I hated the thought of you being alone on Christmas in your little apartment," began Justin.

"I'm only coming for Christmas supper. You and Michelle decided to have your first Christmas dinner together at home, and I'm not going to ruin that special occasion...but I will eat your leftovers!" joked Brady.

"It's been a while now, since we talked, but look-did you ever give any thought to what I said to you when I hired Sue? Are you ready to move on, especially after the County Fair incident?" Justin had really stepped on out a limb when he put Brady in his place. He knew that Brady really needed to man-up and move on, or get down to business and fight for Sue, but he also recognized that Brady was the only one who could know which path was right. He knew after Brady had such a melt-down at the fair, that he definitely had a choice to make.

"I did give it a lot of thought and prayer, and you'll be glad to know that I do know exactly what God's will is for me- at least in one area."

"And that is?" asked Justin in anticipation.

"Sue." replied Brady.

"You're killing me here- what about Sue?" asked Justin.

"She's the one. I can't get away from it. I know that God wants me to marry Sue." confessed Brady.

Justin's frustration reached new levels! His poor friend just didn't get it! "News flash, buddy! She is engaged to another man! They have set a date! They will be married in June, only six months away! Are you telling me that you are gonna try to break them up? Are we going to bat, Sheffield?" asked Justin as if he was looking for a fight.

"Nope, we saw how that worked out back in July, at

the fair," answered Brady nonchalantly. "I'm not gonna have Sue hate me for the rest of my life because I ruined our 'friendship,' her 'reputation,' and her 'engagement.'"

"Well, might I just pry and ask how you plan to marry another man's fiancée? Please tell me that kidnapping is not involved?!" asked Justin.

"I'm not going to do anything-I'm just gonna wait. That's what I should have done to begin with!" answered Brady with complete confidence that God would fight this battle for him.

"Hm. Six months and they'll be on their honeymoon. And you're just gonna wait?" asked Justin.

Brady looked at his friend and quoted, *"Wait on the LORD: be of good courage, and he shall strengthen thine heart: wait, I say, on the LORD. Psalm 27:14"*

"Oh my goodness, you really are serious about this-you've claimed a verse." realized Justin.

Brady continued, *"Delight thyself also in the LORD; and he shall give thee the desires of thine heart. Psalm 37:4"*

"Two verses!" said Justin with a laugh.

"You see-I *know* what I'm doing. God will take care of everything, and I'm not worried about any of it. I don't know how or when; I just know that it's going to happen-she and I."

With that, Justin accepted the fact the God had indeed shown something to his friend, and he was so relieved!

Chapter 15

January came and that meant the spring semester had begun. Brady and Sue had signed up for their courses, and it was again business as usual. Sue had plenty of credits to graduate with her Associates in Arts degree, but she didn't want to blow it while planning her wedding, which would be on June 1st, less than six months away now, so she spent all of her free time studying. Sue could hardly believe it; in less than six months she would be Jason's wife. They would spend a lifetime together. As she remembered the first time they "met" she simply laughed at how they ended up together. She remembered their first "kiss" that night in the Science Lab when they were just about to break out in a knock-down, drag-out fight! The more that Sue thought about how she and Jason had come to be in a relationship, the more strange that their pairing seemed, but she remembered how Brady had given her such good advice-Christian advice, and Sue really felt that God was smiling on their future union.

Classes came, and before she knew it, January and February had come and gone. The weekends were like heaven and were way too short for Sue, as Jason went back to Ridgeway every Sunday night. It was now March, and Sue had begun making some definite wedding plans, but she needed Jason's input desperately, as she so wanted to make their marriage a success and start off on the right foot-together.

That first Saturday of March came, and Sue was scheduled to work. Jason had agreed to pick her up for lunch during their Friday night conversation. He often came into town late, and sometimes didn't even see Sue until the next day. On this day, Sue went in to work, as usual, and then, Justin came to her register. "Here, I'll relieve you for a minute, Sue. You have a phone call in the office."

Sue quickly went to the office. It was Jason. "Hey,

babe," he began, "Listen, you wouldn't mind if we skipped lunch today! The old boys from high school are having a basketball game down at the park, and it's kinda an all day thing-I'll catch up with you tonight, okay?"

Sue's heart fell, and she felt a tinge of anger rearing its head. "Well, it sounds like you've already decided! I was really looking forward to seeing you, J," said Sue as her heart writhed in her chest. *'She couldn't believe what she was hearing! She had waited all week just to see him-she needed him to help her plan their wedding! She lived for their Saturdays together-and now all of that was gone! And he was blowing it for basketball? What was that about?'* Sue thought to herself angrily.

"I will see you-tonight, I promise," said Jason as he hurried to hang up, "Bye, babe."

"Good-bye," said a confused and angry Sue as she hung up the phone. She could not understand how Jason would want to give up his Saturday lunch with her to play basketball! The issue weighed heavy on her, and it showed as she went back to the register.

Hours passed by as Sue tried to remain a cheerful cashier for her customers. She scanned groceries and other items from the discount store, in a monotonous cycle as she tried to pass the day away and keep her mind off of her lonely lunch to come-one without Jason, even though he was here in town! *'Didn't he have to eat too? Surely he couldn't play basketball the whole day through without some nourishment!'* Her thoughts were interrupted as Brady came up to buy a Gatorade to drink while he worked. He immediately saw the disgruntlement in her eyes. He was so trained at reading her. "What's wrong, Sue?" he asked.

"Jason cancelled our lunch date for today. He met some of his old friends for an all-day basketball marathon, or something." she replied.

"Really? Hm." Brady replied. He could already see God at work. *'Things are beginning to happen-maybe it was the miles of distance between Sue and Jason that was beginning to allow them to drift apart-or could it be God's Divine Hand intervening?'* Brady thought to himself.

"What do you mean, Hm?" asked Sue sarcastically.

"Well, I wouldn't be ditching my girlfriend for basketball, especially if I only got to see her on the weekends!" replied a bold Brady. He had decided that he would not purposely interfere in Sue and Jason's relationship-but at this point, Sue had asked him a question, and he definitely felt obliged to answer her, without reservation. He knew that he could help Sue gain some new "perspective."

"Well, smartie, what would you do?" asked Sue. Sue had always thought that Brady liked Jason; after all, it was his idea to have Sue start over and be a good Christian example to him, as she had only just recently recalled. Now it seemed like Brady had something against Jason. *'Why is he acting this way?'* Sue thought.

"I'd keep my promises," answered Brady solemnly. "Tell you what-since you're free for lunch, how about spending your lunch hour with me? We'll go somewhere besides the Greasy Spoon?!" offered Brady. He couldn't believe the words that came out of his mouth! *'You weren't going to interfere, man! Now, you're asking her out? Isn't this cheating? No-it's just lunch between friends-we do this all the time at school?! What's the big deal? Anyone who may see us will also see that we are in Bargain Bin Uniform, and they won't think anything of it. Sue's reputation will be protected.'* Brady reasoned with himself.

"Okay, I guess." answered Sue. Sue had no reservations about taking her lunch break with Brady. After all, they did share lunch at school every day-why would this be any different?

"Well, please don't be excited about it!" retorted Brady, as he tried to prime that smile out of Sue, only this time, it didn't come.

"Oh, I'm sorry. I appreciate the invite, really," said Sue, as she watched Brady walk away. Sue immediately realized that Brady was only trying to cheer her up. She felt so bad for wallowing in her self-pity, and she decided that when their breaks came, that she would do her very best to be a ray of sunshine for her friend.

When their lunch hour came, Brady came and collected Sue, and they left through the front door of the Main Street storefront. "Well, where are we going?" asked Sue.

"You'll see," answered a very secretive Brady.

Brady motioned for Sue to follow him to the deli, but then he stopped her from coming inside. "Stay here-I'll be right back," said Brady. He went straight up to the counter and picked up a large white bag. He had already called in the order, and it was ready to go.

'When did he have time to do that?' Sue thought to herself.

Brady came out and simply said, "Follow me," and the bewildered Sue did just that. Brady led her down the street to the memorial park and offered her the picnic table where they sat and ate lunch.

"Here's your homemade pimento cheese on sourdough, just like you like it," said Brady as he handed her a sandwich from the bag.

"How did you know that?" asked Sue.

"I pay attention," answered Brady.

"So you've told me," said Sue as she remembered the last time that Brady had ordered for her.

"I've been paying attention for a long time," said Brady, as he opened his sandwich.

Sue wondered what he meant by that, but strangely, it didn't bother her. *'Maybe he's just referring to us having been friends for so long-yes; I'm sure that's what he meant.'* Sue thought to herself. Then she realized that she kind of liked the fact that Brady thought about her-at least *someone* was thinking about her and not basketball! She felt that anger coming back, but it quickly turned to puzzlement, as she also realized that Jason had never once ordered for her. She wondered if he even knew what she liked!

The two of them ate their sandwiches and snacks, which took only about thirty minutes. Sue made a note of the time. "Well, I guess we should head back," said Sue as she threw her trash away in the mesh trashcan.

"No, we've got some time left. Let's take a walk," offered Brady.

"You walk a lot, I've noticed. I don't think that I've ever even seen your vehicle," confessed Sue.

"Well, my truck's pretty good on gas, but I have to save as much as I can; besides, I get to think better when I'm walking," Brady replied. "Let's go this way." Brady headed toward a new housing development that was going up across the street from the park. "Let's check out some of these houses."

"Won't we get in trouble for trespassing?" asked Sue, as she looked around to see if anyone saw them.

"Naw, see the 'FOR SALE' signs, the contractors want people to come and check them out so they'll sell! Most of them won't even be locked. Now, come on," said Brady as he took off in a jog towards the first house. It was a two-story house with a carport and a balcony on the back. Sue walked in through the carport behind Brady and began to explore the house. As they walked in, they found themselves in the kitchen. The cabinetry was absolutely beautiful with white, raised panel doors. There was an archway to the left of the kitchen which led to the living room, which was an open space displaying the most beautiful oak banister railing all the way up the stairs and across the upstairs hallway. The evening sunset shone through the front door's stained glass insert which gave a rainbow glow to the unpainted sheetrock walls. On the wall to the kitchen was a beautiful cobblestone fireplace. Sue wondered how different colors would look painted on those unfinished walls. "I love the fireplace here," she remarked.

"Yeah, and I love this balcony off of the master bedroom. It's a good place to think and read," said Brady. "What kind of house do you want, Sue?" he asked.

Sue thought for a moment. "I don't know. I guess I've never thought about it, really; I've only thought about the apartment that Jason has, that's all," answered Sue, as she began to really inventory the future that she was facing. It was a sobering thought as Sue realized that she and Jason had not talked about such things.

"Well, do you expect to stay there forever? If you have kids, wouldn't they need a nice yard to play in?" suggested Brady. Sue began to wonder why she had never thought about these types of things before! She stood still in dismay, for it was occurring to her that she had never spoken to Jason about children, or houses, or any future plans. She had no idea what he expected from their marriage, besides the consummation!

"What do you really want out of life, Sue?" asked Brady.

Sue almost cried. All she had been thinking about was getting married and moving in with Jason in the apartment, and being his wife. She hadn't thought any further down the road than that. She looked around the house, and she couldn't really see Jason anywhere. Maybe it was because she was upset with him for ditching her for lunch, or maybe not! She looked up at Brady, who was standing upstairs, leaning slightly over the banister, looking down at her in the open living room. He looked like home. He looked like comfort. He looked like he belonged there-with her. There was only one problem. The ring on her hand wasn't given to her by Brady-it was from Jason. Her commitment belonged to Jason, not to Brady. She looked at Brady and realized that there was something more to their relationship than just friendship. She wasn't sure what it was, but she now knew that it was getting very complicated.

"I don't really know what I want…" Sue said as her voice trailed off.

*****

Later that night, Jason did pick Sue up from work at the Bargain Bin and took her out for a nice dinner, to make up for their missed lunch. Afterwards, they walked in the park, where Brady had taken Sue earlier that day. Jason sat down on the bench and beckoned Sue to come and sit beside him. He put his arms around her and held her close. "Thanks for understanding about today, Sue. I haven't seen those guys in years," said Jason.

"Speaking of years, Jason, where do you see us in five years?" asked Sue, determined to get some answers.

"Wow! Where did that come from?" he asked in complete fear and shock.

"Well, you know, we've never talked about life after the wedding. I know that you want to move up with the firm, but where do you see us- a house, maybe? What would you like?" asked Sue as she tried to pry some information out of Jason. After all, it was only reasonable to know what he expected out of their marriage.

"I don't know. Let's just get through June," he replied, offering no additional information.

"How many children would you like to have?" asked Sue.

"Whoa! Kids? Just hang on there- who said anything about kids? We aren't even married yet!" said Jason, as he was beginning to freak out.

"Well, we never talked about it, and I think that we should. We should know what we expect out of our marriage, shouldn't we?" asked Sue.

"Let's just take it one day at a time, and let's just see what happens," Jason replied. "Now, it's getting late, maybe I should be taking you home." He tried desperately to change the subject-and fast. It was very obvious that Jason was uncomfortable. *'But why? Jason should be excited about thinking of our future together! Surely he wants a son to carry on his name? Doesn't every man? Doesn't he think about these things?'*

Sue was becoming angry that Jason had not given her any clear answers. *'Who is this man I'm about to marry? Why haven't we talked about these types of things before? Why is he not being open with me?'* Sue thought to herself as she felt her blood beginning to boil.

Jason drove her back to the dorm and kissed her in the car, a quick peck on the cheek; that's all that Sue had offered. He told her that he'd pick her up tomorrow morning for church. He didn't even walk her to the door. Sue was really angry and confused by this time; she was glad he wasn't walking her to the door.

When Sue reached her dorm room, Mari wasn't there, as usual, and so Sue took advantage of the quite time to call her dad, Max. Sue knew that she could always count on her Daddy when she had a problem, and this was turning out to be a big problem.

"Hey, kiddo! What's up? It's kind of late, isn't it? Is everything okay?" Max asked.

"Yeah, Daddy. I just needed to talk."

"About Jason?" asked Max. As the wedding date kept drawing nearer, Max began to anticipate a call from his daughter. He prayed daily for it-not for his daughter's unhappiness, but for God's promise to him that all would be well, and they wouldn't marry.

"Yes, sir. Things just don't seem to be going well right now. I can't exactly put my finger on it, but I'm concerned," explained Sue.

"Has he done something to you, or said something…I'm not sure that I am following you?!" asked Max as he tried to give Sue liberty to talk. He loved his daughter, and he had perfect peace that God was in control of this situation. He only wanted to provide the right advice in this time, without coming across as being on 'someone's side'.

"Well, I was trying to talk with him about the future, and he didn't really seem interested in talking with me about it, stuff like, kids, and maybe a house somewhere. He didn't want to talk about any of it! He nearly fell off of the park bench where we were sitting, and he pretty much cut our date short! Today, he cancelled our lunch date to play basketball with his friends. He's never done that before."

"Well, maybe he's getting cold feet, Sue," Max replied. He tried to take account of the facts that Sue was giving him without disclosing any information from his own prayer life.

"I don't know, Daddy. It seems like it might be more than that, or am I over-reacting?" asked Sue. She had always valued her Dad's advice, and she knew that she could always count on him to give her an honest answer.

"Sue, have you prayed about it?" asked Max.

"Well, it just happened today, so, no sir. I really haven't prayed about this particular issue, but I pray for me and Jason all of the time," answered Sue.

"How are you praying, Sue?" Max knew that if Sue was really praying for God's will, then he and she both would be on the same page.

"I pray for God to work everything out for me and Jason," answered Sue.

"Well, really, that's not how you should pray. You should be praying that God will have His Will done in your life," advised Max.

"I have prayed that way in the past; then I met Jason, and I felt like he was the one for me. It just seems like God isn't answering any of my prayers," Sue said in desperation.

"Maybe He has answered them, but you've just not listened to the answer," replied Max. Sue felt a drop of horror when she realized-that was word for word exactly what she had told Cal, as he confronted her and Jason in the church parking lot at Christmas!

"Sometimes knowing God's will and having a feeling are two different things. When you truly understand God's will, you will have a deep peace that is unmistakable. Pray for His Will, Sue, and God will definitely show it to you. It can be a hard thing to discern God's Will for your life, and it takes longer for some people to figure it out than it does for others. But you must earnestly pray for His Will to be done, and not yours."

"I know, Daddy. Maybe…I've been afraid to do that, but I really do want God's Will, and not mine. I guess I'll go now;" she paused, "I've got some praying to do," Sue confessed. She almost dreaded the thought of praying; it had been a long time since she earnestly prayed. She had asked for God's favor on her relationship with Jason, but she knew that she had not really sought God's Will for her life. Coming to Jesus in prayer now would be like trying to talk to a friend that she had ignored for the past few months, except for a couple of emotionless emails or texts. She was very apprehensive, but she knew that she needed to run back to the Saviour-after all, He had never left her.

"Alright; you know that I love you, and you call me anytime you need me," consoled Max as he said his 'good-bye'.

"Thanks, Daddy. I love you, too." said Sue as she flipped her cell shut.

Sue laid down on her bed, with her arm laid across her forehead. She cried out to God, "Dear Jesus, please forgive me of my sins today, Lord. Please forgive me for not praying more, for not reading my Bible, for ignoring you Lord. I'm so sorry. I've let so many things get in the way of our relationship. Dear Jesus, I want to be a better Christian, and Lord, I want to be closer to You so that I can hear Your Voice. Dear God, please have Your Will done in my life…" and the tears began to flow as she continued, "whatever the outcome may be…" She wept there because she knew deep in her heart that something was about to change.

"Create in me a clean heart, O God; and renew a right spirit within me."

Psalm 51:10

Chapter 16

Weeks passed by, and Sue found herself staring at the calendar crossing off the last days of March. She couldn't believe how fast their wedding day was approaching, but what she found harder to believe was how Jason didn't seem to be excited. He never asked about the plans for their ceremony, nor did he offer any ideas for their honeymoon. Any time that Sue asked him little questions, he would give a nonchalant answer or change the subject altogether. Sue had begun praying more, and reading her Bible more, as she was truly seeking God's Will for her life, and she didn't understand why Jason had not come around! She feared in the depths of her heart that something was not right, but she didn't have the courage to come straight out and ask Jason about it.

When April arrived, Sue decided that it was time to have a serious talk with Jason. This was the first weekend of the month, and they only had eight weeks to plan the major details. Jason had called late Thursday night and told Sue that he had the afternoon off that Friday, and would actually be in at a decent time. Sue decided that this was when she would approach him, and maybe, they could get some concrete plans made. Jason came by Sue's dorm and picked her for a bite to eat, and he didn't really have a lot to say. On the way to the Pizza Parlor, Sue broke the silence.

"Jason, you know, we really haven't decided anything concrete about the wedding. I have some ideas; wouldn't you like to see things, or offer some input?" Sue began.

"No, not really. That's girl stuff. Whatever you decide will be fine," Jason answered rather curtly.

Sue had had enough. It was time to just put it out there. "Look, Jason, you're making me really nervous. You've not wanted to help with one thing in regards to this wedding. It makes me think that you've changed your mind! Don't you want to get married?" asked a nervous Sue.

"Of course! I don't care how we get married, just as long as we say, 'I do'. You know, we could always just fly to Vegas if you want; we'll save so much money that way! The firm has access to a charter jet; we can just pack up and go. How's that sound?" Jason offered.

She couldn't believe what she was hearing! "Horrible!" Sue cried, "I want my family and friends to all be there. I want to get married in my church, not some hokey 'Elvis' wedding chapel. Doesn't that mean anything to you? What about your mom and dad? Won't they want to be there?"

"You want World War III on your hands? That's what it will be like if my mom and dad are at the same place at the same time! No, thanks! Maybe my mom will want to come, but we'll catch up with Dad later." Jason paused and rubbed the back of his neck, as if the subject was taking a great deal of effort to discuss. "Look, I'm sorry that I haven't been very interested. It's just not my thing." He stopped long enough to see the crushed looked on Sue's face. "I tell you what; I'll take care of the honeymoon arrangements. We'll go wherever you want to go-just tell me."

"How about Jamaica, Mon?" said Sue with a laugh.

"Ooh! Jamaica sounds great! I'll take care of the travel plans when I get back to Ridgeway," he answered without so much as a hesitation.

"Are you serious? I was just joking!" said Sue with an unparalleled look of excitement on her face. She couldn't believe that he would really be willing to take such an expensive vacation! How would they work that into their budget? *'Maybe his dad has some connections,'* Sue thought to herself.

"Yeah, like I said, I'll take care of everything. You don't worry, now. Okay?" he replied as he leaned over and gave Sue a hug, in an attempt to reassure her that everything was okay.

"Okay," answered a relieved Sue.

"Listen, can you cover the pizza tonight, I'm a little low on cash." asked Jason.

'How in the world can he afford to take me to Jamaica, but he can't cover the pizza?' she thought. "Why?" she asked as she immediately became suspicious. Jason's firm covered all of his bills, and Jason had not been giving Sue any money for the wedding fund, so why couldn't he cover the pizza? "Didn't you get paid last week? What do you have to pay for? The firm covers just about all of your expenses! Besides, I don't think that I have enough; I've been putting back my money in the wedding fund," said Sue.

"I guess we'll just go find the Value Menu at McDonald's," said Jason as he turned the car around.

Sue was becoming furious at Jason's skilled knack for avoiding her inquiries. "Look, you didn't answer my question. Where's your money going? We need to be saving!" said Sue as she began to release her fury.

"You look-we're not married yet! Why do you have to know what I do and what I spend- it's my business!" yelled Jason.

She sat there with a stunned look on her face. Sue was taken aback from his response. She couldn't believe that the man she was about to spend the rest of her life with was treating her this way. This relationship was supposed to be about trust and being open with one another. She knew this was a problem. "I know we're not married yet, but we are engaged, and we're not supposed to be keeping secrets from each other."

"A little bit here, a little bit there, and you know, it's just gone! Payday's just around the corner-everything's fine," said Jason as he tried to calm Sue down, and change the subject.

Sue let the argument go, but she couldn't help but

feel like something was not right. Jason and Sue ate their burgers and then spent some time in the garden down from the arena where they first kissed, spending most of their time against her favorite weeping willow tree. Sue really didn't want to go there-not after the night that they had had. But it seemed like every time that she was with Jason, she lost all control of rational thought. At least the garden was still a semi-public place, and she felt 'safe' there. Jason always had a way of making Sue forget about their arguments. It was too easy for Sue to get lost in his deep blue eyes as he held her close. Before she knew it, it was already ten thirty, and the dorm curfew was eleven. Jason drove Sue back to the dorm, and they said their 'Goodnights'. As Sue climbed the stairs to her dorm room, she couldn't help but feel a little guilty. How was it that Jason always seemed to divert her attention from the important matters at hand with a little kissing under a tree? She really needed to get to the bottom of things, but he always seemed to have this control over her. She realized that she really needed to get a grip.

Sue entered her room to actually find Mari at home! She was already asleep, no doubt exhausted from working those long shifts for her orthopedic rotation. Sue quickly dressed for bed and laid down, staring at her bedside picture of Jason. *'Why was Jason keeping secrets from her? What was he doing with all of his money?'* Sue wondered, and then it occurred to her. *'He's already been planning the honeymoon! He's probably been making payments, on a trip or something, and now, he'll probably be changing them because I mentioned Jamaica! How stupid am I! He didn't want me to know! I just about ruined his surprise! How could I ever think that something was wrong?'* Sue convinced herself that everything was going to be alright, and she kissed his picture, as she did every night, and rolled over to go to sleep.

The next morning, Sue was scheduled to work at the Bargain Bin. She walked down to her Ford Focus and climbed in, but it would not start. She tried again and again, but nothing happened. Mari had already left at some point and time that morning, perhaps even in the wee hours; Sue had still been asleep she supposed. So she picked up her cell phone and called for Jason. He always stayed at his mom's when he came home on the weekends, which was just down the street. Jason answered his cell phone and agreed to come and pick Sue up for work. Sue sat there and waited for thirty minutes. Jason finally arrived.

"Where have you been? I've been waiting here for thirty minutes! It only takes about ten minutes to get here from your mom's house. What happened? " Sue asked impatiently.

"I wasn't at home. The guys met this morning for an early morning game. We play across town. Sorry. I got here as fast as I could," answered Jason.

"Oh. Okay." *'I absolutely loathe basketball.'* Sue thought to herself. It was becoming a very weak excuse-and barely believable, but she would discuss that with Jason later. "Well, can you pick me up tonight around eight when my shift ends?" asked Sue.

"Sure, I'll be there, and I'll come back and take a look at your car while you're working, okay?" Jason offered, trying to smooth over the incident.

"Thanks," said Sue as they rolled up at the Bargain Bin, "My hero! I love you. See you tonight," Sue said as she tried to rekindle the spark that they usually shared. She then opened the door and stepped out for work.

"I love you, too," said Jason as he pulled Sue back in the car for a quick kiss 'goodbye'.

Sue worked the first half of her shift without any glitches, and also without any call from Jason. Sue thought that surely he would call and at least let her know what was wrong with her car! As she took her lunch hour upstairs in the break area, Sue decided to try and use her time wisely. Her Literature exam was rapidly approaching, and Sue never did like Shakespeare much. Romeo and Juliet was definitely not what Sue wanted to be reading right now-two doomed lovers. Ever since Sue had begun to pray for God's will to be done, she began noticing how she dreaded being with Jason. At times, she felt that she was crazy for putting up with his behavior, but when they were together, it was like magic. He had such an effect on her that when she was in his arms, it was like nothing else in the world mattered. Just as she began to try and focus again, Brady walked up to his locker.

"Hey there, Haybert! Whatcha reading?" he asked.

"Oh, hey, Brady. I'm just studying for my Literature exam. Romeo and Juliet," Sue remarked with raised eyebrows of disgust.

"Oh…the story of Love that wasn't meant to be." Brady was so used to being depressed about the subject of Sue, that he almost got disheartened at the thought of the story. Then he remembered God's promise-'*Delight thyself in the Lord, and he shall give thee the desires of thine heart*'. "Is there anything that I can do to help you?" he asked in an effort to be able to sit and talk with her about anything!

"I kept trying to read this, but it's just so depressing! Especially when…" Sue began, but then her voice trailed off. She always confided in Brady about everything, but now, she suddenly felt strange about talking to Brady about her love life.

"Especially when what…? Sue, you know that you can talk to me about anything," he re-assured her. "And I mean anything!"

"That's just it. We get along so wonderfully!" she remarked.

"And that's a problem?" asked a confused Brady.

"NO! Please-don't misunderstand." Sue paused to gather her thoughts. "Okay! Here it is: I've been praying for God to have His perfect will done in my life..." she began.

"Okay…" Brady answered as he inwardly began to get his hopes up. What was God doing in the life of the woman he loved?

"And ever since then, strange things have been happening," she replied.

"What do you mean, strange?" he asked.

"Well, with Jason. He's changed. Something's not right."

"Has he hurt you, or mistreated you? Do I need to take care of something?" Brady asked as he began to get riled up.

"Easy, boy! It's nothing like that." Sue's face shone of bewilderment. "I can't put my finger on it; but something is definitely not right. I've been going over things in my head, and I…oh…I don't know. Look, I'm sorry that I bothered you with any of this. Let's just forget that I said anything about it, okay?"

"Okay, but, look Sue; I'm always here for you. Whenever you need me-about anything? Okay?" Brady offered.

"Okay. Thanks, B." Sue answered with a quick smile and a hug from her friend.

*****

As eight o'clock came, there was no Jason. Sue called him from her cell phone, but Jason didn't answer. When eight forty-five came, Sue became more frustrated. As Brady walked up from the candy aisle, he could immediately sense that something was bothering her.

"Hey, Sue. Is everything okay? What's wrong now?" he asked.

"Jason was supposed to be here to pick me up at eight, and he's nowhere to be found," said Sue, with anger.

"Do you think he's alright?" asked Brady as he tried to cool her anger. He figured that Jason was just being a no-account, but he did want to give him the benefit of the doubt.

"Yeah, he's probably fine, but I just don't know where he is," Sue answered. "And there's some other stuff too." Sue was a little reluctant to share her suspicions with Brady, but she was about to burst! She had to talk with someone, and, as always, Brady seemed to be there for her.

"The stuff we were about to talk about earlier?" asked Brady, as the discussion had just become interesting.

"Yes. Well, here lately, when he comes home on the weekends, he's broke. He has no extra money, and he spends all of his extra time playing basketball with his friends. He has taken no interest in the wedding plans, or anything. He finally said that he would take care of the honeymoon travel plans, but, I don't know…" confessed Sue.

"Well, maybe he's just saving up, same as you! Maybe he wanted to surprise you, kinda like Justin and Michelle." said Brady as he tried to console Sue.

"I thought about that, but, I just have a feeling, you know, in the pit of my stomach that something's not right. Now, he's not here, and I just..." Sue said as her eyes filled with tears.

"Hey, don't do that-I hate to see you cry-you can't be doing that around me, now…" said Brady as he put his arm around Sue, "Look, gimme about fifteen minutes, let me take this stock to the back room, and if you don't mind riding in a dirty old Ford Ranger, I'll take you home. Okay?" said Brady.

"Okay, thanks, Brady," Sue paused as she hugged him. "You've always been such a good friend. I appreciate the help."

"You've been my chauffeur many times; it's about time that I returned the favor!" said Brady with a laugh. "I'll be right back," said Brady as he gave Sue a quick squeeze and returned to the candy aisle. *'A good friend. Maybe not for much longer...Maybe it's time for God to move our friendship to the next level...'* he thought to himself as he pushed the cart of boxes back to the stock room.

Sue sat down on the end of her counter to wait on Brady. *'Huh, a Ford Ranger'* Sue thought to herself. *'Imagine that-A Ford man!'* She began to straighten the magazine racks just to kills time. About five minutes later, Jason drove up in front of the store in Sue's car and came knocking at the glass doors. Sue was furious. She didn't even want to see Jason, and now he was here to take her home. Sue came and unlocked the door, not saying a word, except for telling Jason to wait there, and she'd be right back. She'd remembered Brady's offer to take her home, and she needed to let him know that she was leaving. Sue walked to the back room to tell Brady that she was going. It was the least that she could do since he offered her a ride home.

Brady was standing on a stepladder, placing a box on the top shelf, and he didn't hear Sue coming up behind him. She called his name, and he turned around too quickly, falling onto Sue, boxes and all!

"Oh, I'm sorry, I'm so sorry!" said Brady as he quickly stood up, and extended a hand to Sue to help her up. He pulled Sue to her feet. She landed standing close to him, stumbling a little-but he reached his arm around her waist to steady her. He then noticed her hair was coming down out of her ponytail. "Your hair, it's...," he said as he took his hand and pushed the strand of her hair back behind her ear, and then he caressed her face. Brady looked at her, like he never had before. Their eyes locked, and they leaned in towards one another, neither one of them speaking for a moment. Finally, Sue stopped and broke the silence by clearing her throat. They both moved back.

"Um...Brady... Jason's here. He just showed up. So, I just, I don't need for you to take me home." She paused and began to become nervous and fidgety. Brady remained as still as a pond after the rain. "Thanks anyway, though.

I'll…um…see you tomorrow at church," said Sue as she slowly backed away.

"Tomorrow," answered Brady, as he watched Sue's every move, making her way out of the stock room. Brady couldn't believe what had just happened between them and how right it felt. There was not a doubt in his mind that God intended for Sue and him to be together-until death they did part. As he turned to pick up the boxes, he played the events over and over in his mind. He remembered the soft touch of her hands as he lifted her up, the feathery texture of her hair, and the velvety feel of her face as he caressed it. He closed his eyes as he savored every moment and prayed, *'Dear Lord, I can see that Your hand is in this; You are bringing us together-and please Lord, work quickly!'*

Chapter 17

The next day at church, Brady watched Sue and Jason together, and it nearly ate him alive. He had peace in his heart that God was going to give him Sue, but he didn't enjoy seeing them together at all. He prayed for God to give him strength to make it through. All that week, as Sue worked at the Bargain Bin, Brady couldn't keep his mind on anything but the incident in the stock room. He wished that he could have taken her in his arms right then, but he knew that it wouldn't have been right. She still belonged to another man. The days were ticking down to Jason and Sue's special day, and Sue stilled seemed determined to marry him. Brady kept reminding himself of God's promise, '*Delight thyself also in the LORD; and he shall give thee the desires of thine heart.*' He knew that God would keep His promise.

The next Saturday, Sue was scheduled to work, but Jason promised to pick Sue up for their standing Saturday lunch date; much to Sue's surprise, he was actually on time. She had been very sorrowful all week, with all of her suspicions, and she was looking forward to seeing Jason, so that he could make everything better. They went to a Jack-in-the-Box for a quick bite, and Jason picked a booth in the back corner of the restaurant. Sue thought she would feel relieved to see Jason today, but instead, she felt tears filling her eyes. As they sat down, she felt the warm tears silently flowing over her checks.

"What's wrong, Sue?" asked Jason.

"I don't know! I can't explain it, Jason. I've felt this way all week. I've felt totally alone and deserted, and like I couldn't breathe!" said Sue as the tears really began to fall.

"It's probably just your nerves, baby, that's all. You've been working, and studying, and trying to plan a wedding all by yourself, no wonder you're about to crack! I'm sorry, a lot of this is my fault, I guess. Look, eat your lunch and dry your tears; everything will be alright- it's almost over," said Jason.

'That's what I'm afraid of..." Sue thought to herself as she bit into her burger. Sue had no idea why she was feeling this way, but she knew that something had to give. She was tired of feeling like Jason was hiding something. She used to trust him completely, but now it was so different. She couldn't explain it, and part of her didn't want an explanation-she was afraid of what it might entail. She just wanted it to stop.

Jason drove her back to the Bargain Bin to complete her shift, and Sue promised that she'd be better company after her shift was over, that perhaps she was just a little tired. Jason told her that he'd be back at eight o'clock to meet her for a little 'quality time' together. Sue smiled and went back to work. Sue felt no relief as she worked the rest of her shift. The confrontation weighed heavy on her heart, and she found herself dreading meeting Jason that night.

Eight o'clock rolled around, and Sue had counted down her till, locked the door, and had the front end ready for Monday morning. She went to her car and sat on the hood, as it was a beautiful, cool, spring evening. She waited there for about thirty minutes, but Jason never showed up. At about eight forty-five, Brady came out of the back door, where he and Sue had parked their vehicles. He had finished the stock early and was about to leave. He saw Sue sitting on the hood of her Ford Focus, and he knew immediately what had happened. Jason had stood her up again. "I thought that you had already gone!" he said.

"Well, I was waiting on Jason. He was supposed to be here at eight o'clock," said Sue, as she slid off of the car's hood and began to walk towards Brady.

"Let, me guess, he hasn't called either?" said Brady, as his anger mounted. "And he doesn't answer his cell..."

"That's about it." answered an extremely frustrated Sue.

"Why do you keep on going like this? Can't you see what he's doing?" asked Brady, as Sue looked at him in bewilderment. "He's cheating on you, Sue, and you can't even see it."

Sue was appalled. She had had suspicions of some sort; she knew that something was going on, but she never thought that it could be this! Her mechanisms of denial quickly kicked in. "He is not cheating on me! We are getting married in less than seven weeks! He's planning our honeymoon trip to Jamaica for crying out loud! He's not cheating!" she argued.

"Yes, he is cheating! He comes home broke as a joke, and his company pays all his bills. You wanna know where his money is going? He's spending it on other girls-dinners, hotel rooms, whatever! He hardly calls you during the week; he spends all of his extra time here 'playing basketball,' or so he says, when he should be spending his time helping you and loving you. Instead you're the one killing yourself working and trying to get ready for exams, while he plays around on the weekends like a kid. "

"I don't see you with a girlfriend! How are you such an expert in relationships? What do you know about it? " said Sue as the tears filled her eyes. She didn't know what to believe.

"I know that he doesn't really love you, Sue. If he did, he'd be here right now. I've been here for you, Sue. I've always been here..." Brady said as he snubbed back his tears. Months of keeping quiet and holding in all of his emotions came rushing to the surface as Brady finally let go. "I've been in love with you for months now, and....I've always prayed for a girl like you...I've always been there for you when you needed someone, and I've been invisible to you, Sue-invisible! You've never even considered having me." Brady paused to wipe the tears that were now streaming down his face. He had held his feelings back for so long; even though he was angry, pouring his heart out lifted a huge burden. "I never wanted to interfere; I told myself I'd never interfere, but, Sue, if you marry him...you'll be making the biggest mistake of your life, and you know I'm right."

"Stop..." said Sue, as she broke down sobbing, "I don't believe you! You're making it up!" she cried as she was beginning to see that Brady was absolutely right. She knew deep in her heart that she and Jason were not meant to marry, but for some reason, perhaps her pride, she was holding on to an empty, dead-end relationship. She was denying it in her own mind vehemently, even though she knew that Brady was more than likely right.

"Sue, you told me these things with your own lips-your own beautiful lips! You just can't see it...You're so blind...I can't take it anymore. I can't take watching you two together, knowing what he's doing to you. I know what he tried at the hotel that night. I'm not stupid. Michelle and Mari just gave him an earlier opportunity. I was there for you then, and you wouldn't see me then either. You could have told me all about it, and I would've sent him on his way right then. I wanted to do it anyway, but at that time it wasn't my place."

"What makes you think that it's your place now?" she asked, delving for the reason that Brady had suddenly snapped.

Brady dared not answer her truthfully then; she wouldn't be able to handle that fact that God had shown Brady that he and Sue were to be married; he suddenly felt like this whole episode had been a mistake. He begged God in his heart to get him out of this situation without ruining anything. "He's not right for you Sue. Justin knows, and Michelle knows. Even if you never look my way, even if you never speak to me again, please believe me-he's doing you wrong, Sue. Don't marry him. You'll regret it every day," he said as he got into his truck and cranked it up, "I'm not gonna sit here and watch you ruin your life. I'm outta here…" he yelled to Sue through the passenger side window as he sped out of the parking lot.

Sue leaned on her car and buried her head in her arms. She sobbed uncontrollably. *'Is Jason really cheating on me?"* she wondered, *"Can it really be true? And Brady…how could I have been so blind? God, are you showing me Your Will for my life? Is it Brady? Has it been Brady all along? He has always been there for me, and now I've lost my best friend-and maybe Your choice for me!"* Sue remembered being with Brady in that newly constructed house that night and gazing up at him standing by that banister-and it felt right. She didn't understand it then, but now she wondered, *'Is Brady the one You have for me Lord? Is this Your path for me?'* Sue was so confused and upset, and then she realized, *'Dear Lord, I can't lose my best friend,'* Sue then decided that she was not going to let that happen. She opened her car door, got in, and slammed the car in drive to take off after Brady. When she stopped at the end of the driveway to check for on-coming traffic, it was then that she heard the thunderous crash.

"What time I am afraid, I will trust in thee."

Psalm 56:3

Chapter 18

Sue raced down Main Street, and onto Maple Street, which led to Justin and Michelle's apartment. She thought that's where Brady might be heading. She knew that Brady was distraught and that Justin was the shoulder that he had leaned on all these months-his friend here on this side of Heaven, but the One that had gotten him through it all was the One that Sue had begun to pray to when she first saw the twisted pile of metal that once resembled Brady's truck. She found the truck mangled and wrapped around some trees. The airbag had deployed, but Brady was pinned in the driver's seat, covered in blood and semi-conscious.

"Oh, God, please help me," Sue prayed as she dialed 911 with her hands shaking. It seemed to take forever for dispatch to pick up the line. Finally, once the operator had answered, Sue relayed the scene as she saw it, through hysterical words. It was a wonder that the operator was able to even secure an address. The dispatch operator then asked her to remain on the line until the first responders arrived on the scene. Sue couldn't bear the thought of standing helplessly by while Brady suffered. Only the Lord knew what the extent of his injuries were, so she set her phone to speaker and laid it on the sidewalk behind her and immediately began to try and free Brady. She pushed and pulled on the door, but it was no use. It had been mashed in as the truck appeared to have spun around, hitting one tree before crashing into the others. Sue touched Brady through the shattered driver's side window. "Brady! Brady, can you hear me? It's Sue!" Brady didn't answer. "Brady, please, I need you, don't do this..." Sue cried as she heard sirens coming closer. "Brady, please wake up..."

Brady began to moan, but he never opened his eyes. Sue continued to tug and pull on the crushed truck door, as she noticed people running towards the wreck. "Step away,

Ma'am. We'll take it from here," said a firefighter as he stepped towards the wreckage and began to try and revive Brady. The fire chief then arrived and took Sue by the arm, and tried to lead her away to ask her some questions, but Sue fought him all the way. "Ma'am, please, let them do their jobs. Listen, did you see what happened?" asked the chief.

Sue finally stopped resisting the chief. She realized that at this point there was nothing that she could do for Brady. Nothing physically-but she could pray. She kept her heart in an attitude of prayer and beseeching from the God on high. *'Please God spare his life…'* She finally focused on what the chief was asking her. "No, not really. We were arguing and…." Sue stopped as she realized the catalyst of the event she saw playing before her eyes. "This is all my fault. Oh, Lord, this is all my fault…" said Sue as she grabbed her head and began to become faint.

"Ma'am, please sit down and breathe." The chief took Sue by the arms and held her still. "Listen, is there anyone we should call?" asked the chief as he tried to console her, and keep her from passing out. They sat down on the small hill next to the sidewalk.

Sue thought for a moment. "Yes…please call Justin and Michelle Rhodes…They live down the street here a ways in the Meadowbrook Apartments…" said Sue in a daze as her eyes desperately found the wreckage again to see what was happening with Brady.

"We'll put that through to dispatch," replied the chief as he followed Sue's eyes towards the wreckage. "It looks like they're getting the Jaws of Life. We'd better move back," said the chief as stood and led Sue back to the fire truck. The firefighters cut the door off of the Ranger and pulled Brady from the wreckage. Sue desperately peered over the hood of the fire engine to try and make out Brady's condition. He was so surrounded by men and women working on and assessing him that she couldn't discern what his condition was. They loaded him into the ambulance, and one of the paramedics came over and asked if Sue was going to ride with them or follow them to the hospital. Sue decided that she would drive. As Sue sprinted to her car, the chief received a message from his lapel radio. "Dispatch has reached your friends. They are going to meet you at the hospital. I really wish that you'd wait and let them drive you," he pleaded.

"Thank you, but I don't want to wait," Sue answered as she climbed into her car, pulled towards the ambulance, and waited for them to leave. *'I've waited too long now as it is...'* Sue thought to herself as the images flashed through her mind of all of the times that she should have realized how Brady felt about her. All that mattered now was getting to Brady and taking care of him, as he had taken care of her since she arrived in Sunset. Sue could see how God had provided someone to befriend her; and to take care of her, and now, she could see that perhaps God had sent him there to love her as well.

Sue slammed her car into drive and began to follow the ambulance as it sped away from the scene. As she followed the ambulance, she pulled out her cell phone and called her dad, Max.

"Hey, kiddo, what's up?" asked Max.

"Daddy..." Sue said through her tears, "...there's been an accident." she began.

"Sue! Are you okay?" Max asked in a panic.

"Yes- It's not me, it's Brady. He's hurt really bad. Please pray, please. Please call Pastor Creighton, too. Dispatch has already put a call through to Justin and Michelle. They're meeting me there," explained Sue as the stinging tears made their way down her cheeks.

"Do you need me to come over there?" asked Max.

"No, just please pray, Daddy, and I'll call you back and keep you posted." Sue tried to focus on the road, but all she could think was the worst. She didn't need any other distractions.

"Okay. If you need me to come over, I'll be right there…" implored Max.

"No, really, Daddy; I'll be okay. Just please pray. I love you," said Sue as she flipped her phone shut.

Sue arrived at the Emergency Room bay and stumbled into the registration area. The desk attendant seemed to be moving at a snail's pace. Sue finally caught the eyes of a young red-haired medical assistant. "I'm here for Brady Sheffield, have they brought him in yet?" she asked. Just as the words left Sue's mouth, Justin and Michelle came rushing in through the bay doors, up to the registration desk. Michelle grabbed Sue and hugged her.

"What happened, Sue?" she asked. "Where's Jason?"

"I don't know, and I don't care right now. I'll explain later," said Sue. She directed her attention to the nurse at the desk, "Has Brady Sheffield been brought in?" she asked. At that moment, a doctor came out from the back.

"Brady Sheffield?" he called across the waiting room. The three ran across and identified themselves. "I'm Dr. Ennis. We're working on Brady right now. It appears that there are several internal injuries, and we are going to have to operate to stop the bleeding. They are prepping him now. We'll let you know how he is as soon as possible."

"Thank you, Dr." said Justin, as he led Sue to a nearby chair. Michelle sat beside Sue and put her hand on Sue's back. The touch of a friend caused Sue to melt and sob uncontrollably as the images of the argument prior to the accident flashed in her mind like scenes from a really bad movie. Michelle gave Sue a minute to get it all out, and then the questions ensued. "Now, Sue, tell us what happened," said Justin.

"I was waiting for Jason to meet me after work, and he never showed. I waited until Brady finished up at the store. We started arguing…and…" Sue began crying again.

"Arguing about what?" asked Michelle.

"Brady said that Jason was cheating on me. I didn't...I don't believe it. I don't know what to believe. Anyways, he broke down and told me that he loved me, and that marrying Jason would be a mistake." Michelle and Justin looked at each other. "He also said that y'all knew..." Sue said as she looked at Michelle.

Michelle looked at her friend with eyes of love and compassion. "We did know. He's loved you since you came here, but he never wanted to get in the way of God's Will. He's been praying for a long time, Sue. I guess watching you and Jason together just got to be too much for him."

Justin had not shared with Michelle Brady's confession concerning God's Will for he and Sue to marry. As far as Michelle was concerned, Brady's love for Sue was still unrequited-as far as she knew, Brady was still seeking God's will. She didn't know that he had found it.

"I'm so confused. I truly began praying for God's will a couple of weeks ago, and everything has gone downhill from then on," said Sue as she hung her head.

"Maybe it's really going up..." said Justin. "Nevertheless, we know that Brady needs prayer. Let's pray for him now." Justin, Sue and Michelle all joined hands, as Justin prayed. "Dear Lord Jesus, we come to you with heavy hearts for our friend, Brady. Please have Your will done in all of these matters, Lord. Please heal and give the doctors wisdom and direction. We turn this over to you, Dear Lord. We love You, Dear Jesus. In Your Name we pray, Amen."

Sue felt a strange calm rush over her soul as Justin prayed. How wonderful it was to have friends-good Christian friends-that could take you right before the Throne of Grace with their prayers! Sue was so grateful for their prayers, as she knew that her soul was so tired already from the evening's events. Sue had begun to pray for answers from God, and now she was unsure of everything-except for one thing-Brady had to survive. He had to pull through. There was so much that was left badly between them, and Sue had to make it right. She couldn't leave things the way there were. Brady couldn't go into eternity believing that she didn't care. Sue knew that she did care, and she knew that their relationship was changing. Where it was going was something that she was still unsure of, but she knew that things between them would never be the same.

The three friends waited for hours. Finally, Dr. Ennis came out with the report. They all stood in anticipation for the doctor's words. "We were able to stop the bleeding, but we did have to remove his spleen. He is stable, and in Intensive Care. We will be watching him closely, but we expect him to make a nice recovery."

The three friends breathed a sigh of relief. "Thank you, doctor," said Justin as he walked over and shook his hand. "God bless you."

Before the doctor had a chance to walk away, Sue jumped forward; "Can I see him?" she asked.

"Only one person is allowed at a time. He is still unconscious, but I believe that he can hear you, if you speak to him. I believe that it helps people heal when they know that they had friends here waiting on them," said Dr. Ennis.

"Could you take me to him?" asked Sue.

"I'll get a nurse for you. I must be getting back to complete the paperwork," said Dr. Ennis. Then he motioned for a nurse to come over and take Sue to Intensive Care.

"Thank you again, doctor. For everything," said Justin as he reached out and shook Dr. Ennis's hand again.

"You're very welcome," said the doctor as he returned through the bay doors.

"Before we do anything, we need to thank God for His mercy for our friend," said Justin, and he began to pray. Sue closed her eyes and silently prayed, *"Dear Lord thank you for sparing his life. Please help me to not take him for granted. Thank you for sending him to me. Please continue to help him to recover fully."*

Justin worried that Sue would try to rehash the evening's arguments with apologies that might cause Brady distress. He tried to get her to go home and return tomorrow, hopefully when Brady became conscious. "Sue, you should go home and get some rest," begged Justin.

"No, not until I get to see him," said Sue. "I have to see him." Sue was persistent. She needed Brady to make it. There was so much that was left unsaid between them. She knew better than to hash the specifics in his unconscious state, but she had to let him know that she was there-and that *she did care.*

The nurse walked up and took Sue, Justin, and Michelle to the Intensive Care Unit. Sue saw Brady lying there with tubes and lines running in and out, and she became weak. Justin had to grab her at the elbow to keep her standing. She finally regained her composure and was able to stand on her own two feet.

The nurse reminded them, "Now, only one person can go in at a time, but do speak to him-I know that it helps the patient if they know that someone's there; but only stay for a moment. He does need his rest." said the nurse, as she returned to her station.

Michelle directed her attention to Sue. "Okay, girl, can you make it in there?" she asked.

"Yes, I'll be fine," said Sue. She slowly walked in and took a seat on the rolling stool beside the bed.

"Let's give her some privacy," said Justin, as he took Michelle by the arm out to the waiting area.

Sue took Brady's hand in hers, and then she brushed his hair back from his forehead. "Brady, I am here. I don't know if you can hear me, but I'm so sorry." The tears began to flow. "This is all my fault. I'm sorry for everything. Deep inside, I knew that you were right. That night that we were in that new house being built, I couldn't see Jason being at home with me... but you were there. I feel so 'at home' with you. You gotta wake up. We've got a lot to talk about," said Sue, as she kissed his hand and left.

Sue walked out to the waiting area and met with Justin and Michelle. She was now indeed exhausted and felt that she would collapse now that the rush had passed. "I'm gonna go home now. I'll be back first thing in the morning."

"Well, I'm gonna stay tonight, just in case he wakes up; someone needs to be here. Can you take Michelle home with you?" asked Justin.

"Sure. See you tomorrow," said Sue. Michelle said her 'goodnight' to Justin, and the two girls headed for home. Michelle and Sue were silent during the ride. Michelle wondered how Sue must have felt-being the first one on the scene of the accident and feeling so helpless-and then feeling that she had indeed caused the accident. She decided that when Sue was ready to talk about it she would assure her of the fact that it was just an accident, no matter what the prior conversation had been.

Sue winced as she drove by the scene of the accident. She stared at the truck that was now loaded on a flat bed tow trailer, waiting to be taken to the junk yard. The memories were just too vivid now, but she snapped her eyes back to the road and determined that she would blot if from her mind. She had to-she needed to be at the hospital first thing in the morning for Brady.

Sue finally made it to Justin and Michelle's small apartment. Michelle hugged Sue one last time and begged her to get some sleep. Sue promised her that she would do her best and then wished her friend a 'goodnight'. As soon as Michelle made it inside, Sue drove away, heading back to her dorm room. When she arrived, she found that Mari wasn't there, as usual, and Sue was glad. She felt drained, and she slept so much better when she was alone. Sue dressed for bed and laid down. Her eyes caught her bedside picture of Jason, whom she realized had never shown up! He hadn't called or tried to find Sue. *'Who knows where he is right now?'* Sue thought to herself. Remembering Brady's accusations, Sue decided that for right now, she didn't want to know. It was well past midnight, and Sue didn't feel like talking about anything anyways. She decided that she would fill Jason in on the situation tomorrow. She would get to the bottom of the matter, after she had seen Brady and knew for herself that he was okay. She took another hard look at Jason's picture, and then, without her 'nightly picture kiss' just rolled over and fell asleep.

"Trust in the Lord with all thine heart; and lean not unto thine own understanding. In all thy ways acknowledge him, and he shall direct thy paths."

Proverbs 3:5-6

Chapter 19

It seemed like Sue had barely closed her eyes when the alarm clock went off at six a.m. She wanted to be up and ready when visiting hours started. She got up and realized that once again Mari had not come home. She probably had another shift with the orthopedic clinic. Sue made her way down to the showers, and thankfully, most of the girls were sleeping in today; then it hit her-it was Sunday Morning! No wonder the showers were empty! She got ready, and went back to the room to grab her purse, and she noticed that her cell phone was about to vibrate off of the desk! She had forgotten to change the ring tone back to loud after leaving the hospital last night. She wondered how many calls she had missed. The caller ID showed 'Jason.' Sue reluctantly answered.

"Sue, we have to talk," started Jason, without even a 'hello.'

"Look, I don't have time to talk right now, I really need to go," said Sue.

"Sue, this is important," Jason paused, "Look, there's no easy way to say this... but...it's over." said Jason. "The wedding is off."

Sue sat in silence on the edge of her bed, as Brady's words came back to haunt her. "What? Why? What's going on?" she asked.

"We are just too different, you and I. You've been asking about kids, and I don't even want kids. I think that we just want different things out of life, Sue, you know..." explained Jason.

Sue's rage engulfed her as Brady's words seared her mind. "What's her name?" she asked. Even though she knew that she and Jason had their differences, Sue felt that Brady's accusations had been right on.

"What do you mean, what's her name? There's no one else," he said as he tried to play dumb.

"Don't treat me like I'm stupid. Tell me, ***what's her name***?" Sue screamed into the phone.

Jason sighed. "It's Mari…"

As soon as the words came through the receiver, Mari walked in. Mari knew that Jason was calling this morning to end it with Sue, and she just couldn't resist being there to take in the show. Sue heard Jason saying something, but it all sounded muffled, like white noise. Her eyes were fixed on Mari as she pranced over to Sue's bedside picture of Jason.

Mari picked up the picture, and gave it a kiss, just like Sue had done every night since Jason had moved. "How did you sleep last night? I've been sleeping good for months now…" said Mari, as she smiled wickedly at Sue.

It was then that Sue understood. Jason hadn't waited for her. He had been sleeping with Mari the entire time-probably ever since the trip with the baseball team, Sue imagined. Sue came out of her daze, grabbed her purse, and threw her cell phone it while running down the stairs. All of the images raced through her mind. *'Orthopedic Clinics? Were they even real? Had Mari been spending all of those nights with Jason? Did she just come from his bed this morning? How could he do this to me? I was ready to spend the rest of my life with him, and he's stabbed me in the heart. Is this how Cal felt, when I left him? No, I think it's worse! Jason knew I made a vow to God, and he didn't wait for me.'* Sue ran into the bathroom downstairs, and straight into a stall, heaving, as the memories made her nauseous. Then it occurred to her, *'I never even asked him if he was a virgin. How they both must have laughed at me-at the fool I was. How could I have been so blind? And how close did I come to giving him the most precious gift that I had to give?'* Sue stared at her diamond and at her purity ring underneath it. She immediately took the diamond ring off and placed it in her wallet. She'd figure out what to do with that later. Right now, Brady needed her.

Sue regained her composure as she ran to her car in the dorm parking lot. Sue drove to the hospital, sobbing, but, the closer she got to the hospital, the more she felt like a burden had lifted. She felt free for a moment, and then she thought about Brady, and the guilt flowed over her. This was all just so much to process at one time. Sue knew that she needed the Lord's help. She pulled into the hospital parking lot and bowed her head. *'Dear Lord,* she prayed, *'Please forgive me Lord, for being so involved in a man that I couldn't see what was important. And thank you, Lord, for keeping me from making the most horrible mistake of my life. Please help my friend, and please show me what You want for my life. In Your name I pray, Amen.'*

After taking a moment to put the events of the morning behind her, Sue walked into the hospital. She made her way to the Intensive Care Unit, to find Justin still there asleep in the corner chair. She walked up to Justin and gently touched his knee. "Justin, wake up."

Justin slowly opened his eyes and looked over at Brady, who was still out. "Morning, Sue."

"How did it go? Did he wake up at all last night?" asked Sue.

"Not that I know of. I stayed awake as long as I could. If he did wake up, he didn't say anything-and I didn't hear anything, so…" Justin said as he yawned.

"You wanna go stretch your legs? I can take it from here." said Sue

Justin then noticed that Sue's eyes were red from crying. "Hey, are you okay?" he asked.

"I'm fine. It's a long story, but I'm gonna be fine. You go on ahead; I'll be okay in here." She answered as she made her way towards Brady.

"You talked me into it. Thanks, Sue," said Justin as he walked out of the room.

Sue took her place by Brady, on the same rolling stool on which she had sat last night. She held his hand, and began thinking. *'What a fool I've been. What agony have I put you through, parading my relationship with Jason around in front of you? And for what?'* Sue began to sob again at the very thought of what she had done. Brady had always been there for her when she needed him, and even when she didn't realize that she needed him, like that night at the hotel. He was right there, watching over her. What could she possibly do to help him now? Then she remembered something Brady had told her-that he loved to hear her sing. She needed to let him know that everything was going to be alright, that God was in control-or maybe she needed to convince herself. She leaned in close to his ear and sang to him, *'So let the storms rage high, the dark clouds rise, they won't worry me for I'm sheltered safe within the arms of God;'* as she stroked his hair. The tears began falling again. She laid her head down near his on the pillow. She missed it when Brady opened his eyes.

"Didn't I tell you that I hated to see you cry?" said Brady with a weak smile. His words startled Sue who was still crying on his pillow.

"Hey, you!" said Sue as she lovingly looked at him. "How are you feeling?"

"Like road kill. But I've been having the most amazing dreams. I dreamed that I died and went to heaven; there was this beautiful angel, singing, just to me," he said with a weak laugh.

Sue smiled. He was getting back to being Brady already! "Listen, Brady, I'm sorry..." Sue began.

"Sorry for what?" said Brady as he quickly cut her off. "You've done nothing wrong." He paused to take a breath. "I'm the one who should be apologizing to you. Let's just forget all about it, okay?" asked Brady.

But Sue didn't want to forget I, and the thought of forgetting it struck a pang of fear in her heart. Sue, even though crushed from this morning's events, realized how close she and Brady had already become. She was now so hurt from the morning's betrayal that she couldn't bear the thought of Brady not being there for her. She had already wondered, as she rode up to the ICU only moments ago, if God was truly bringing them together.

At that moment, Dr. Ennis walked in with Justin on his heels. "Good morning, folks. Our patient seems to have awakened," he said. He then directed his attention and words to Brady. "Good morning, I'm Dr. Ennis. You were in a car accident. Do you remember anything?"

"I remember enough!" replied Brady, as he rubbed his head, remembering the words that had flown between he and Sue the night before.

"We had to operate and remove your spleen. But your prognosis is good," informed the doctor.

"Well, that's good to know," answered Brady with a laugh.

"Let's have a little check on our patient here," said Dr. Ennis as he checked Brady's chart and filled in the vitals. Sue walked to the other side of the room and turned her back in order for Dr. Ennis to examine Brady. He checked his incisions for redness and swelling. "Looks like you're doing fine, and you might be able to get out of here in a few days."

"That sounds great, doctor. Thank you for everything." said Brady, as Dr. Ennis left the room.

"How about that? You'll be back to stocking those shelves in no time!" joked Justin.

Brady laughed harder this time, and realized that it would be a little longer than that, as he hurt so when he laughed out loud. Brady looked at Sue. "So, what's new in the world today?"

Sue realized that Brady didn't know that anything had changed with her and Jason since last night, in fact, no one else knew, and she wasn't going to tell anyone just yet. She decided that she would wait until Brady was home and recuperating. "Oh, nothing much, just getting over the heart attack you gave us all last night," she said with a laugh.

"Where's that television remote, I'm sure we can find a cartoon for you to watch, Brady!" said Justin with a laugh, as he began to flip channels in an attempt to embarrass Brady. "That's what you always watch at our place. He thinks he owns the remote or something." Brady gave another weak smile and looked around at his best friends and thought, *'Thank you, God for sparing my life, and for Your Divine Providence,'* as he remembered every word that Sue had said to him the night before-everything about them being together in that new house and her feeling 'at home' with him. He wondered if he would ever get to hear those words again.

As the three of them sat watching the Flintstones, Max and Irene walked in. "Brady, my boy, it's good to see you awake!" said Max as he patted Brady's foot.

"Mama! Daddy!" said Sue as she jumped up and ran to her Daddy's arms. She knew that God had sent someone to help her this morning!

"We just couldn't sleep. We had to see you, Brady, and know that you were okay. Sue never did call us back last night," explained Irene. "We imagined that it was very late, and you all were just plain exhausted!"

"It's good to see you both; I just hate that you came all this way," said Brady weakly.

"Well, now that we see that you're okay, we'll give you a break before the nurse comes in here and runs us all off," said Max with a laugh. "We'll come back in a little while."

"I don't think that Sue's had breakfast yet, Mr. Haybert. I could hear her stomach growling from all the way over there!" said Brady with a smile.

"Did not!" yelled Sue in utter shock!

"He's coming back around," said Justin as he tried desperately to hold back his laughter.

"Sue, go on with your parents and get some breakfast, before you faint of hunger," Brady teased.

Sue scowled at him and then she followed her parents to the door. She looked at Brady and returned, "I'm not coming back now-how about that?"

"Yeah, you are!" Brady answered with a smile. "You just can't get enough of me."

Sue rolled her eyes and followed her parents to the elevator. Brady watched her every move and wished that his words were true.

As Sue rode the elevator down with her parents; the weight of the morning suddenly came crashing down on her. She burst into tears. "Sue, what in the world is the matter? Brady's gonna be alright! There's no need to cry now!" said Irene, as she put her arm around her daughter.

"It's not that Mama. It's Jason," Sue replied.

Max and Irene looked at each other. "What is it?" asked Max.

"He called this morning. The wedding is off," answered a tearful Sue.

Max didn't smile, as his daughter was obviously hurting; but deep in his heart, he was so relieved. He had trusted that God would take care of the situation, and He had. "What happened, sweetheart?" he asked.

"Daddy, he was cheating on me, and I didn't even see it," Sue explained as her tears continued to flow. At this point, Sue was surprised that she had any tears left to cry at all.

"Susan, I am so sorry," said Irene, as she stroked her daughter's hair. "I can't fathom what you're going through."

"He called me on the cell phone-***the cell phone***. He didn't even have the guts to say it to my face!" said Sue, as she moved closer to her mother's ear. "And even worse-he was sleeping with my roommate, Mama, right under my nose!"

Irene took her daughter to the side. "Sue, you didn't sleep with him, did you?" asked Irene out of earshot of Max.

"No, Mama," whispered Sue. "I held out, and I know that's what drove him away. I feel so cheap, and so used," said Sue as she began to sob again.

"But, you're not, honey; you're not. You did right! Thank God you did right!" Irene whispered as she pulled her daughter near in embrace. "We've been praying for you, Sue. I'm so sorry that you're hurting, but honestly, I think it's for the best," consoled Irene.

Sue looked over at her Daddy, as he began to cry with her. "I've prayed and prayed for you Sue. It just wasn't meant to be, kiddo."

"I know it, Daddy. I *really know* it. I prayed for God's will to be done, and I know now that it wasn't meant to be," Sue replied. "What do I do now?" she asked.

"Well, that's between you and the Lord. We'll support you in whatever you decide. But I'm sure that I can get a partial refund for your room and board from the school. We'll set that up for you in a trust to cover your rent on an apartment if you decide to stay here; you definitely won't be staying in the dorm anymore with her," offered Max.

"Thank you, Daddy. I'll pray about it and let you know," answered Sue.

"We'll spend the night here in a hotel tonight, and you can stay with us until tomorrow, until we make the arrangements," said Irene.

"Thank you both so much; I love y'all," said Sue as she hugged her parents. "Now, I really am hungry, but my stomach was *not* growling!" said Sue with a laugh as she wiped the tears from her face. It was just like Brady to supply humor at the most devastating time of her life.

"That Brady! He sure is a character!" said Irene with a laugh.

"Yep-he sure is…" answered Max, as he smiled strangely.

Chapter 20

Brady only spent one more day in the Intensive Care Unit and then he was moved to a bed on the hospital's pediatric wing, as all of the other beds in the hospital were full. Justin promised that he would never let Brady forget it either. "Now you can watch cartoons all day long, if you please!" Justin had teased.

In the meantime, Sue called Pastor Rhodes to see if anyone else in the church had any apartments for rent; Sue and her parents had wisely determined that Sue should not go back to the dorm, even if Mari hardly ever stayed there. It just so happened that Widow Johnson's son had just finished the bonus room over her garage, and Pastor Rhodes made a call. She was more than willing to let Sue rent that space. Sue would be able to come and go as she pleased, as the access door was in the garage and not in the house. Sue was very grateful, and she quickly accepted. Max and Irene took care of the financial arrangements, and Sue reassured them that she and Michelle could handle the rest from there. She thanked her parents for all they had done for her, and then saw them off back to Campbell's Grove.

Sue realized that she needed to tell someone else besides her parents what had happened between her and Jason, and she opted for Michelle. Sue called and asked if Michelle could drive to the dorm and help her with something, but she couldn't tell her what. Michelle agreed but didn't understand all of the secrecy.

As Michelle pulled up in the Grand Marquis, she almost jumped out of the car while it was still running. "Hey! What's so important, and what's the big secret? What's going on?" she asked.

Sue explained everything, and when she had finished, she had to restrain Michelle. "Look, I prayed for God's will to be done, and this is obviously it. Jason and I are finished. I don't see Mari's car anywhere, but would you please go up first and make sure that she's not there? I just want to get my things and go. Just call me on my cell if the coast is clear," begged Sue.

"Okay, but if I find her up there, you may have to call 911," threatened Michelle. Michelle went up and, fortunately for Mari, she was nowhere to be found. Michelle called Sue and told her that it was safe to come up. The two girls packed up all of Sue's belongings, except for Sue's bedside picture of Jason. Sue took her silver heels from the wedding and cracked the glass, several times and threw the remains on Mari's bed. Then the girls packed Sue and Michelle's cars to the gills, and left for Widow Johnson's.

The room was great, and Sue was looking forward to her new found privacy. The room had its own bathroom, and Sue really liked that! No more hiking down to the showers every morning! Widow Johnson had given Sue permission to decorate the room any way she cared to, but Sue really didn't feel like putting much up yet, as she wasn't sure what her plans were. She had enough credits to graduate with the Associates degree, but, settling for her two-year degree seemed pointless now. She should have never wanted to settle for anything! She and Michelle talked, and Sue decided that she would stay at ACU and keep going. As the two girls unpacked, Michelle asked the question that Sue was hoping she wouldn't.

"Sue, so now that Jason's out of the picture, what about Brady?"

"I don't know, Michelle. I really haven't had time to take it all in. I've never really thought about him that way, but there is something there," Sue confessed. She really felt like God was bringing them together, but she didn't want to rush into anything. She had made that mistake with her last relationship, and she wasn't about to make any mistakes with Brady-if indeed that what was God wanted. From now on, Sue would fervently seek God in prayer for everything!

"He is devastatingly handsome!" said Michelle as

Sue gave her a sideways look. "Hey, I'm married-not blind!"

Sue continued. "The other night we shared a lunch break, and he took me on a 'tour' of a new housing complex. Michelle, this house was so beautiful! But the sad thing was, I looked around, and I couldn't imagine Jason and I together in a place like that; but, I looked up at Brady leaning over that banister, and I can't really put my finger on it, but it felt right. I felt like I was at home with him-that's really the only way that I know to describe it. I don't know if I'm ready to rush into another relationship right now, but I do know that we share something. At the hospital, when he first woke up, he apologized to me for the argument that night, and then asked me to just forget about it-just to forget about the fact that he told me that he loved me, like it never happened."

"You mean you didn't tell him that you and Jason broke up?" asked Michelle, with her eyes as big as golf balls!

"NO-I didn't want to over excite him; and I don't want you to tell him either, or Justin. I will tell him eventually, but I want to wait at least until he gets back home," answered Sue.

"I can understand that. So much went on that night." Just then, Michelle's cell began ringing. "Hang on, it's the hubby," she said as she answered the phone. Sue mouthed the words, *'Don't you tell him…'* to Michelle, and then she kept on working to give her privacy.

After a quick muffled conversation, and then what Sue was sure sounded like several sickening pet names, Michelle flipped her phone shut. "Justin said that Brady gets to come home on Saturday, so I guess you can tell him sooner rather than later!"

"Well, I'm off then, so I'll meet y'all at Brady's on Saturday and fix lunch. I'm glad to have this place, but I really don't feel like being by myself right now."

"Sounds great," said Michelle as she hung up some more clothes. "Speaking of lunch, girl, I'm getting hungry, but I'm a little low on cash."

"Well, I haven't stocked this mini fridge yet, and I have a good idea on where to get some quick cash," answered Sue.

The two girls drove down to the Pawn Shop. Sue took the diamond ring out of her wallet and presented it to the shop owner, along with the golden locket that Jason had given her for Christmas. He offered her one hundred dollars for a ring that was worth at least a thousand, but Sue didn't haggle. Then he offered her only fifteen dollars for the locket. She knew that a hundred fifteen bucks would cover lunch and get her some groceries for her new apartment-as well as a special gift for Brady, so she accepted the offer. After the broker gave her a check, she ran by the bank and cashed it. Then she and Michelle enjoyed the Pizza Hut buffet before stopping in at the Bargain Bin. Sue just had to pick up some Fred Flintstone Pajama pants for Brady to recuperate in!

*****

That Saturday, Sue waited in her car parked in front of the house that held Brady's apartment, as she was unsure of which one was his. When Justin and Michelle drove up, Sue grabbed her grocery bags and waited for them to get out. Justin had to help Brady out of the car and up the steps. Sue just followed behind. Brady hadn't spoken to Sue yet, and it made her nervous. Justin got Brady set up on the sofa, as Sue and Michelle brought in all of the cards, balloons, and stuffed animals that people had sent Brady in the hospital. It was obvious that Brady was loved by many at Pastor Rhodes's church.

As Sue was setting flowers around the living room, Brady finally spoke. "I didn't expect to see you here today-it's Saturday. Don't you have a date?" he asked.

Michelle looked at Sue, and then at Justin, who was clueless. There was a long silence. Then Sue showed Brady her hand, which was only wearing the purity ring, and said, "No, that's over."

There was complete and utter silence in the room-Michelle put her finger on Justin's chin and pushed up to close his wide open mouth! Then the silence was broken by Brady as he sang to Sue, *"I'm Sorry, so Sorry..."* and the room erupted with laughter! Sue picked up a stuffed animal and threw it at Brady on the sofa. Brady smiled and thought to himself, '*Game on*'.

"Just for that, I don't think that I will give you this gift!" teased Sue.

"You got me a gift? Do tell!" said Brady as he continued his game.

Sue pulled out the Flintstone lounge pants, and Brady's head just dropped. The crew had always teased him because he loved cartoons; he'd sit and laugh for hours as he watched them just like a little kid!

"Stomach growling? Please! Don't mess with this vixen-you'll lose every time!" said Sue as she pranced towards the kitchen.

Brady yelled to Michelle, "Don't let her touch my food!"

Sue joined Michelle in the kitchen to prepare the lunch, and Justin stayed with Brady to have a little 'chat'. "I don't believe it. I just don't believe it," said Justin as he sat on the floor, leaning against the sofa. "I didn't see that coming."

"I did. I suppose you know that's what Sue and I were arguing about before the accident. I was just so tired of seeing him treat my wife that way!" said Brady with a smile.

"Yeah! Now, what are you going to do?" asked Justin.

"Well, I'm gonna take it slow. I imagine she's not looking for anything right now. She'll need time to heal, and you know there will be trust issues, no doubt. We'll just take it one day at a time," answered Brady.

"That sounds about right," said Justin as he shook his head. "I wonder what happened with them?" asked Justin.

"She'll tell me in her time, I'm sure," Brady said. He decided that he would not rush her to explain.

"My guess is that Michelle already knows. She went somewhere with Sue yesterday and was gone for hours, but she said that she couldn't tell me where she was. That was hard to take, being that she's my wife and all; I'll find out in a little bit. I figured that if she was with Sue though, I shouldn't worry."

"Yeah, but now you've got me wondering; find out sooner, would ya?" said Brady, as he peeked over the sofa to see if either of the girls were listening. "I have a feeling that Jason won't take kindly to not having Sue around. I don't know who broke it off, but I know Jason enough to know that this won't be over and done with just like that. He's very possessive, and in case you hadn't noticed, there's not much that he has ever done without. We really need to keep our eyes open, you know?"

"Okay. Duly noted. But hey bro, there's no need for you to worry about anything. I'll schedule Sue some time off and conveniently schedule you some more time off as well," said Justin as he smiled at Brady.

"I appreciate the help," Brady said as the girls called for them to come to the table.

Chapter 21

Sue really enjoyed the new room at Widow Johnson's as she studied for the final exams for her spring courses. The way she figured it, if she enrolled in the summer courses and took another fall and spring Semester, then she would have enough credits to graduate with her Bachelor's Degree in Independent Studies if she took a full load. This way, she would stay at ACU until she walked for graduation. She had no wedding to plan, no boyfriend, and only a small part-time job, so, even though the work would be difficult, she knew that she could handle it.

Before Sue knew it, spring exams were underway, and the threshold of summer was upon her. Brady had made plans with Sue to meet Justin and Michelle for a victory lunch after the last exams on that Friday. Brady said that he would meet her at the student union in his new 'surprise ride.' Sue was excited, but yet, nervous, as she and Brady had not yet had a serious conversation about the accident-actually about the argument before the accident, or about the break-up.

The Friday after she finished her last exam, Sue walked towards her car to drop off her backpack, and she found an un-welcome visitor leaning against it waiting for her. It was Jason. Their eyes met, and Sue turned and walked away towards the Student Union.

"Sue, please, I've got to talk to you," said Jason, as he followed Sue.

Sue kept walking and added briskness to her steps. "The way I see it, you've lied to me, broke my heart -over the phone, no less. You didn't even have the courage to say it to my face, and you cheated on me only about seven weeks before we were supposed to get married, which I am actually thankful for. You saved me from the biggest mistake of my life, so I'm thinking that we've got nothing to say to each other." Sue answered. Jason grabbed Sue's arm to stop her from walking away.

"Sue, you are right. I was unfaithful..." Jason started.

"Hum." Sue laughed sarcastically. Before she lost what little composure she had, Sue began walking toward the Student Union building again, chiding him as she walked. Unfortunately, Jason was on her heels. "Unfaithful-you try to make it sound so much less than what it is! You were ***engaged*** to me! You made a solemn promise to me that we would be husband and wife. Then, you sleep with my roommate, not once, but for months, according to her, and you simply want to call it ***'being unfaithful'***? I guess that's where all of your money has gone!" Jason could only hang his head in shame. "Hotels are costly, as are romancing dinners. Basketball! How stupid did you think I was? You must be insane! Actually, I was the insane one for not seeing what you really are-"

"Sue, I love you, and I made a mistake. I want you back!" begged Jason.

Sue stopped dead in her tracks. "Look, no matter how I might have felt about you, I will ***NEVER*** be able to trust you again. Like you said on the phone, *'it's over.'* I'm moving on."

"Sue," called a voice from the parking lot of the Student Union. It was Brady wearing Sue's favorite Atlanta Braves T-shirt with his arms crossed-showing off his biceps-leaning against a brand new, shiny, black Mustang Cobra, and to Sue, he had never looked so good. His glare screamed protection, and his eyes seemed to dare Jason to make a false move.

Jason looked over and saw Brady waiting for Susan.

"I see," said Jason as he realized that he had no chance of winning Sue back.

"Thanks, though," said Sue with a pause, "If you hadn't been such a low life, I would've missed out on a really wonderful man." This wasn't a lie, even though she and Brady were not 'together.' She had never considered Brady as a love interest, the way she considered him now, as she believed that God had orchestrated in both of their lives to bring them together, if Brady would only have her. Then with not so much as look of 'goodbye,' Sue boldly walked towards Brady and the Mustang, leaving Jason standing there watching the treasure he had lost walk into another man's life.

As Sue approached the car, Brady called to her, "Are you okay?" He never took his eyes off of Jason even as Sue walked towards the passenger side of the car.

She looked at him with resolve and love in her eyes and answered, "Yes-I'm gonna be just fine-by the way, sweet ride."

Brady walked around to her side of the car. Sue waited, as she was unsure of what he was doing. "Don't get too excited; I'm only test driving it. I've really been a truck man all of my life, but I thought I might try something new." He stopped in front of her and reached for the car door to open it for her. "You know there's definitely something to be said for trying something new," he continued as he closed the door. He glared at Jason one last time, and then he walked around to the driver's side and got into the car.

"Indeed there is," answered Sue, alluding to the possible relationship with Brady, if he would have her. Brady started the car and backed out of the parking lot. He turned onto the highway and began driving towards the restaurant.

Brady and Sue sat in silence for a moment, with the memory of the unwanted visitor still looming in the air. Finally, Brady broke the silence.

"Well, now that things are over with Jason, what do you plan to do about your degree? I've got three more semesters left. If I take classes this Summer, Fall, and Spring, I can walk in the Spring graduation with my business degree," said Brady.

Sue already knew the answer to this one; she was definitely going to finish her degree-but Brady didn't need to know that this instant; remembering how Brady asked her to forget about their argument before the accident, Sue thought she'd fish a little bit. "I have *thought* about staying..." she mumbled with a subtle hint of innocence.

"Can't you think of *any* good reason to stay?" asked Brady, as he did a little fishing of his own.

"I can think of one..." she answered, staring down at her hands. This new prospect of Brady as her love interest felt strangely exciting. She knew how he felt about her, but there was still the question of whether or not he was willing to have her, after the way that she had treated him. She had been so blind. Would he be willing to forgive her for being so stubbornly blind?

Brady smiled as he continued driving. He suddenly felt that things had turned in his favor. *'Thank You, Lord,'* he whispered in his heart. *'I knew You would keep Your Word.'* Just then his curiosity got the better of him. "So...Sue, you never did tell me what happened with you two. You, uh, don't mind me asking, do you?"

"No, I don't mind." Sue began. "You already know the answer. He was cheating, end of story."

"With some girl from up where he lived?" asked Brady.

"No-with Mari," answered Sue.

"Mari? Are you kidding?" Brady never expected that, but in retrospect, he understood how that probably happened, remembering his blind date with Mari.

"Nope. He was fooling around on me right here under my nose, and I couldn't see it," answered Sue with a twinge of dismay.

"Don't be so down on yourself. You were in love and love is blind," said Brady in an attempt to console her. Brady dwelt on the word 'were'-the past tense!

"Love! What is love? I was ready to spend the rest of my life with someone that I really didn't even know. I don't even think that I know how to love," said Sue as she pulled down the vanity mirror to check her makeup.

"Oh, I think you do." Brady mustered the courage to let Sue in the loop-only partially of course. *'Baby steps…'* Brady thought to himself as he stepped out on that limb. "Someone once told me that they felt 'at home' with me." Brady's words fell on Sue like a ton of bricks, and her breath caught in her chest. She had no idea that Brady had heard her say those things when he was unconscious in the hospital. Noting her reaction, he continued. "And they say home is where the heart is; don't you believe that?"

"I do," Sue answered with a thoughtful pause. She really didn't want to mess this up. She treaded lightly and stepped out on that same limb that Brady had teetered on. "I just don't know how to start over." Sue wasn't sure how to put her feelings into words, but she did the best that she knew how to do. "It's strange-my heart aches, but it's not totally broken," she said in an attempt to let Brady know that she was interested. She wanted to belong to Brady, but at the same time, she was afraid to step out there so quickly.

"You know how I feel about you, Sue, but I know enough to know that you need time to heal." Brady paused as he offered her his heart, in the wisest fashion possible. "I'm all for taking things slow, if that sounds like something you're interested in?" offered Brady.

"I do have strong feelings for you, Brady. I've been a fool for never seeing it before. I see you now, and I really like what I see," Sue managed to fumble out as she reflected on her words. *'Does he understand?'* she thought.

"The feeling is definitely mutual," said Brady, as he reached for her hand. Sue smiled, and felt assured that he did understand her. Brady understood her better than anyone; he always had. Sue held onto his hand for the duration of the ride to the restaurant. She held on for joy-for security. His warmth emitted the promise of a future, one not yet charted, but a future that Sue desperately longed for.

The couple finally arrived at the restaurant and Brady squeezed Sue's hand before they got out of the car, "You're gonna be okay, Haybert."

"As long as I have you, Sheffield," she answered.

Brady ushered Sue into the Denny's and checked behind them as they entered the glass doors. He thought that he had seen a Red Toyota Yaris following them a good ways back, and then he was sure that it passed by the restaurant. Now that Jason was aware of Brady and Sue's relationship, Brady knew that he had to be extra cautious when it came to Sue. It was unlikely that Jason would let the matter go, even if he did instigate the break-up. Brady had felt that immediately when he learned that Jason and Sue were no longer together. Today's confrontation in the parking lot proved that.

As Brady and Sue entered the restaurant, Michelle and Justin waved to them and motioned for them to come to their table. Michelle was almost giddy as she watched her Sue-walking hand-in-hand with Brady. She looked at Justin, and their eyes silently agreed. These two belonged together.

The couples enjoyed their meals and talked and laughed anticipating a great summer together. When they were done with their celebration, they all four walked out into the parking lot to call it a night. Brady immediately noticed the car leaning down in the back. He walked to the back of the Mustang and saw right away what the problem was. Someone had slashed his tire-and not even his tire, as he was only test driving the car! He began to look around, and he shot Justin a look. Things were going too well to have Sue become edgy. Brady decided that he needed to keep her in the dark on this one, and he reacted quickly. "Hey girls, why don't you go by the Blockbuster and rent us a movie to take to Justin and Michelle's to watch. Justin and I have some things that we need to take care of, okay?"

Brady asked, as he ushered Sue over to Michelle's side.

"Well, okay." Sue said as she and Michelle opened the doors to the Rhode's Grand Marquis. "Whatever you want to do is fine with me," Sue replied as she climbed into the car. Brady leaned in and looked into her eyes. "We will be along soon! No worries." he said as he hugged her, and then closed the door, hoping that they would leave quickly without noticing the slashed tire.

As Michelle drove away and headed towards the Blockbuster down the street, Brady nodded, directing Justin's attention to the slashed tire. "I saw it too when we walked out, and I remembered what you said at your apartment the other day," said Justin as both men squatted down to take a good look. "He's definitely up to no good."

"And that puts Sue in danger. If you wouldn't mind, could you give me a hand in changing this tire? I hope that the dealership doesn't make me buy this Mustang tonight! I wanted a little longer to think about it! But I'll definitely pay for the tire, no questions asked," Brady offered. "I thought that maybe Sue would be happier with the car, instead of a truck. You know, it's not just about me anymore," Brady continued, as he began pulling the jack and spare out of the trunk.

"Bro, it's never been about you-even I know that. Trust me, she'll be happy with you…no matter what you drive!" answered Justin as he began rolling up his sleeves to help his friend.

"Well, I've always been a truck man, and I'm thinking now that being back in my element might be a good thing. I need to be extra vigilant." Brady paused for a moment. "If he ever hurt her, well, I'd…"

Justin cut him off. "Look-this is only one event. Now, this could be where it ends, and then he'll be on his way. There's no need getting all worked up about it tonight. Let's just get this done and retire to the Rhode's Castle for the duration of the evening." said Justin as she attempted to lighten the mood.

"Alright, but I'm begging you, please help me keep watch. I can't let anything happen to her. She's everything to me," Brady said as he stopped and looked at the ground.

"I know...I know," answered Justin as he rolled the spare tire over to Brady.

*****

The sultry weeks of summer passed by, and Justin kept his promise of helping Brady guard Sue, without her being the wiser. The summer was filled with several informal dates between Brady and Sue, some with Michelle and Justin and some with just the two of them, but most of them in public places. She never realized that she was being guarded.

But there was something else that was bothering Sue; she noticed that Brady never seemed to want to be totally 'alone' with her. All of their dates had been to either the park, the mall, or to Justin and Michelle's, or somewhere with them. One evening, Brady took Sue to eat at the China Palace, the most exquisite restaurant in Sunset. The evening was perfect-a moonlight stroll after dinner, walking hand-in-hand being totally enthralled with each other. Sue thought most assuredly that Brady would take this opportunity to kiss her, but much to her dismay, Brady ended their date at the apartment steps with a tender embrace. Sue wanted to linger there in his arms, but Brady let go too soon, at least, too soon for Sue! Brady continued to court her, and he was always very sweet to her, and very considerate.

When the two month anniversary rolled around Sue became alarmed. Sue kept wondering why he hadn't kissed her yet! She knew that they were going to take it slow, but she felt like Brady was trying to just be her friend and not her boyfriend. She was very confused. The Fall Semester had already begun, and one day as she and Michelle were shopping, Sue confided in her friend. It was somewhat of an uncomfortable subject, and Sue found herself a little embarrassed, as she wondered whether or not Brady found her appealing. The best way to get some information, Sue decided, was just to jump out there and ask Michelle's opinion.

"Michelle, when did Justin first kiss you?" she asked.

"Why? That boy hasn't kissed you yet? Y'all have been dating for like two or three months now!" gasped Michelle.

Sue was relieved that she wasn't imagining things! "I know! We talked about taking it slow, but, this is kinda ridiculous! We only go to the park and the mall, or out with you and Justin. There was this one date, you know, to the China Palace?"

"Yes, I know-Justin got him reservations there!" Michelle answered as she was most proud of her husband. "He is such a romantic thing!"

"Oh, thanks, by the way! That was an awesome place! But, back to the subject, it was so awesome, that I thought surely that would be the night, and yet, just a wonderful hug. Maybe I'm missing something, but I'm just getting a little concerned. Do you think that he's not as in love with me as he thought?" asked Sue.

"No way! Maybe he just wants your relationship to be solid, you know, not based on the physical," replied Michelle.

"It seems that was all Jason and I had was physical. Our talks were always kind of shallow," confessed Sue.

"What can you expect from a Toyota driver? I told you not to mess with him," Michelle gloated.

"I know, I know. But look, really-do you think that's all it is? Or, do you think that Brady's changed his mind, and he's just too afraid that I'll get hurt again if he breaks it off?" asked a serious Sue. Sue couldn't bear the thought of losing another boyfriend, but only this time, it would be losing two persons in one-her boyfriend and her best friend.

"He has definitely not changed his mind. I know that it's not a lack of love. You should've seen him Sue, while you and Jason were together. He was pitiful," Michelle explained as she remembered the forlorn looks on her friend's face as he watched Sue and Jason at different functions. She was relieved for both Sue and Brady that they had finally decided to get together.

"I can't believe that I didn't see his love for me. I'm so glad that he finally got it in him to tell me. I would've made such a mess of my life," Sue confessed.

"Yes, you certainly would have. But look, I'll talk to Justin and see what I can do for you," said Michelle.

Sue was suddenly aghast. "No! Don't you say a word, Michelle-not one word to him about this, please? Promise me you won't talk to Justin about this," begged Sue.

"Okay, I promise," said Michelle as she thought to herself, *'I won't say anything to Justin, but she didn't say that I couldn't talk to Brady...'*

*****

Later that evening, Sue was scheduled to work, but Brady was off for the evening. Michelle decided to take advantage of the situation, and invited Brady over for dinner. She was determined to light a fire. Justin, Brady and Michelle all sat at their kitchen table, and it was relatively quiet as they ate. In the silence, Michelle seized the opportunity. "Brady, we've gotta talk."

"What about?" he answered, nonchalantly. He couldn't imagine what Michelle could have to talk to him about.

"It's about you and Sue," she answered.

"What's wrong?" he asked swiftly with a gasp of worry. The men had been very alert over the past two months, but Brady immediately thought the worst. Justin had managed to keep Michelle unaware of the slashed tire incident and of his watchman's eye when it came to Sue. She didn't suspect that anything was amiss, if indeed, anything was. The past weeks had been uneventful in that respect.

"Sue talked to me-she told me not to talk to Justin about her problem, but technically she didn't say that I couldn't talk to you; so-here it is: She's concerned that you haven't kissed her yet," said Michelle very matter-of-factly, and then took a huge bite of chicken.

At first, Brady breathed a sigh of relief. He was glad that no other strange 'event' had occurred. Then the words that Michelle had spoken floated down like bubbles, as he realized what Michelle had actually said, and a new kind of horror overtook him. "We're taking it slow…" began a rather embarrassed Brady.

"Sounds to me like you're not taking it anywhere!" said Michelle with a laugh. Poor Justin just sat in the crossfire as she continued. His head just kept moving back and forth, like he was watching a tennis match. "You've got to do it," Michelle demanded.

"Look, I want our relationship to be…" Brady paused as he fumbled for the right words. "I want her to know that we're about more than that. I love her. She needs to know that a relationship is about more than the physical aspect."

Justin finally chimed in. "Yes, but, she also needs to know that you, as a prospective husband, are also interested in her physically, and not just spiritually."

"Well, I remember how she and Jason were together, and I don't want us to be like that," Brady said with confusion.

"I can promise you…that you two are nothing like they were," Justin continued. "You need to let her really know that you are interested. You've been dating, but like you're friends. Even I've noticed that. The friendship is extremely important, but you need to take the next step, Brady, really," advised Justin.

"She's beginning to doubt your feelings," Michelle chimed in.

"How can she think that? After all that we've been through..." rebutted Brady.

"Yes, with all that you've been through, and you haven't even kissed her, not once!" said Michelle as she cut Brady off.

"I've never kissed..." began Brady, and then he stopped.

And then it all became clear. "Oh, my Lord, you've never kissed a girl at all?" Justin said in horror.

Brady sat there, embarrassed. But finally he spoke. "I've been saving my first kiss for my wife," he admitted.

"Well, since you know that Sue will be your wife, there's no problem then," said Justin as Michelle's jaw dropped. Justin had never revealed to Michelle that Brady had received confirmation from God-that he and Sue were meant to marry, but he quickly related the details, much to her delight.

"I've wanted to kiss her several times, even before the breakup; every time she speaks, all I can think about is her lips-her beautiful lips! But, I also didn't want to make her feel pressured, because we're ***taking it slow***."

"Well, I think that it's time to pick up the pace," said Justin. There was an unusual silence until Justin and Michelle saw the light bulb appear above Brady's head.

"Her birthday is coming up next week, and I wanted to do something extra special on that day. Maybe that will be a good time to...as you say... 'pick up the pace,' but I need some help from you two. Are you in?" asked Brady.

"You bet we are!" answered an eager Michelle, as she grabbed a pencil and paper.

Brady began, "Okay...here's what we need..."

Chapter 22

It was Sue's birthday, and everything had been the same with she and Brady, and it was causing Sue some sleepless nights. She wondered daily if Brady was only hanging on because he did not want to hurt her. Ever since the break-up with Jason, Sue had become very paranoid. She was so happy with Brady; he was the best thing to ever happen to her. She just found herself having a feeling in the pit of her stomach that something bad was waiting around the corner.

It was just like Sue to feel this way. She remembered feeling that same feeling of paranoia when she declined Cal's marriage proposal, and her mother tried to make her feel guilty about it, but eventually Sue escaped that dark cloud of impending doom and managed go on to college looking forward to a wonderful, adventurous experience. Now, Brady was the experience she was enjoying, and she had never been so happy! However, that dark cloud was beginning to form again in Sue's suspicions, as she waited for his kiss-the facet of their relationship that had not yet developed; it was really worrying her. She almost regretted mentioning anything to Michelle, but the matter concerned her so.

Sue and Brady shared their lunch at the Greasy Spoon, just as they always did. Brady had been sort of quiet while they ate, and that seemed to depress Sue even more. It was her birthday for crying out loud, and Brady hadn't even mentioned it! This seemed to make matters that much worse. After their uneventful lunch, Sue ventured on the library. She had to finish working on an essay for her Western Civilizations class and ended up staying a little longer at the library than she had planned.

Sue glanced at her watch and noticed that the time was already 5:15 pm. She wrapped up her studies and thought to herself, that since she and had not heard from Brady, she would be spending her birthday at home alone. But, as Sue was beginning to leave the media center that afternoon, the librarian stopped her. "Sue, this message was delivered for you."

"Thank you," she said she opened the slip of paper. It read:

'Once a year, it is your special day
Go home and get ready-We're going away'

Sue smiled in anticipation, as she practically ran out of the door and jumped in her car. Even though it was not signed, she knew that her Brady had something special in store! As she approached her car, she noticed something in the passenger side of the front seat. It was a bouquet of a dozen red roses, with another note which read:

'A rose's beauty, like yours, is unsurpassed
Please make it home safely, and don't drive fast.'

Sue threw her head back in laughter as she started her car and began to drive home to her small apartment. Sue wondered, *'what in the world has he got up his sleeve tonight?'*

When she arrived at home, Widow Johnson was watering her mums, looking rather suspicious. Sue held up one of the notes and looked at her and said, "Have you, by chance..." she asked as she was cut off.

"I see nothing, I know nothing..." she said with a smile.

Sue returned the smile and ran up the stairs to her room, and there was a note on the door:

'To look in your eyes is a glimpse of heaven;
Don't take too long, your ride will be here at seven.'

Sue could not believe what was going on! She opened the door and found, lying on her bed, her bridesmaid's dress from Justin and Michelle's wedding, along with the platinum wrap, her silver strappy heels, and yet another note:

'Your day is so special; it's one I'd never miss;
You look wonderful in anything, but please wear this…'

Sue's curiosity was at its peak now! She looked at the clock, and it was already five forty-five. She knew that she would have to have to hurry! She showered and curled her hair with the curling iron, and fixed her makeup. She checked the clock, and it was six forty. She breathed a sigh of relief, knowing that she had made it. She quickly flipped open her cell to call Michelle and clue her in on what was going on, but Michelle didn't answer at her house phone. She quickly dialed Michelle's cell, which she didn't answer that either. Then, Sue became very suspicious. *'Did she and Justin have something to do with this?'* she wondered as she slipped into her dress. She grabbed her wrap and purse just as she heard a horn blowing for her in the driveway. She lighted down the stairs, and almost fainted at the sight that awaited her. There sat a white stretch limousine parked in the driveway, with the driver standing at the door, waiting for her.

"Miss Susan Haybert?" asked the driver. Sue only nodded as she stood speechless. "This way please," said the man as he opened the door for her and gestured for her to enter the car.

"Thank you," Sue managed to get out as she slipped into the long car. She could barely believe what was happening. Sue barely felt the car leaving the driveway as she was busy checking out all of the rings and bells in the limo. She then noticed that the windows had been darkened, and she couldn't see where the car was going. She saw that the window was down between her and the driver, and she asked, "Excuse me, can you please tell me where we're going?"

"I'm sorry miss; I have strict orders not to," he answered.

Sue felt a tad bit of apprehension, but she knew that Brady would never disappoint her. "Well, can you tell me how long we will be?" she asked.

"I can only tell you, and let me read it from this little paper so I get it right:

'Don't let my little mystery bring you any sorrow.
Enjoy the ride-You won't be back 'til tomorrow'

If you get hungry miss, there are some snacks there in the bin to your right and some sodas in the cooler panel on your left," said the driver with a smile.

Now Sue was on pins and needles! She had absolutely no idea what was going on-all she knew was that she was too nervous to eat! She closed her eyes and tried to rest, but her whole being was full of butterflies!

After about thirty minutes, Sue felt the car making some turns, after they had been driving pretty much straight ahead for a while. Then she felt the car begin to slow down and eventually stop. It was now getting on to about eight o'clock, and the sun was just beginning to go down. The southern fall had just gotten underway, and the sunsets were still late and beautiful. As soon as the driver began to open the door, Sue smelled the air-the salt air-and she knew that she was at the beach.

The driver opened the door, and Sue found a hand extended to help her out of the limo-it was Brady, dressed in a tuxedo. "Did you enjoy your ride, Miss Haybert?" he said with a huge smile. He nodded to the driver in a 'thank you,' and gave Sue his arm of escort.

"Brady, this is extraordinary. I can't believe that you went to all of this trouble," said Sue as a small tear trickled down her cheek.

"Didn't I tell you not to be crying around me?" he said with a laugh as he handed her his handkerchief. Brady led Sue down a boardwalk between the Hilton and the Sheraton hotels that led to the beachfront. The evening breeze that rustled through the palmetto trees lining the boardwalk blew Sue's hair back ever so slightly. As they reached the end of the boardwalk, Brady led Sue to a white lattice gazebo on the beach that was decorated with white lights and greenery. Inside was a small bistro table set for two inside, complete with two silver dinner trays. Brady pulled out Sue's chair and seated her, and then he took his own seat. He looked at Sue, but she could barely look at him; she was so nervous.

"Let's see," said Brady as he reached under the table. "I'm sorry that they wouldn't let me bring any candles into this gazebo, as that would be considered a fire hazard, so this will have to do," said Brady, as he plopped an LED Coleman lantern in the middle of the table!

Sue and Brady both burst into laughter! Sue was glad he had done something to break the nervous tension. That was so like him! He always seemed to have the perfect words to break the tension when Sue was at a loss. But then again, he knew her, and he could tell when she needed to be put at ease.

"And one more thing," said Brady as he picked up a small remote to turn on the small boom box setting on the rail of the gazebo, which played some Kenny G.

"Well now, I think we do have everything," said Susan.

"No, not everything," said Brady as he reached under the table for a long velvet box. "Happy Birthday, Sue" said Brady as he flipped open the box to reveal a golden necklace with a beautiful sapphire pendant, that was surrounded by two diamonds on the side. "May I?" he asked as he took the necklace from the box.

"Yes…" Sue managed to say as she found herself again wiping tears from her eyes. Brady's hands sent shots of electricity down her spine as they brushed against her neck and shoulders while her affixed the necklace for her. Sue's back still tingled as Brady made his way back over to his seat.

"Are you hungry?" he asked.

"Yes, I'm starving! I was too afraid to eat anything in the limo!" she answered.

Brady extended his hand to Sue for prayer. "Dear Lord, thank you for this beautiful evening that you've given us, and Dear Lord, thank you for this wonderful woman that you've given to me…" he prayed as he held back the tears, "please help us to honor You in all that we do. Please bless this food to our bodies and our bodies to Your service, Amen."

"Amen," Sue said as she realized that God had indeed given her a wonderful man, and she deeply hoped that she would spend the rest of her life with him.

Sue lifted the silver dome over her plate to find prime rib, and a baked potato along with a salad on another other small plate. "Brady, this is wonderful. How in the world were you able to do all of this?" she asked.

"Well, I had a little help," Brady confessed as he pulled something from his inside coat pocket. "Here;" said Brady as he handed Sue a small paper envelope with a card in it. "Put this in your purse," he said as he handed Sue a key card to room 215 at the Hilton, which was the tall building to the right of the gazebo. "This is your room key. You're in 215, I'm in 219, and my accomplices are in 217."

"Justin and Michelle are here?" asked Sue with surprise as Brady smiled.

"Yes, I couldn't have done this without their help. Michelle has packed you a bag-it's in your room," he explained.

Sue smiled and shook her head, as she could just see

Michelle rummaging through her clothes trying to pack her a bag! Brady and Sue ate their meals, laughed, and talked. Sue thought to herself that it was so good to be able to enjoy the companionship of someone of the opposite sex without any pressure. She so enjoyed spending her time with Brady- any time that she could! *'Surely,'* Sue thought, *'Surely anyone who would go to all of this trouble to make me feel so special does indeed care for me deeply. I can't believe that I doubted Brady's feelings for me, even if he has never kissed me!'* Just as the thoughts had floated through her mind, Brady interrupted them and suggested that they take a walk on the beach. Sue smiled in agreement, remembering her thoughts of the moment. She took off her strappy heels, setting them in the corner of the gazebo. Brady took her hand, and he led her through the gateway which led through the dunes straight down to the beach.

It was dark by then, and the moon beamed on the ocean, as a gentle breeze blew. Sue grabbed her wrap, and Brady helped her pull it around. As they walked along, Brady looked towards the ocean. "Look, there," he said as he pointed out to sea. There was a schooner sailing across the silver-tapered waters. "I wonder what it would be like to sail for a living?" he asked.

"I would imagine that it is like anything else, a job to supply your needs. One would have to love it though-it's hard work," Sue answered as she stared at the boat gliding through the waves.

"And yet it all means nothing if you have no purpose, no one to provide for, no one to care for," Brady uttered. He continued to lead Sue down the golden strand. He remembered for a moment, what it was like without Sue. He felt how that void in his heart had been filled, and he thanked God for every moment that he had with her.

They continued on towards the nearest pier, hand in hand, without another word between them. Sue became lost in the sound of the waves crashing on the shore. She could have only dreamed about the evening that Brady had shown her! She felt so blessed to have a man with a true sense of romance, chivalry and gentility.

Brady suddenly felt knots in his stomach, and Sue noticed that his palms were beginning to sweat. As they walked underneath the pier Brady stopped her. He took Sue by the arms and turned her to him. "Sue, you know that I love you…" he started.

Sue took her finger and placed it on his lips. Brady then moved in towards her slowly, and their lips met. Brady felt Sue go limp, and he reached his arm around her to catch her fall. Sue had never felt like this before, not with Jason, or Cal. His kiss made her literally weak in the knees. He held her there for a moment, until Brady himself was almost light-headed. As they pulled away from each other, he began to regain his composure. "I'm sorry that I've taken so long to show you how much I really do care. I know that words can only express just so much. I just wanted you to know that I respect you, and that my love for you is real and true, not lustful," explained Brady.

"I knew that, Brady-I'm just so glad that you wanted to kiss me at all! I thought that perhaps you discovered that you weren't as 'in love' with me as you thought. I didn't want to even think about that possibility, but, I couldn't help but think the worst. Everything has been going so well for us, that I thought it was too good to be true. Then I guess my mind just ran wild…" Sue confessed.

"How could you ever think that? You are the reason that I wake up every morning-the reason that I breathe. I've dreamt about your lips a thousand times."

"Well, now you don't have to dream anymore," Sue answered as she reached for him again.

"No-now I'm living my dreams," Brady replied as he kissed her once more, and then took her hand, leading her back down the shoreline and towards the hotel. *'That's about all that I can handle right now, without totally losing control'*, he thought to himself as they strolled along arm in arm. Brady walked her to her room; and in the dim lamplight, becoming totally addicted, he kissed her once more at her door, followed by a long embrace. Sue whispered in his ear, "I love you, Brady…" as he held her tighter, and she continued, "…forever."

"Let him kiss me with the kisses of his mouth: for thy love is better than wine."

Song of Solomon 1:2

Chapter 23

The next morning, Justin and Michelle joined Brady and Sue for breakfast in the Hilton restaurant. The couples had a great time playing volleyball on the beach and shopping; they even took in a show. Sue hated for the trip to end, but the couples left Saturday evening to be back at home for church on Sunday. Sue was amazed at Brady's love and understanding. He had always thought of her in everything that he did. Sue had fallen deeply in love with him, but she still found herself just waiting for something bad to happen-even after Brady had proved his love to her by such an elaborate birthday surprise, and he had kissed her and opened a whole new facet of their relationship. She really felt like Michelle had blabbed, but it was so magical, she really didn't care if she had! But even though things were still going so well between her and Brady, Sue still waited for the worst to happen. She wondered if she had fallen too hard and too fast. She had been hurt so when Jason broke off their engagement, that she found it difficult to trust anyone, but she was learning. Brady was working hard to help Sue learn to trust again. She had been earnestly praying for God to have His will done in her life, and every day she grew to love Brady more. She was sure that God meant for them to be together-almost. Most days she felt like she didn't deserve something this good-that she didn't deserve a man like Brady. She wanted so for everything to work out, and she didn't want to ruin anything. She dared not ask any questions about the future; she had decided to leave everything to Brady. She knew that if they were to marry, God would let Brady know.

Thanksgiving was upon them, and something very rare had occurred! The North Carolina campus of Atlantic Coast University was covered in snow! It happened only once or twice every five to ten years, but this year, it served to prevent Brady and Sue from traveling home to

Campbell's Grove to enjoy the traditional Macy's Parade and Turkey dinner with the Haybert's. Instead, Justin and Michelle opened the doors of their home to their best friends.

After dinner, the crew launched themselves into the snow for a long snow ball fight! Soaked to the bone and freezing, Brady managed to help Sue across the ice without 'falling' and into his F-150, to take her back to her apartment. He did love the Mustang, but he gave in to his desire to remain a truck man and had purchased the new truck, partly with the insurance payout from the accident. After lovingly bidding his Sue a 'goodnight,' Brady made his way back to his own small apartment.

When he reached his door, he grabbed for the knob, only to find that his door was in fact open, with the door only pulled to. He made his way back to the truck, grabbed his softball bat from behind the driver's seat, and made his way slowly into the apartment. Stealthily, he searched each room, so as to surprise any intruder who may still be inside. After making absolutely sure that no one else was in the apartment, Brady reached for his cell phone and called Justin. "Hey-I need you to do me a favor. How about ride over here and meet the police when they get here." Brady said as he walked carefully back to his truck.

"Why? What's happened?" Justin asked.

"I've got to get to Sue. He's been in my apartment."

"What do you mean?" asked Justin, as walked into the bathroom and shut the door to privatize his conversation.

"Jason-he broke into my apartment, and totally trashed the place. Spray painted the walls; there's broken glass, and ripped pillows and cushions everywhere!"

"No way! How do you know that it's him? It could've been anyone!" said Justin as he sat on the edge of the tub, for sheer support!

"I know that, but I've got the only thing in the world

that he wants but cannot have; that's a considerable vendetta against me! Now, go on over there. I'm riding over to Sue's to make sure that she's alright. Look, tell Michelle that you're going out for milk and bread and meet the cops at my place, alright."

"Okay. And I know-don't tell Michelle where I'm really going. I know."

"Thanks. And…uh.. I'll pick you up some milk and bread after I know that Sue's okay. Tell them I'll be there in a moment," Brady said as he flipped his phone shut and pulled up into Widow Johnson's driveway. He bounded up the garage stairs leading to Sue's apartment, and banged on the door.

Sue, already dressed for bed and wearing her hair in pink sponge rollers and cleansing her pores with cold cream, donned her bathrobe and raced to the door, expecting Widow Johnson. As she opened the door, shrieks rang out from both parties!

"Brady! What are you doing here?" cried Sue as she ran to her bathroom.

"Sue! What's that on your face?" Brady screamed as he followed her inside, forgetting his reason for hurrying to her door. Then, as he waited for her to come out of the bathroom, he took a quick look around. There was no evidence of disturbance or of any vandalism, and he quickly checked her closet, as Sue came out of the bathroom.

"What are doing, looking in my closet? Your Christmas gift isn't in there!" said a clean-faced, and much more beautiful Sue.

"Oh, I'm just checking the place out. I was running an errand-I need to pick up some milk and bread for Justin and Michelle. I just wanted to see you one more time," he said as he picked her up and swung her around in a big and earnestly relieved bear hug.

"Well, I guess you saw the real me!" answered Sue with a laugh!

"And she's even more beautiful than I could have dreamed," he answered.

"Smooth, Sheffield, very smooth!" Sue answered as she showed him the door. "Goodnight, love!"

"Goodnight, Sue;" he replied as he bounded down the stairs.

*****

Brady drove back to his apartment and met Justin with the police. The crime scene unit had already dusted for fingerprints; they were waiting for Brady's report. Since no one had been hurt, and none of the events directly involved Sue, the police would not provide protection for her. Brady and Justin knew that they would have to continue to be extra vigilant on their own.

*****

Christmas came, and Brady came by to pick Sue up for the trip back home to Campbell's Grove. Brady drove up in his F-150 and loaded Sue's luggage in the crew cab. The couple drove home to the Haybert residence, where they were greeted with open arms. Brady had made arrangements with Brother Connery and his family again, much to Irene's dismay. The Haybert's had invited Brady to stay with them, but he politely declined in an effort to *'abstain from all appearance of evil'*; besides, knowing that Sue was right down the hall, might have been too much temptation for even Brady to handle.

Christmas day was a very suspenseful day for Sue. She was unsure what Brady had in store for her, after her surprise birthday trip. She secretly hoped for a diamond ring and a proposal. But just as much as she wanted that, she tried to put it out of her mind-*'not my will, but Thine,'* she reminded herself. As the family gathered to open their gifts,

Sue presented Brady with a camouflage Bible cover and matching wallet, along with a bottle of Nautica, his favorite cologne. As Brady presented Sue with a small velvet box bearing a bow, both Sue and Irene held their breath. Sue opened it slowly, and without even knowing it, she closed her eyes before opening the box, as she just knew that it was a diamond ring. As she slowly opened her eyes, she found the most beautiful pair of sapphire earrings that matched the necklace that Brady had given her for her birthday.

Irene was disappointed deep down, not in the gift, but that there had not been a proposal. She and Max loved Brady, and they were very pleased that he and Sue were dating. Sue shared her mother's disappointment; even though she didn't mean too, her face fell when she opened the gift. She really loved the earrings, but she was expecting something else. Irene was not the only one to notice her changed countenance. Brady noticed it as well. "I hope you like them, Sue."

"Oh, they're beautiful. Of course I like them," she replied as she kissed his cheek, "They are the perfect match," she continued as she hugged him. Brady whispered in her ear, "Just like me and you."

Brady had an idea of what Sue expected. He knew that they would be together, but he also knew that it wasn't the right time to propose. He had to establish himself and make it possible to take care of Sue; he wasn't about to propose without having a way to support his wife.

*****

Christmas passed, and the couple traveled back to Sunset, as they were scheduled to work for New Year's. The ride home was rather quiet, as Sue found herself beginning to worry, again. Brady had just proved to her that she meant the world to him, and she was already allowing her mind to create problems that just weren't there. She began to think that maybe since Brady hadn't proposed at Christmas, that he wasn't going to propose at all. As soon as the thoughts entered her mind, she scolded herself for even worrying about it. *'A girl isn't supposed to be trying to figure out when and if her man is going to propose. I'm not supposed to have anything to do with it! Brady is so good at surprises; why am I trying to mess it all up? Think, Sue, think,'* she said silently to herself. She reached into her purse and took out her Bible. She turned to where she had inadvertently placed a bookmark-in book of Isaiah. Her eyes fell on chapter forty and verse thirty-one: "But they that wait upon the LORD shall renew *their* strength; they shall mount up with wings as eagles; they shall run, and not be weary; *and* they shall walk, and not faint." Sue silently prayed, *'Lord, please help me to wait on You. I know that You are in control.'*

New Year's Eve came, and Brady, who was so good at surprises, had another one for Sue. He and Sue had spent the evening with Justin and Michelle watching the ball drop after their shift at the Bargain Bin had ended. When the clock struck midnight, Brady gave Sue the customary 'New Year's kiss.' He couldn't believe what he had missed out on for so long, but then on the other hand, he was so glad that he had waited for his first kiss to be with Sue. She had the keys to his heart, and he was sure that she was the best kisser in the world.

Sue remembered the last 'New Year's kiss' that she had with Jason, and she thanked God again for His divine intervention and for bring her and Brady together. When Sue opened her eyes, Brady presented her with another velvet box-this one a little bigger than Christmas. Sue could tell right away that it wasn't a ring; inside was the sapphire bracelet that belonged to the same set that Brady had given her for her birthday and Christmas! "You are so good to me," Sue began as she felt a tear running down her cheek, "I don't deserve you."

"Hey, what am I always telling you?" asked Brady,

as he looked at her in a mocking scornful look.

"'Don't be crying around you'-well, stop making me cry!" said Sue as she laughed at him.

Outside, the sounds of fireworks and the neighborhood kids playing in the street caught Sue's attention. Brady softly turned her face back towards him. "Let's start this new year right," said Brady as he reached for her hand to pray. "Dear Lord, thank you for a wonderful year. Thank you for all You've done for me-for sparing my life," he prayed as he felt Sue grip his hand, "for giving me the most wonderful woman in the world, and most of all, Lord, for Your salvation. Everything else means nothing without you, Lord. We ask that You would please have Your will done in our lives in this next coming year, and for every year to come. Please guide and direct us, and help us to always honor You in all that we do. In Your name we pray, Amen."

As Brady prayed, Sue felt the Lord calming her heart and giving her assurance that He was indeed in control, and that He was also The God that kept His promises. Sue had read in her Bible for devotions that morning Psalm 37:4, *"Delight thyself also in the Lord, and he shall give thee the desires of thine heart."* Little did Sue know that God had shared with her the same verse that He had given Brady to confirm His will in Brady's life-the truth that he and Sue would indeed marry.

*****

As January got underway, so did Brady and Sue's Spring classes. This would be their last semester at ACU. As Sue got up that first morning of class, she read her Bible and prayed that God would keep her emotions in check. She thought about the end of the semester-graduation-and how their lives would change. There would be no more daily lunch dates at the Greasy Spoon. Soon, she would resign her job at the Bargain Bin and be going home, or at least she thought. She then reminded herself, that she was not going to get ahead of God, or Brady, for that matter. She remembered Proverbs 3:5 and 6, *"Trust in the Lord with all thine heart, and lean not unto thine own understanding. In all thy ways acknowledge him, and he shall direct thy paths."* Sue decided that she would lean on God to help her keep her mind on the here and now, and not on the future events, even if they were only six months away!

February came, and that meant Valentine's Day. This was Brady and Sue's first Valentine's Day together, and Sue found herself getting her hopes up again. As the day neared, Sue became anxious. She wondered, *'Would this be the day? Will Brady propose now?'* When the cell phone rang on the night before, she thought that she'd jump out of her skin! It was Brady calling to wish her a good night. She answered her phone with the most cheerful 'hello' she'd ever given.

"Well, 'hello' to you, too!" Brady replied.

"What are you doing tonight?" asked Sue in anticipation.

"Well, I'm calling to say that I'll be picking you up for a Valentine's lunch instead of a Valentine's Dinner," said Brady, with a strange tone.

"Why? What's going on?" asked a very surprised Sue.

"I have to go out of town," Brady paused, "I have a job interview."

"Oh, really, where?" asked Sue as her hopes picked up again. If God gave Brady a job, then that might mean great things for the two of them-like a proposal!

"I can't tell you. It's really hard for me to say that to you, Sue, but I really can't tell you," he said as he waited for her response.

Sue held her breath. The memories of Jason and his lies and deceitfulness came flowing over her. *'Why couldn't*

Brady tell her where he was going?' Sue thought to herself.

"Sue, are you still there?" Brady asked.

"Yes, I'm still here…Um, okay. Lunch sounds great," she replied as she tried to sound chipper.

"Sue, do you trust me?" asked Brady.

Sue answered a little reluctantly, "Yes….I do."

"Then know this-everything is fine, and everything will be fine. I'm not Jason." Brady replied as he tried to comfort Sue. At this point, Brady could sense the need to keep things on the down low. He knew that the situation would trouble Sue, but he also knew she would grow from it. He knew some of the details, but he also felt that at this point, they were facts that Sue simply shouldn't know, for both their sakes. With Sue's paranoia everything could be ruined.

"Oh, I know that everything will be fine. I'm okay, really…I'm sorry…I didn't mean to doubt," Sue apologized.

"Well, then I'll meet you at the deli at noon," decided Brady. "I love you."

"I love you too. Goodnight," said Sue as she closed her cell phone and dressed for bed. Sue tossed and turned all night, as her 'wheels of terror' began to spin! Why couldn't her brain leave well enough alone? Why did Brady have to keep a secret from her? But then again, wasn't he being honest about the secret, in that he let her know that he had a secret to keep? Her mind did the paranoia polka all night long, and she barely got any sleep at all, which showed on her face the next day.

*****

Their Valentine lunch at the deli was relatively quiet, and Brady could sense that Sue was still a little worried. He could see that she had hardly slept at all last night, as she had so many bags under her eyes that she could have packed for a week's stay somewhere!

Brady was somewhat anxious about leaving Sue like this, but there had been no strange occurrences since Thanksgiving, and Brady had made arrangements with Justin, to keep an eye out for anything, or anyone suspicious. Brady paid the bill and then walked Sue out to her car; he put his arms around her and held her in a tight embrace. "Don't worry. I'll call you when I get there."

"Get where?" she asked, hoping to get some more information.

"Now, you know I can't tell you." Brady replied, as he himself struggled with withholding information from her.

"Why? You've never held anything back from me before. I don't understand!" said Sue as tears filled her eyes.

"Please just believe me when I tell you that this is for the best; for both of us. If everything works out like I think it will, then you'll find out soon enough. It has to be this way, Sue. You'll understand later," said Brady as he hugged her one last time and then walked to his truck. "I love you, girl."

"I love you, too," she replied as she wiped the tears away and slipped into her car and drove away, without looking back. It would have hurt too much. She fought desperately against the doubt and concern that kept creeping into her thoughts. Then she would scold herself for comparing Brady to Jason. She knew that she needed help-help from God. When she arrived back at her apartment, she took out her Bible and began to read. God helped Sue while away the hours by taking her mind off of the situation, and by giving her one simple instruction from Psalm 56:3 – *"What time I am afraid, I will trust in thee."* Sue knew that she needed to trust in God. He knew all about where Brady was and what he was doing, and she knew that Brady trusted God completely. Brady was in tune with the Lord, and he wouldn't betray her.

Later that night, Sue studied, still trying to keep her

mind off of Brady's mysterious job interview. In the middle of her preparing her speech for Public Speaking Class, her cell phone rang. It was Brady. Sue grabbed her phone. "Hello..." Sue answered in nervous anticipation.

"Hey, girl! Boy, do I miss you!" Brady said in a cheerful voice.

"How did it go?" asked Sue.

"It went well. I'll know something soon. I really have a good feeling about it. I think that I'll get the job." He answered, with hope in his voice.

"That's great! Now, can you tell me where you are? Please?" begged Sue. She forgot for a moment that she was supposed to be trusting in Brady and in God, and gave in to her flesh!

"No, I still don't think it's a good idea, yet. Sue, you've got to learn to trust me, really trust me. I love you, and I would never do anything to betray that-don't you know that by now?" he asked.

"I do, it's just so hard..." she answered truthfully.

"I know it is, but I must say I am impressed. You didn't call my cell phone a hundred times. You did good, girl," he told her with a laugh.

"Well, it's not because I didn't think about it!" said Sue as she laughed in return.

"I'll be back tomorrow, and I'll take you out to a real belated Valentine's dinner, how's that sound?" Brady asked, changing the subject.

"That sounds wonderful," Sue replied as she allowed her mind to drift to the evening to come, which helped her to relax.

"I'll pick you up after your shift at the store, okay?" he offered, as he could sense that he was successfully distracting her.

"Sounds great," she answered as she remembered, *"What time I am afraid, I will trust in thee."*

"Well, I'm really tired, and I need to sleep. I'll see

you tomorrow, girl. I love you. Sweet dreams," said Brady as he yawned.

"Goodnight, I love you, too," said Sue as she closed her cell phone.

Sue tried to lie down and get some rest for herself, but that was just about impossible as her eyes caught her road map of North Carolina. She knew that she really needed some beauty sleep, but she couldn't help but pick up the map and begin to study it. *'Hum,'* she thought, *'he got there in one day, so, let's see where he could be?'* as she drew a big red circle around Sunset.

*****

The next evening, Sue was very eager to see Brady, who she had planned to meet after her shift at the Bargain Bin. The plan was that Brady would meet her at the store on his way back into town, and they would go out from there.

She finished working and preparing the front end for business on the next day. Sue then decided that she would wait for Brady at her car, knowing that he would be there on time. Justin had offered to stay with Sue until Brady arrived-he hated to leave her there alone-but she insisted that Justin go on. Michelle would be waiting on him, and he really shouldn't keep her waiting, she emphasized! Sue preferred to greet Brady alone.

She walked to her car, with her keys in hand, and as she stood at her door, she felt an eerie shiver up her spine. Sue shuddered, and then looked down to unlock her door. It was then that she heard the click, and a felt a warm body suddenly standing behind her. His hot, sweaty hand covered her mouth, masking her scream-and then she felt his other hand press the cold steel to her face. "Are you waiting for him?" asked the man in a growling voice, that Sue suddenly recognized as he spun her around.

"Jason, what are you…" she began, but she was cut

off as he kissed her forcefully. Sue pushed and shoved trying to fight him off, but it was to no avail. Jason had waited to grab Sue at her most vulnerable moment.

Jason finally released his mouth from hers. "There's never been anything that I've wanted, that I didn't get," Jason bragged.

"Well, this will be a new experience for you then, because we are done," said Sue as she spit in his face. Jason snatched her head back by her hair. Sue winced in pain. "We'll see about that. I know he'll be here soon; don't even think about trying to warn him," Jason said as he reached into her pocket, where he knew that she kept her cell phone. He took it and threw it into the row of shrubs that outlined the parking lot.

"What are you doing, Jason?" asked Sue, as she began to get nervous.

"I'm here to get you, babe, to take you back," he answered, "and to take care of all of the loose ends. I'm gonna put a bullet through his heart, just like you did mine."

Sue remembered, *'What time I am afraid I will trust in thee.'* She mustered the courage to speak freely. "Jason, you were the one that broke it off-you were the one who cheated-you threw me away-you were the one who called me early that morning and just threw me away like a piece of trash. I felt worthless and used, like I was nothing. You've turned me into a paranoid wreck!" Sue realized as the words had left her mouth that she had lied. Jason hadn't turned her into a paranoid wreck; she'd done that on her own. She was the one who had failed to trust Brady, and the Lord. She would try her best with God's help not to let that happen again. She found more of that emboldened spirit and continued. "And then you showed up thinking that I'd take you back? I'll never go back with you…" Sue paused for breath as she saw the anger and tears filling Jason's eyes. He knew that he had hurt her and that his actions were not amendable. "Brady loves me-he really loves me-our love isn't based on lust, Jason. We have a real relationship," Jason tightened his grip on her and dug the gun into her ribs now. Sue moaned in pain, "You're not even half the man he is."

Jason began to grow angrier, and he was beginning to lose his temper. "What do you know about ***that***? I know that you haven't 'given your gift' to Brady yet! You're too much of a Christian for that!" said Jason as he meant to insult her, but his insult empowered Sue even the more to stand her ground with God's help. She ***was*** a Christian, and she took pride in the label.

"No, I haven't slept with him. That's not what makes you a man; respect, true love, and compassion make you a real man. You need the Lord, Jason. I don't know how you could have sat through all of the preaching and services with me and truly not know the God I know. What's wrong with you?" she said as she felt anger began to rise.

"Shut-up. Don't say another word. I don't wanna hear anything of that. What has God ever done for me? I believed on Him, and then He let my parents' divorce and split up our family. My life has been meaningless ever since my parents divorced-until you. You were the only thing good in my life, and I messed that up. Now I'm here to fix my mess."

Sue looked at him in fear and disbelief at the words that Jason rambled. *'What is he planning to do? He knows that I'll never turn to him again. He needs some serious help.'* Sue thought to herself as Jason continued.

"You know, my Dad always showered me with gifts, money, whatever I wanted- but I really needed him. But even though he was never around, he taught me one thing- stop at nothing until you get what you want," he said as he stroked her hair with his free hand. The act sent chills down Sue's arms, as she hated his touch.

"He didn't teach you this. God didn't do those

things to your family, Jason-Satan did. Look, why don't you just let me go? We have no future together..." Sue pleaded as she felt his grip lessening, and she tried to walk away slowly.

Jason slung her around and slammed her back against the car. "Get back here...Don't move." Sue cried out in pain, as Jason twisted her arm behind her. She didn't know how much longer her strength would hold out. Jason was strong; it was one of the traits that had attracted her to him, and now he used it against her. "We'll wait for ole' Brady to come driving up, and what a show we'll give him. The last thing he'll ever see, before I put a bullet in his heart, is me claiming what is rightfully mine," he said as he reached down to grab her skirt, to try and force himself on her.

"I don't think so," said Brady, as he came running into the parking lot.

"Brady, stop," screamed Sue. Deep inside she felt immediate relief, as Brady had come to her rescue, but it was quickly replaced with fear, as she knew what Jason would do to him. He would take her true love's life, just to hurt her.

Jason spun Sue around, and held the gun to her head. "Well... well... well. Your hero has arrived. He's always been there to protect you, hasn't he, Sue? At your church the very first time I went there, at the hotel that night-Brady, you know, you've always been there ***in my way***-but not anymore," Jason said as he put Sue in a tight head-lock, and pointed the gun at Brady.

Sue pleaded as she gasped for air, "Brady. Please leave. He won't hurt me. Please-if you love me, please, just leave!"

"Sue, do you trust me?" Brady yelled.

"What?" she screamed.

"Do you trust me?" Brady yelled. Sue nodded *'yes'*. "Then ruuuuun," Brady screamed as he charged them. As

Brady lunged for Jason, a softball came flying at Jason's head from the side, hitting him, and knocking him unconscious.

As Jason fell, two shots fired. Sue dropped to the ground, and the next thing that she remembered was Justin staring at her; his lips were moving, but she couldn't hear anything except but her ears ringing. Justin sat Sue up with a quick inspection, and then subdued the unconscious Jason, as the police cars began to pull into the parking lot.

Sue tried to stand, but her legs were like rubber. She desperately turned her attention to finding Brady, as her hearing was beginning to come back. He was lying on the ground a few feet away, with blood pouring from his right shoulder. Adrenaline took over, and she ran to him, kneeling down beside him.

He immediately caught her eyes. "We've gotta stop meeting like this…" Brady uttered with a laugh. Sue took off her smock, and applied pressure to the wound. "Well, the Good Book says, *'Greater love hath no man than this, that a man lay down his life for his friends,"* Brady said as he tried to bring in his humor, even at a time like this!

"Don't be talking like that…you're not just my friend, you're my everything!" Sue said as she sat Brady up. "And besides, I haven't got any insurance on you; I'd get no cash payout, so you gotta make it," she said with a smile.

"Ahhh…you're learning!" Brady answered with a slight smile. As he struggled to keep sitting up on his own, he began coughing. Sue helped prop him up, leaning his head on her lap. "I'll be alright," Brady assured her.

"It looks like the bullet went straight through, but there's still just so much blood!" Sue said as she tried to control the bleeding. She began to feel lightheaded from jumping up too fast. Just then, a paramedic came up to relieve her, and it was just in time, as she had to drop her head between her knees to breathe. The paramedic gave Brady a shot of morphine for the pain.

Sue scooted over giving the paramedics room to

work; she looked over to see the police picking up Jason and placing him into the police car. Justin walked over to her, squatted down, and placed a blanket from the ambulance around her shoulders. Sue had a dazed look in her eyes as she looked over at Justin. "He took my cell. How did you know that I was here?" she asked.

"I didn't feel right about leaving you here alone Sue. Things had happened, Sue. The evening that Brady picked up the Mustang, someone slashed the tires, and then on Thanksgiving, someone broke into Brady's apartments and trashed it. He thought that it was Jason the whole time, but no one could prove anything. Anyways, we've both been keeping a vigilant watch over you since then. I knew not to leave you alone, so I drove around the corner, but then I went and sat over there in the park, where I could see you," Justin told her as he pointed to the park bench. "I knew you and Brady needed your privacy, and I was gonna leave when he got there, but then I saw Jason grab you. I called Brady first to head him off, and then I called the cops. Brady parked down the street and met me here; he was only a few minutes away. I'm glad that we had a moment to plan something, or this may have turned out differently." Sue shivered as Justin's words brought horrible images to her mind. "Are you gonna be okay?" he asked. Sue simply nodded her head, and Justin continued. "I went around back with the softball. I didn't know what else to do! The softball was all that Brady had in the truck," Justin said, as he listened to how ridiculous it was to use a softball as weapon.

"I'm sure glad that you didn't miss!" said Sue with a slight laugh. "I'll be fine. I just won't be sleeping for a couple of nights," Sue said. She shuttered again and turned to check on Brady, who was being treated in the ambulance. She stood up, unwrapping herself from the blanket and ran over to the rig.

She stood outside the van to check on Brady. "It

looks like it was a clean shot, ma'am…" began the paramedic, "…we're gonna take him to the ER and let the doc patch him up. You'd better get your words in fast, 'cuz that morphine's gonna kick in soon," he said as he offered a hand to pull Sue up on the rig.

Sue looked at Brady with mixed emotions. He was always there to protect her, and this time it almost got him killed. "What were you thinking?" Sue asked Brady.

"I…I couldn't let him hurt you, bottom line. Are you okay...he didn't hurt you, did he?" Brady answered, as his words were beginning to slur.

"No, I'm fine. He could have killed you, you know. I can't even think about what could've happened. I can't lose you, Brady. Please don't scare me like that anymore," Sue pleaded.

"All I could see…was him hurtin' you…or worse…and I hadn't even…asked you…." Brady said as he trailed off to sleep, courtesy of a morphine cocktail.

Chapter 24

Brady's words rang in Sue's mind like church bells on Sunday! She just knew what Brady was going to say-he was going to ask her to marry him-she was certain of it-or was she? The thoughts tormented her as she tried to sleep at night; they tormented her when she was with Brady, and when she wasn't; it was killing her! Sue found herself thankful to have this issue to ponder, instead of flashbacks of Jason's assault. Sue decided to never question Brady about not letting her know about Jason's vandalism. She knew that he only had her best interests in mind. Sue knew herself well enough to know that she would have been a nervous wreck, always looking over her shoulder. She realized how blessed she was to have such a protector as Brady Sheffield. Remembering Jason's assault, and the fact that Brady had *almost* asked her to marry him, sort of, Sue calmed herself. With both issues in mind, she finally came to the realization that God is in control, and that He would never let anything happen to her that she couldn't handle. Sue rested on one fact- God had yet again spared Brady's life, and she knew that it must be because Brady was to be her husband. Sue prayed daily that God would give her rest in her soul and the ability to turn that matter over to Him.

Brady's shoulder healed quickly, and before he knew it, he was back to stocking the shelves at the Bargain Bin again. Justin teased him often about 'the lengths that Brady seemed to go to in order to avoid working! Brady preferred his night shifts, especially the ones that he got to work with Justin. One evening, Justin seemed troubled. He explained to Brady that Michelle's and his first anniversary was rapidly approaching, and he was at a loss for what he could do for her. He had surprised her with a trip to Niagara Falls for their honeymoon, but now he was drawing a blank.

"Maybe you should take her to the Caribbean," suggested Brady as he and Justin worked up the back stock late one evening.

"A cruise? What happens if she gets sea-sick? What happens if I get sea-sick?" worried Justin.

"Fine, what about Disney World?" suggested Brady.

"No, that's too many..." answered Justin as Brady cut him off in frustration.

"Too many what?! Look, I don't understand what the problem is! You've always been a romantic devil-I've stolen several ideas from you. What's really eatin' at you?" asked Brady.

Justin paused. "It's too many kids. What if she wants to start a family?" said Justin, as his voice dropped, "I don't know if I'm ready for that."

"Well, I've always heard that for young married couples, it was kinda like tires-give yourself one 'Goodyear' before having a baby," answered Brady with a laugh.

"Look, this is serious. I like the way things are now. Maybe that sounds selfish, but I want her to myself a little longer," Justin confessed.

"There's nothing wrong with that, I guess. Has she said anything about wanting to start a family?" Brady asked.

"No, but I caught her looking at baby clothes in Wal-Mart the other day, and I started sweating. Evidently, I went pale, too, cuz' she asked me if I was okay. I think I got my color back when we made a stop in the sporting goods department-but anyways, I do want children, just not right now."

"Justin, I must say that I'm surprised at you. For a man who was so close to God that he knew who his wife was going to be when he first met her, you sure do seem to be worryin' about this. You're a prayin' man! Pray about it," advised Brady.

"I know, I know. But what if God says that it is time?" asked Justin, still with a tinge of worry.

"Then He'll give you grace to get through it. The Bible says '*As arrows are in the hand of a mighty man; so are children of the youth. Happy is the man that hath his quiver full of them.'* replied Brady.

"Yeah, but everything will change." Justin said sadly.

"Yeah; everything does change. That's life. Speaking of 'change', I got a job," Brady informed Justin. "I won't be starting until after graduation, but, it's a good job."

"Where? Who will you be working for?" asked Justin.

"I'd rather not say. It's in everyone's best interests," replied Brady, "but it is out of town."

Justin couldn't believe his ears! "You're not telling me? You've never kept a secret from me before, Brady Sheffield. I've been your own personal mall cop when it came to looking out for Sue these past few months; now the least you can do is level with me! Come on. Spill."

"Nope; because I don't want Sue to know, and if I tell you, Michelle will torture you until you tell her, and then it's all over."

"So true," confessed Justin.

"So, sorry, my friend, you're just gonna have to wait like everyone else," explained Brady. "Disney World can be romantic, in its own way-maybe you really should reconsider it," offered Brady as he changed the subject.

"Michelle would look cute in a pair of Mickey 'ears,'" said Justin as his mind suddenly began to drift. "Hm. Let's get this done so we can go home," he decided.

"Oh, are ya in a hurry now?" teased Brady.

"It's your fault..." said Justin with a laugh, as they got back to the boxes.

*****

The next three months went by like a whirlwind. Sue was busy studying for her final exams before graduation, and she found herself once again, getting emotional. She knew that her life was about to change, yet again. Her chapter of independence was coming to an end, and boy, what a ride it was! There were still so many uncertainties about the near future. It made Sue's head spin thinking about it, so, to keep her sanity, she opted not to think about it. She would let the Lord handle it.

Brady studied for his exams and worked on his other life plans as well. There were several times that he had to go out of town, and Sue worried at first. But, after she saw that Brady took the time to call her, and kept his word about when he was coming home, and where he would meet her, she respected his secrecy and understood that it must be for the best. This was a huge step for Sue, considering her past. There were several nights that it really nagged at her, and she wondered where he could be. She would stare in the red circle on her North Carolina map, and come up with quite a list of possibilities, but in the end, she would rest in the promise of Brady's love for her, and her fear would leave.

Widow Johnson had told Sue that she could rent that small studio as long as she wanted to. Ms. Johnson had become accustomed to Sue living there, and it made her happy to have someone around. Sue conveyed her thankfulness, and told her that she was in no hurry to pack up for home. She was unsure of what Brady's plans were at the moment, and she had learned that *'when you are unsure of what to do, stand still.'*

It was the night before graduation, and Brady had just called Sue to wish her a goodnight and to take care of one additional small order of business.

"Hey there, beautiful! Listen, I've got a few things to take care of after graduation tomorrow, and I want you to come with me, okay?" he asked.

"Oh, Brady, can't we do it later? You know Mama and Daddy are coming over for the ceremony and then out to dinner!" she replied.

"Well, it's like this, Sue. Right after graduation,

there's gonna be a reception for the recipients of full-ride scholarships. The graduates will be meeting their benefactors to thank them, and tell them all about their promising futures."

"Are you telling me that your scholarship donor will know about your new job before I will?" Sue asked.

"Now, come on, don't be like that! I know that it will be terribly boring, but I really want you to come with me; after all, you're the best thing that's happened to me since I've come to ACU! How can I not show you off to the scholarship donor as part of my promising future?"

Sue's breath caught in her chest! Was he actually hinting now? Was this the right time? How could she turn down his request now!

"Oh, okay, when you put it that way!" Sue happily agreed, and the two said their goodnights.

The next morning, everything went so fast. Sue's parents were at her door at eight a.m. to take her to breakfast. They wanted some time with her alone before graduation. Max and Irene had survived the 'empty nest syndrome' with flying colors, but they did miss their Sue. Max was all in tears with pride for his only child-the first college graduate of the Haybert family. Fortunately for him, Irene had a plenteous supply of tissues in her purse! Sue was also proud of herself, but not too proud. She realized that the only reason that she had made it through college was because the Lord was with her. She realized daily that she couldn't even wake up in the morning if it weren't for Him! Sue and her parents enjoyed their breakfast, and then the family made their way back to ACU.

Sue arrived at the college auditorium and met with Michelle, Justin, and Brady outside by the fountain. "Congratulations, Miss Haybert," offered Brady, as he reached out for a quick hug and peck on the cheek. Max and Irene approached, and Brady immediately greeted them. "Mr. Haybert," he said as he reached out to Max with a firm handshake. "Mrs. Irene," Brady said as he extended his hand to Irene for a handshake, but that wouldn't do today! Irene reached out and grabbed Brady in a huge bear hug that even made Sue laugh!

"It's good to see you again, Brady," replied Max.

"You are coming to dinner with us after the ceremony, aren't you, Brady?" asked Irene, as she finally let him go!

"Yes, Ma'am, I'd love to, but I'll be a little late. I've got to run a quick errand, and then I'll be right along," answered Brady, with a quick glance at Max.

"Well, I think it's time to take our places," Sue said as she grabbed Brady's hand.

"We'll go take our seats and see you kids later," said Max, as he and Irene left for the auditorium, with Justin and Michelle following behind.

"I'm proud of you, girl. You made it. I knew you could do it. Nothing is impossible with God!" Brady said as he hugged her. "I love you so much, you know that right?" started Brady.

"Yeah; I know!" she answered, with a sly grin, teasing him. He knew that her heart belonged to him. "And come to think of it, I'm kinda proud of me, too!" said Sue with a laugh. "You never cease to disappoint me, Mr. Sheffield. I never doubted that you'd graduate with flying colors!"

"Alright, let's go," said Brady, as he tried to walk away, but Sue clung to his hand, "It's such as long way from 'H' to 'S'," she said with a smile.

Brady paused and looked at Sue, rather strangely, she noted. Then he asked, "Do you trust me?" Brady asked, with a raised eyebrow.

"With my life..." she answered with love in her eyes, as she released his hand, and he turned and walked away to his seat.

As the ceremony ensued, Sue began to get nervous as they got down to her name. As she stood there waiting in line, images began to flash in her mind of the time since she had begun her college career. She remembered first seeing Brady in her English class and being glad that God had sent her a friend. *'Little did I know that God had sent me so much more in Brady Sheffield.'* she thought. She also remembered Jason and his stupid Yaris- *'dumb Toyota driver,'* she thought to herself. Michelle had such wisdom, if only she had listened! What heartache could she have saved herself? Michelle-she remembered her friend- and all of the happiness and the home that she found with Justin. Perhaps if Sue had not come to ACU, then they may have not met at all. Then she remembered how Brady had been there for her. He was always there-watching over her-protecting her-loving her-from the very beginning. She remembered Brady being there that night at the hotel. She could have kicked herself for being so blind to his love for her even then.

All of a sudden, Sue heard the dean call her name: *'Miss Susan Leigh Haybert-Bachelors in Independent Studies.'* She was almost bursting inside, and a tear streamed down her face as she accepted the degree from the Dean. She paused for her picture, and then shakily descended the stairs with such a sense of accomplishment. She floated all the way back to her seat, and waited to watch her Brady walk across that stage. She had come to the end of the great hallway of her college career, and now there appeared two huge doors of change, and she was still unsure which door of the two would open to her this day!

Sue was right-it was a long way from 'H' to 'S' and it seemed to take forever! Finally, Sue saw Brady standing at the edge of the stage waiting to hear his name called. "Mr. Brady Leroy Sheffield-Bachelors in Business Management" called the dean as Brady walked across the stage and accepted his degree. ***"LEROY!!"*** gasped Sue mentally, as she envisioned a small, brown-eyed toddler running around the yard with his grandmother chasing him-*'Come back here, Leroy!'* She laughed out loud at the thought. No wonder he never told me his middle name! We definitely will not be naming our son 'Leroy'! *'Oh, there I go again, Lord. Please put the brakes on me!'* Sue thought to herself.

After a speech by a local business owner who was ACU alumni, the graduates were announced, and tassels were moved. Sue understood that the speakers always tried to inspire the graduates, but their speeches were always so boring; Sue really had better things to do. She wanted to get to Brady as fast as she could and find out what part of his 'promising future' she played. But then she remembered the scholarship ceremony-just another road block in the day's events.

After the final declaration by the dean, the graduating class of Atlantic Coast University was introduced, and the students were finally free! Brady quickly made his way to Sue and scooped her up in his arms; he held her there for the longest time, as he knew that their future together was well under way. Their moment was interrupted by Sue's parents and Justin and Michelle. Irene had her camera, steadily snapping pictures. Max was blubbering so much that his handkerchief was sopping! After wringing it out, he began pulling tissues out of Irene's purse.

"I'm so proud of you, kiddo," Max told Sue as he hugged her. He held Sue almost as long as Brady did! Max was so proud of his daughter, and what she had accomplished there at ACU, not only in the classroom, but how she had endured the trials that came her way. She survived a devastating breakup, nearly losing her best friend, who was now her boyfriend, and escaping harm at gunpoint. The average person would have been a shattered, broken mess, but Sue had the Lord, and His grace was sufficient.

After the all of the pictures and hugs, Max and Irene

excused themselves and told the young people that they would meet up with them at the restaurant. Justin and Michelle decided to follow behind them. Brady and Sue made their way to the reception hall. "Do we really have to go to this thing? Can't we just go with Mama and Daddy to the restaurant?" asked Sue.

"It's part of the stipulations of the scholarship. I definitely don't have thousands of dollars to pay the school back, so yes, my dear, we do have to go!" answered Brady emphatically. "Don't worry, as soon as I sign in, it won't take long."

Sue and Brady walked into the dining hall, and Brady stopped by at the registration table. Sue walked a few steps ahead to the refreshment table and picked up a glass of punch. As she waited for Brady, she sipped on her drink and scanned the room. Over in the corner, sat someone resembling her dad, Max; then Sue looked a little closer, and realized, it ***was*** her dad. Sue approached him, assuming that he was looking for her. "Dad, what are you doing here?" she asked. "I thought you and Mama were gone!"

"I sent your Mom to the restaurant with Justin and Michelle. I had a small matter to tend to before I could go." Max paused as he gathered the courage to tell his daughter the truth. "You know, the Lord blessed us with a thriving business, but only one child to send to college. God began to deal with me about sharing with someone else. Sue, I would like you to meet the recipient of the Max's Automotive World scholarship…" began Max as the scholar walked up behind Sue… ***"Mr. Brady Sheffield."*** Sue stood and looked at them both in disbelief. She was so shocked; she didn't know what to say, much less feel. "You see Sue, when Brady's grandmother died, God burdened my heart for him. Here was a young man in the church, who had lived for God and displayed strength beyond measure in taking care of his family, to the end." Max's words were touching, and Brady stared at the floor in humility. "After counseling with Pastor

Creighton, and much prayer, I contacted the school, and they in turn contacted Brady," explained Max.

"When did you know about this?" asked Sue as she turned to Brady.

"I found out when I received a job offer from..." he began as he was cut off by Sue.

"Let me guess, from Max's Automotive World?" she asked sarcastically, as she could feel her blood beginning to boil. Even after weeks of learning to trust Brady and to leave her apprehensions behind, Sue's mind was already working overtime, trying to destroy the moment. She remembered how worried her Mama was about her going off to college. How she suspected that she would 'go wild'. Had her mother really been that wrong? Wasn't her relationship with Jason a little out of character for her?

"Yes; I thought it best that you didn't know right away." Brady replied carefully, sensing Sue's paranoia beginning to claim control of her. Sue had spent so much time worrying that something would happen to deter their relationship. At this point, Brady was concerned that Sue was a little more than shocked at her father's actions. She was angrily suspicious. Yes, Sue knew that she had made some bad choices in these past few years, but God had forgiven her, and she had moved on. Now to find out that everything was a set-up? Sue was livid.

"It's time for me to retire, kiddo, and I can't think of another person who would be better at taking over the family business. The interview was really only a formality. This job is his," said Max.

"So, let me get this straight." Sue began as her anger got the better of her. "I go away to college, to live a life on my own; now, I've learned that my own father sent a spy to watch over me." She directed her anger at Max. "Didn't you trust me, Daddy? Did you think that I couldn't make the right decisions on my own?" She pointed at Brady. "Did you tell him to ask me out, too? Did you 'select him for me' after I brought home Jason? I know that you and Mama didn't like Jason, but I didn't know that you'd try to manipulate me into a relationship?!" Sue threw her hands up in disgust, and then realized that she was about to cause a scene. She continued her ranting in hushed tones and tears. "I knew this was all too good to be true. I knew that I could never really be this happy," said Sue with tear stained cheeks. She turned and ran out of the dining hall and to the courtyard bench, where she had sat many times before.

"I was afraid this would happen, Mr. Haybert. Sue has been so paranoid since Jason. For some reason, it seems like she's been living under a little black cloud, just waiting for something 'bad' to happen. But, she was finally learning to trust me, so I thought," confessed Brady.

"She's always been that way. She trusts you, Brady; she really does, and that's why she's hurting so right now. She trusts you, but her uncertainty is taking over her judgment. Let me talk to her, son," offered Max.

"No sir, let me. I've gotta straighten this out. She's got to know without a shadow of doubt that I love her-that God has truly brought us together, otherwise..."

"I know, son...I know," answered Max as he watched Brady follow after Sue.

Brady found Sue crying on the bench in the courtyard. "Sue, scoot over; let's talk." Sue sat there in silence, staring at the ground, snubbing from the tears. Brady waited for a moment. "Alright," he said as he knelt down in front of Sue, peeking up at her face. "Sue, I only found out about all of this when I received word that your Dad wanted me to come and talk to him about a job at the store. I was just as surprised as you were about the scholarship." Brady peered up at Sue through her cupped hands. "Remember when I told you that I didn't remember applying for the scholarship? It was because I didn't apply! Your dad didn't send me here to spy on you, and he certainly didn't send me here to fall in love with you. You're the one responsible for that." Sue looked up at him, her cheeks stained with tears, as he continued. "I prayed after Grandma died that God would show me what to do next. I had spent so much time taking care of her, that I didn't have a clue what to do with my life. I chose to pursue a business degree only after I came to school here so that I could move up in the Bargain Bin Company! I had no idea that your Dad would offer me a job...but the bottom line is this-God has provided, Sue. This has all been His Master plan! I'm taking the job at your dad's store, and I'm leaving Sunset at the end of the week. I'm not going home alone; *am I*?" he asked, as he presented Sue with a small velvet box containing a two-carat princess-cut diamond, resting between two princess-cut sapphires. Sue gasped. "Looks familiar, doesn't it? I had this set designed for you at the jewelers. It took them a while, but they had it ready at your birthday. It's been killing me holding on to it all this time, but I had to wait until God let me know that the time was right." Sue began to shake. "I can't offer you much, and I don't know what's up the road for us Sue, but I can offer you a lifetime of love in this world and the next. I know that you believe me, Sue. I know that you trust me. You've showed me these past few months that you've learned to love and trust again. I watched God remake your broken heart and place it in my hands, and I promise that I will handle it with great care, with God's help," Brady paused. "Susan..." he began as he caressed her face, "Be my wife. It's time to go home-come home with me," pleaded Brady, as he slipped the ring on Sue's trembling fingers.

Sue's head whirled about, and she felt dizzy. She knew that Brady really loved her. The only problems that existed were the ones in her own mind-only created by her lack of faith. God had given Sue the best man that she could have ever hoped for, and she was about to mess it all up with her foolishness. She couldn't speak one word; she simply threw herself into Brady's arms, in complete love and trust in him and God.

"I'll take that as a 'yes'," said Brady, as she squeezed him tighter.

"Yes, I'll marry you," Sue answered as she pulled back and looked deeply into his eyes, "Take me home."

“Therefore shall a man leave his father and his mother, and shall cleave unto his wife: and they shall be one flesh.”

Genesis 2:24

Chapter 25

The graduation celebration quickly became an engagement celebration as Brady, Sue and Max arrived at the restaurant with the others. Max had kept Irene in the dark about all of the 'business' matters: the scholarship, the job offer, and Brady's request to marry Sue during his 'job interview'. Irene was so relieved that she became lightheaded. She thanked God so loudly that people were beginning to stare!

Sue looked at Brady in a different light since he placed that huge diamond ring on her finger. She no longer looked at him as her 'boyfriend'. When she looked at him she saw her protector, her soul mate, and her friend; then it occurred to her-as she glanced at her purity ring underneath her diamond-he would also soon be her lover. She felt a light flutter as her mind turned to the thoughts of how it would be waking up next to him-as his wife.

Brady interrupted her thoughts. "So, Sue, how fast can you plan a wedding?" he asked with the biggest grin on his face. Sue immediately blushed! *'Was he reading my mind?'* Sue wondered, and the look on her face was like she had been *'caught'!*

An excited Michelle jumped in. "Brady, we can plan this wedding in two weeks if you want us too!" She barely paused to breathe. "Sue, I can take you to all the places that I went and we can pick out everything together and...."

"Now, just wait a minute. I'm gonna need a little more time than just two weeks," Brady said as he looked at Sue, "I need about four weeks."

"Oh, you do?" Sue remarked. "What's so special about four weeks?" she asked.

"Nothing really special, per say, but there are a few things that I need to take care of. Some loose ends that need tying up, that's all." he answered very covertly.

Justin finally spoke up and waved his hands to make

himself known, as Michelle and Sue had been ignoring him in all of this. "Hello? And what am I gonna do at home alone while you're down in Campbell's Grove helping to plan a wedding?" he asked.

"Oh, you can find something to do at the store. Just schedule yourself to work," Michelle said apathetically, waving him aside with a laugh.

"Well, that's just fine!" said a disgusted Justin! His frown turned back to a smile quickly as Michelle whopped him aside the head with her purse!

"I do have one question, Brady-if Daddy gave you the job right away, why did you have to take all of the other trips?" asked Sue with her 'detective eyes' on.

"Don't look at me, kiddo," replied Max. "I only had one interview with Brady. I only asked him home that one time."

Sue stared at Brady in disbelief, along with Michelle who was tapping her foot waiting for an answer, as if it had anything to do with her! Sue continued, "You said that you had to go away for the *'new job'*; Care to explain?"

"No, not really," Brady said with a smile. "Don't you trust me?" he asked Sue.

Sue stared at him with a sarcastic look on her face, "Yes, but you're pushing it."

"Well, there were some things that I had to take care of, and that's all you need to know," he replied as he squeezed Sue's leg under the table. She jumped, startled at the daring physical contact! After he quickly moved his hand, she felt that spot on her leg tingling, at the remembrance of where his hand had laid. But, she knew Brady well enough to know that this was an event that would likely not happen again, until their wedding night! He simply wanted to shock her off of the subject at hand for a moment! And it had worked! She knew that Brady was up to something, and she *really* wanted to find out what is was, but until then, she would be content to let her mother and

Michelle plan out her first few days at home.

*****

That Saturday, the moving caravan was deployed. Justin drove the U-Haul from Brady's apartment to Sue's studio. Widow Johnson was disappointed to see Sue go, but at the same time, she was excited to hear that she and Brady were about to start a new life together. Justin, Michelle, Brady and Sue emptied Sue's small studio apartment, and then the crew started off for Campbell's Grove. Sue was elated to be moving on, and to have her uncertainties about the future alleviated! But at the same time, she looked around her small garage apartment, and she knew that she would miss her days there. As the four friends gathered to their vehicles, Sue hugged Widow Johnson and thanked her for being part of God's plan for her!

Justin drove the U-haul; Sue drove her Ford Focus; Brady drove his F-150 pickup truck, and Michelle followed behind in their Grand Marquis, so that she and Justin could return to Sunset at the end of the weary day. It was then that Sue began to think about life without Michelle nearby, and it grieved her. She was so excited to be getting back to Campbell's Grove that she had only thought about that fact just then-Michelle would still be in Sunset with Justin. *'Back home to Campbell's Grove'*-that was something Sue never thought she'd be longing for! She remembered when she couldn't wait to get out of town-to find adventure in her new college life-*'and boy did I find it,'* Sue thought to herself.

Finally, Justin stopped the moving truck at the self storage lot on the edge of Campbell's Grove. Brady had made arrangements with the Connery's to stay with them until the wedding, so he rented a small storage unit for his and Sue's things. Sue and Brady had decided that *'wherever'* they would live together, neither one would move in first; they would spend their first night in their home together.

Brady was so thankful to the Connery's for helping him during the past years since he had gone to college. They had practically adopted him!

The gang unloaded Brady's furniture and items all but his suitcase, and then they unloaded Sue's unnecessary furniture. Sue never thought that she could find such cheap items of furniture for her studio at the local thrift store, but she had found quite a few good pieces. However, they would be clutter at home in her room at the Haybert House.

When they had finished, they dropped off the U-Haul at the local service station and grabbed a quick burger. Fatigue shone on the faces and bodies of the four young people, as they fell into the booth at the What-A-Burger! It never took so long for the young people to eat a burger and fries, but they were simply too tired to chew! After finishing their supper, Justin and Michelle were quite 'give out' and decided that they would start back for Sunset, but Brady had other plans. He asked Sue to drive her car home to her mom's and said that he'd meet her there. She did just that, as she was too tired to argue.

Brady picked her up, as promised, in his F-150.

"Where are we going? I'm so tired!" sighed Sue as she climbed into the truck.

"You're tired of me already? Girl, we're in this for the long haul!" joked Brady.

"You know what I mean!" she answered as she rubbed her own shoulders.

"I've got an early wedding present for you, and you have to have it tonight," he said as he pulled out a blindfold.

"Are you kidding me? Really!" Sue said in rebuttal.

"Don't you…" Brady began as he reached towards her with the blindfold.

"If you ask me if *'I trust you'* one more time, I think I'll beat you to death," Sue threatened.

"***Alrighty, then,***" Brady answered in a surprised tone. He realized that Sue was so tired, that he'd better tread lightly. "Please, put this on," asked Brady politely.

"Okay. But I can't promise you that I won't fall asleep under this thing." Sue said as the slapped the blindfold on and laid back in the seat.

"Are you sure you can't see anything?" Brady asked, teasing her and waving his hand in front of the blindfold.

"BRADY!! JUST DRIVE!!!" shouted Sue, as her patience was running out.

Brady did drive, for several minutes. He took several turns, and almost made Sue a little motion sick with the blindfold on. Finally they came to a stop. Brady ran around to her side of the truck and helped Sue out. He took her by the hand and led her up a slight incline, guiding her every step of the way. Then he asked her to stop and be still. Sue was beginning to wonder if she should duck and cover or brace herself, as she could sense that she was standing in a large area with nothing close around her. She heard some rattling in the distance, and then Brady's, or at least she hoped they were Brady's, footsteps coming towards her. In one swooping motion, Brady picked up Sue and began carrying her.

"Brady, what are you doing?" she screamed, as she began to laugh. She threw her arms around Brady's neck and held on for dear life, as she still couldn't see anything. "Where are you taking me?"

"Just hush and we'll be there in a minute!" he said as she squeezed her arms even tighter. Sue could tell that he had brought her in from the outdoors, and he gently placed Sue's feet on the floor. He waited until she had steadied herself; "Now, don't move until I tell you to," said Brady as she sensed him walking away. Suddenly, Sue saw the blindfold become lighter, as Brady had turned on some lights. She heard several 'hollow' footsteps as Brady ascended the stairs. "Okay now-take off your blindfold," said Brady, as he watched Sue from upstairs, leaning over the banister.

Sue took off the blindfold and opened her eyes to find that they were standing in an un-finished house-an exact replica of the house that she and Brady had 'toured' that night on their lunch break back in Sunset. It was there that Sue realized that she and Jason really had no future together, and that she and Brady were becoming more than just friends. It was there that she saw Brady looking down at her from that same banister; him dreaming about a life together with her, and wishing that he could tell her about it.

"Welcome home, Susan," Brady said as he held his arms open wide to present the whole house to her. "This is why I kept coming home for my *'job'*. It is my *'job'* to take care of my wife, and that's what I've been doing. I've been meeting with the contractors making sure that everything was built just right-just like…"

"Our house in Sunset," said Sue as she tearfully finished his sentence. "Brady, it's perfect-the banisters, the fireplace, everything just like we saw it that night."

"It's got the balcony, too! Wanna see?" he offered.

Sue nodded 'yes' and ran up the stairs, practically tripping over her smile; she followed Brady to the master bedroom. "I did make a few little changes here and there, but I tried to think about what you would like." Sue followed him, speechless and amazed. She walked down the opposite end of the hallways first to glance and the Jack-and-Jill style rooms, with a shared bathroom in between the two rooms. Both rooms had access to the bathroom from their rooms. Sue looked over the rooms and imagined blue walls with baseballs and gloves, and dump trucks. *'Hum. I'd be proud to have a little Leroy running around this room!'* she thought with a laugh! Then she looked into the other room and thought about a little girl, if God would bless them. *'Pink walls, lacey curtains, and teddy bears…'* she thought again.

"Sue," called Brady, as he ran towards her on that end of the hall. He could read her thoughts and simply smiled at her, as she lovingly smiled back at him. He took her hand and led her out to the balcony. They stood there together, arm in arm, in the dusk of the evening, and Brady pointed out over the meadows and line of trees that held some dense forest. "Look out there-it's all ours."

"What do you mean?" she asked.

"We own the land all the way back past the forest line, there. Fifty acres in all," said Brady as he pointed over the green rolling hills of their 'backyard'.

Sue was surprised and elated, but then she came back to reality for a moment. "Brady, how can we afford this on an Auto-World salary?" Sue asked.

"Well, remember I told you that I was going to sell Grandma's house?" Brady began.

"Yeah," answered Sue, anticipating his explanation.

"Well, what I didn't tell you was that her house was so close to town, and she owned such a large tract of land, that some commercial developers were interested. I think I could've gotten more, but what I did get was a small fortune! It seems that the developers want to build a Target and a small strip mall there, so I was happy to part with it."

"Brady! You didn't tell me anything about this! I don't know what to say!" She paused and remembered their conversation about selling the house that day at the Greasy Spoon. "And to think I gave you such a hard time that day about selling your Grandma's house!" Sue reflected thoughtfully and realized, "You wanted to tell me then, didn't you? We weren't even together then! You've known that long ago that we'd be together?" Sue said as she began to cry.

"Well, I was praying earnestly then, just like I told you that day. But it wasn't long after that, God gave me peace in my heart that we would be married-I just had to wait for you," Brady answered, as he took Sue by the hands.

"You're so wonderful; I don't deserve you," Sue said through her tears.

"Well, just say you love me, and we'll let it go at that!" he said with a laugh. Sue playfully slapped him on the shoulder.

"You know I do," said Sue as she then jumped into Brady's arms, and he swung her around.

"This place is paid for, and then it cost a little bit to have your jewelry made special-like that, and of course I set aside enough to take you on a nice, long, honeymoon; your Daddy said that I could take all the time that I wanted to, and he'd wait to 'retire' until we got back," said Brady as Sue's eyes got bigger and bigger. She couldn't imagine Brady and her Daddy discussing her honeymoon plans! "And that's not all-the rest is being invested, so that you will never have to work a day in your life, unless you choose to, but Lord willing, it won't be because you have to. I personally thought that you'd like staying at home with all those babies that we're gonna have-the ones you were seeing down the hall there just a minute ago," Brady said as Sue realized that Brady had indeed read her thoughts. They both wanted a family, and strangely, she wasn't embarrassed talking about it with him, because it was right-in God's way.

Sue stood there with her hands over her mouth. She was so stunned; she really didn't know what to say! She just stood there in awe of what God had done for her and her future husband. She couldn't believe it. Finally, she found her voice. "I've read the verse a thousand times, and it's never really hit home-*'Delight thyself in the Lord,'* she began, and then Brady finished it with her as they held each other in a long embrace, *'and he shall give thee the desires of thine heart.'*

"Now, we'd better not stay too long," Brady reminded her. "There should be some paint samples down on the hearth of the fireplace. You need to pick out the colors that you want for the walls, the patterns for the countertops, and the carpet. I've been waiting for you to make this house your own," he explained.

"But it's our house-don't you want to help me pick them out?" Sue asked.

"Yeah, but I was waiting on you. The contractor said that he could have everything finished in four weeks, which will put us moving in when we get back from our honeymoon. Tomorrow we will pick out the appliances, and I've also included an allowance for some new furniture. I know that the pieces that you picked out from the Thrift Store were nice, but..." Brady said as Sue cut him off.

"YARD SALE!!!" Sue yelled as she ran downstairs to check out the samples.

"Wait for me!" yelled a smiling Brady as he ran down behind her.

"Except the Lord build the house, they labour in vain that build it:"

Psalm 127:1a

Epilogue

Sue and Brady made all of the choices for their new home. Blue for the one Jack-and-Jill room, and pink for the other! For their Master Bedroom, the couple picked a soothing Peninsula Blue from the Sea Side collection-a reminder of their time spent together on the beach. After completing the details on the house, they turned their attention to the wedding plans. Sue had no idea that a man would care so much about flowers-but only about hers; he insisted on picking out Sue's bouquet, and only fresh red roses would do. To complement the red roses, Sue decided to go with red evening gowns for the ladies-long A-line sateen gowns with short cap sleeves, complete with long white gloves.

The sanctuary was decorated in white lilies, and gladiolus, and the Matron of Honor's bouquets was of red tulips, tied together with a single red ribbon. They were, 'simple, but elegant' Sue insisted. Sue had placed a beautiful arrangement of red roses on the communion table on the Groom's side of the sanctuary in remembrance of Brady's parents and his Grandparents.

Sue decided to have a small wedding party, only composed of Michelle and Justin. They were more special than friends, they were family; God had used them mightily in their lives. There was no one that Brady and Sue wanted to share this day with more than them. Before Sue knew it, it was rehearsal time. Pastor Creighton and Pastor Rhodes would both be officiating the ceremony. The wedding party was all assembled for the rehearsal, complete with Sue's grandparents and Mr. and Mrs. Connery, who were to be seated in honor of Brady's parents; The Connery family had done so much for Brady through prayer and the opening of their home, that he thought of them as his foster parents. Pastor Creighton prayed to begin the practice, and everything went smoothly.

The Connery's and the youth group banned together and cooked supper for the party, as it was customary for the groom's family to provide the rehearsal supper. Brady thanked them earnestly, realizing that they had practically adopted him, and after all, 'that's what family was for' insisted Brother Connery. After the fellowship hall was cleaned up, Brady approached Sue.

"You wanna take a walk?" asked Brady.

Sue looked at him in a rare look of admiration. "You often provide me with the most amazing walks," Sue replied as she followed Brady outside. The Haybert home was only a few blocks from the church, and Sue had ridden to the church with her parents, so a slow walk home sounded just right.

The summer night was warm, but breezy. The wind blew through the trees along Main Street, whisking the fresh scent of the magnolias down the sidewalk while they strolled in silence, taking it all in. Sue remembered how Brady said that he loved to walk, and how it helped him think. She was beginning to become a fan of walking as well! All that she could think about was how by this time tomorrow, they would be on their honeymoon! Finally, Brady broke the silence.

"Well, I don't have any houses up my sleeves, or new cars or anything, but I do need to tell you something," Brady said, with a pause. Sue began to shiver in suspense. "I got a call from the District Attorney's office in Sunset. Jason has pled guilty to the charges and has already been sentenced. Those high priced lawyers that his dad hired for him must have pulled some strings. Usually the process takes longer. There may be a possibility of parole, but it will be a long time before he sees the light of day again. Since he pled out, there was no need for any of us to appear in court."

Sue was immediately relieved. "Oh, thank goodness. I don't ever want to see him again, for any reason. I'm glad that's finally over," said Sue as thanked God for taking care of the matter.

"And if by chance, he does make parole, and comes looking for trouble, he'll definitely find it," Brady stated in the way only he could. Sue trusted him wholly to take care of her in every way. She trusted him to be the spiritual leader of their home and to be the protector of their family. She was so thankful for God's choice for her. "But I don't think that he will. I believe that we've seen the last of him." And with that, he promptly dismissed the matter, turning to a more pleasant subject. "Now, put your mind at ease, my beautiful bride-there is one last gift that I need to give you, but it's not really a gift for you. It will make you happy, but it's really a gift for someone else!" explained Brady.

"Now you're confusing me. What's up?" asked a perplexed Sue.

Brady stopped dead in his tracks. "It's a secret-you can't tell anybody yet-only me and another person know..." informed Brady.

"Okay-mum's the word," answered Sue as she looked at him quizzically.

"I mean it-no telling anyone!" Brady re-iterated. With Sue's nod, he continued. "I'm extending the hours at the Automotive World, and that will require a night shift manager," began Brady.

"Justin and Michelle???" asked an excited Sue.

"Yes. Michelle doesn't know yet..." Brady's words were choked out by Sue's immediate bear hug. "Release, Release!" Brady managed to get out!

"Sorry!" Sue said with a laugh, as the two began to walk again.

"Like I was saying, Michelle doesn't know about it yet. Justin said that the job change would be a good thing, and the pay raise will definitely be coming in handy now."

"What do you mean? I thought they were doing fine?" asked Sue.

"You remember that Justin took Michelle on an early anniversary trip to Disney World, right?"

"Yeah..." answered Sue.

"Well, evidently they brought back a little more than souvenirs!" replied Brady with a smile.

"Uh-Uh! Are you for real? My Michelle's gonna be a mama!" Sue said with a smile.

"And she doesn't want anyone to know yet," Brady interjected, emphasizing the need for secrecy. "She didn't want it to take away from our wedding, so she had not told you even you yet. You'd better act surprised when she tells you! And remember, not a word to anyone else!" admonished Brady.

"I promise." said Sue as she took Brady's hand and continued their stroll. "Wow! I'm so excited for her! I'll be able to help her do so much! I can't begin to thank you for telling me about all of this."

"Oh, I can think of a few ways that you can 'thank me'-tomorrow night!" said Brady with laugh and a sly look as they walked up the driveway to the Haybert house.

Sue stopped and looked at Brady. "You know-you're always giving me things, and I really don't have anything to give you, per say, but, I want you to have this," Sue said as she slipped her purity ring off of her finger. "You've always been there to watch over me. Even in the parking lot at Clover when I was breaking up with Cal, you came to my rescue. But most importantly, you were there that night at the hotel, watching over me, helping me to protect this most special gift-*which I will be giving you tomorrow,*" Sue reminded Brady, as if he needed reminding. She reached over and placed the ring in Brady's shirt pocket. He closed his eyes, sensing the touch of her hand on his chest; he took her hand and held it there, protecting the ring. "Keep it there," she said, "close to your heart-I won't need it come three o'clock tomorrow. You'll get the rest of the gift tomorrow night, when we go to...?" asked Sue as she snuggled up to Brady, to 'persuade' him to give her a clue to their honeymoon destination.

"Nice try, Haybert. You're not gonna find out where we're honeymooning-at least not until we get on the plane tomorrow! Your mom packed your bags-you're good to go," teased Brady.

"A plane?" asked Sue.

"And that's all your getting outta me!" said Brady as he gently kissed Sue under the porch light and turned to walk away. "See ya at the altar!" he called back to her, and thought to himself, *'Hawaii bound, with the hammer down'.*

*****

Sue didn't sleep a wink that night. She knew that she needed to sleep, but so many thoughts raced through her mind. *'The dresses, the flowers, the procession, the reception, and then…it will be just Brady and me-time.'* It seemed like she rolled over and saw every hour on the alarm clock, as she eagerly awaited it to sound! When it did sound her feet hit the floor, and the hours seemed to fly by. Before she knew it, it was time for the "Bridesmaids breakfast," which seemed a little silly, as it was just Sue and Michelle, but Michelle insisted that Sue do things right! Then, in what seemed like a blink of the eye, Sue suddenly found herself standing in front of the mirror in the bridal room of the church, gazing at herself dressed in her wedding gown and waiting for the cue to join her Daddy. She couldn't believe that the day had actually arrived. It all seemed so surreal. Sue had been very quiet all that morning as she followed through the motions with all of the activities. She thought about Brady, and the love that they shared, and how it was so different from the relationship that she had with Jason. She and Brady had a connection on a spiritual level, as well as a physical. She could hardly believe that in only minutes, she would be joining her life together with her best friend, her confidant, and the love of her life. Brady had loved her even when she didn't love him. Sue thanked God that Brady had never stopped loving her. She then prayed and thanked God for never letting her make the biggest mistake of her life by marrying another man.

The wedding director came and brought Sue to the foyer where the bridal procession had begun. Max was waiting there for her. He extended his arm of escort, and he pulled Sue close. "Hey; the car's running kiddo, in case you've changed your mind!" Max said with a chuckle.

"Oh, Daddy, really! This is the best day of my life," Sue replied. "I never thought that anyone could love me so much," Sue said with a slight pause. "You know, when Jason broke it off, I felt so broken-so used. Then I realized that Brady had always been there; he loved me when I felt un-loveable." It was then that the Holy Spirit impressed His truth on Sue's heart, and her eyes welled up with tears. "I guess that's how it is with God. We as sinners are all used goods-just broken, dirty vessels, but Jesus loves us, and remakes us into what He knows that we can be; He loves us when we can't love ourselves!" said Sue as a small tear ran down her cheek.

Max was so proud of his daughter at that moment that he could have burst. "God is so good to us, Sue. We all deserve hell and death, but thank God that He did make a way. Now, don't go messing up your makeup and all that; this is a happy day," said Max as he wiped her tear, "That's a love that will never die-one that is based on Christ. I know that you and Brady have Jesus at the center of your home, and I couldn't be prouder of both of you," said Max as he shed a tear of his own.

"It's time," said the wedding director as she had the ushers open the doors. The wedding march began to sound as Max ushered his only child down the aisle. The church was filled with friends and family, but Sue only saw one person in the whole room-Brady. He was standing on the platform, with Justin at his side, grinning from ear to ear. There was her groom-the man who loved her, who had protected her, and who had already made her dreams to come true. She remembered back at the beginning of her college days, which seemed liked such a long time ago, thanking God for bringing Brady into her life. She needed a friend then. Sue giggled to herself at the thought that God had His Master plan all this time and had brought her husband to her at the very beginning!

On the way down the aisle, one couple did catch Sue's eye-Cal and Bethany. Sue thanked God for giving her the gumption to break up with Cal, in the parking lot that day at Clover High. As Cal watched Sue walk down the aisle, he squeezed Bethany's hand and thanked God for his *'unanswered prayer'* knowing full well that he was in the perfect will of God!

As Max reached the altar with the bride, Brady stepped down to stand beside Sue; then Pastor Rhodes began his portion of the ceremony. After a beautiful oration about God creating a help meet for man, Pastor Rhodes asked, "Who gives away this woman to this man?"

Max tearfully answered, "Her mother and I," as he kissed his daughter and placed her hand in Brady's. Brady held Sue's trembling hand and helped her up the steps to the platform where Pastor Creighton would perform the rest of the marriage.

"Would you please join hands?" asked Pastor Creighton. Sue turned and passed her bouquet to Michelle, who had tears in her eyes. Michelle smiled at Sue; she was beaming with joy for her best friend, and Sue was beaming right back, keeping her friend's secret of joy-the baby to come. She could hardly wait for the little one to arrive. She had always confided in Michelle, and she valued her advice. She thanked God for such a wonderful friend. Michelle had always loved the Lord and had always seemed to keep Sue in line, in her own fun-loving way-all of her jokes and advice based on cars! Michelle tried to wink at Sue, but the tears rolled out of her eye when she did, causing both girls to laugh!

The pianist began to play, and the soloist stood to sing what had become Brady and Michelle's favorite song by the Whisnant's: *'I delighted in the Lord and He gave me you…You were the desire of my heart…"*

Sue's hands continued to tremble, and Brady leaned in, whispering as the music filled the room, "Are you nervous?"

Sue gained her composure and answered with a smile, "Nope-I've a got a Ford Man."

The Beginning